Fate's Betrayal

Beth Ann Stifflemire

Published by Waldorf Publishing
2140 Hall Johnson Road
#102-345
Grapevine, Texas 76051
www.WaldorfPublishing.com

Fate's Betrayal

ISBN: 9781943093144
Library of Congress Control Number: 2015936353

Copyright © 2015

Printed in the United States of America

Dedication

Eternally grateful to my own fated love and soul mate. As your wedding band's engraved, *To My Sunshine*, you truly are my light in any dark day.

Just for you, Hank: "have you seen the magic time machine?" – *Not Sure*

<u>Chapter One</u>

"Brooke, isn't that your hot tea ready at the counter?"

"Yup, that's mine." I rose from the deep couch in the coffee shop and headed for the counter, twirling a piece of my recently-colored chocolate hair through my fingers. After picking up the steaming green tea, I sweetened it up at the condiment bar, squeezing a few globs of honey into the cup and stirring until the lazy thick swirls disappeared. Returning back to the mammoth turquoise couch, I carefully settled into it next to Tessa, maneuvering in my pencil skirt until I found a comfortable position. Tessa's beautiful strawberry-blonde hair only emphasized her rich hazel eyes in the now-fading daylight. Her tapered black pants and blush-colored sweater showed off her petite physique.

"Can you believe it's already spring break?" she asked, her voice full of enthusiasm. It was an enthusiasm I equally shared. As we were teachers at the same school, this had been a hiatus before summer that we had eagerly looked forward to.

"Tell me about it. My kids couldn't escape fast enough after the final bell rang today, and neither could I!" My mind drifted back to a few hours earlier when my second-graders had scurried out for their week-long vacation. Minus the tasks of grading a few math tests and science projects over the break, I was definitely ready to relax.

"Any plans next week?"

"Don't really have any. Been feeling tired this past month. I think I'll lay low, maybe do some yoga and take Alf for his walks, clean the apartment; nothing too exciting."

Tessa's eyebrows furrowed. "Feeling tired? Are you taking all your meds?" she questioned.

"Yes, Tessa," I sharply replied, staring at my tea. "You *know* I always do. My doctor adjusted some of them last time, maybe that's all it is." Reminded of my condition, the world around me momentarily disappeared. I hated what I couldn't help, living with a constant reminder that my heart was frail. I listened to the doctors, took my medications, went light on the physical stuff—blah, blah, blah. Yoga had become a good outlet for me, but it was about all I managed. Tessa meant well, but it annoyed me a little when she brought it up. I wasn't a five-year-old! I took care of myself and opted out of many activities I might have been able to do, just to be on the "safe" side. My moment of self-pity wore off and I looked up at Tessa to make sure I hadn't been too harsh, but she was focused on the café entrance.

Following her gaze, I caught a glimpse of Julie striding through the door. She scanned the dimly-lit shop then smiled and waved after spotting us.

Julie's luscious dark hair bounced in loose tendrils against the snug white turtleneck dress she'd partnered with knee-high boots. Work was her life, other than playing the typical dating game of a twenty-something woman in Austin. She logged long hours for a nearby local marketing firm but harbored no shame in the sea of men that naturally gravitated to her striking looks.

"What's up, ladies?" she said in a giddy tone.

"Well, aren't you chipper," Tessa laughed.

"Got a hot date tonight... guy I met at Fire Fly's last week."

"Wait," I interceded. "Isn't that where you went on your date last week?"

"Yes, but the bartender caught my eye, and he convinced me to give him my number."

"Oh, well then, what about the date you were on?"

"Old news... boring," Julie said, sarcasm written all over her face and a phony yawn to push the point.

I had, in a secret way, always envied Julie her openness to meeting people and dating. Even though I didn't give myself the opportunity, dating a little here and there, mainly in my days at the University of Texas, it wasn't like I didn't want to. I wanted to go out, let my hair down, but all I really seemed to focus on these days were

3

my little second-graders, dog, and health. Keeping up with second-graders was a chore in itself, but one I loved. With my inability to stay up past ten, and tendency to veer towards the mundane, what would dating matter anyway?

"Well, I guess we'll hear about this date next time we meet. Plus the new date you'll probably get on this one," Tessa laughed. I couldn't help but giggle along with her commentary. Julie held her head confidently, appearing to take slight pleasure in Tessa's judgment. Tessa and Julie always gave each other a hard time in a fun, sisterly sort of way. Clearly, they were quite different but seemed to love that about each other, the whole yin and yang concept, I suppose.

Contrary to Julie's dating escapades, Tessa had been in a very serious relationship for several years; a bit old-fashioned, but I expected to hear any day that Lowell had popped the question. Tessa was a woman who was one hundred percent certain she wanted two things in life: a husband and a family. She'd found that in Lowell.

I vividly remembered when she'd met him our sophomore year at U.T. He was a baseball player and right up Tessa's alley: cute, with sandy blond hair, sincere and gentlemanly. He was not as macho as his teammates. He and Tessa desired the same things in almost every possible way and had been a couple for nearly five years, living together for the last two.

Julie chimed in, "If you girls are up for it, we could head over to Virgos in a little while before I meet up with my date."

Tessa and I replied, virtually in sync, "Not tonight."

"Um, nope."

"Oh, come on, ladies, a little night scene won't kill you," Julie argued.

"Lowell is headed home from a business trip. I want to spend some time with him when he gets home from Dallas," Tessa sighed.

"Are you kidding me?" Julie rolled her eyes and laughed. I think Tessa and Lowell's relationship was a little much for Julie's free-spirited ways to handle at times. "You two have been together for what, nearly half a decade now, and a few days away from each other is that unbearable? Must he okay your every move, Tessa?"

"Well," Tessa went on the defensive. "It's not that, *Julie,* I just happen to miss him a lot when he's not around. Maybe someday you'll find that in your many dating games."

"Oh, please, Tess—"

"Come on, ladies," Sensing a squabble about to unfold, I stuck my nose in. "Let's just drop it, shall we?"

"Fine with me," Julie answered curtly. "I need to go grab a coffee anyway." With one final eye-roll, Julie headed for the counter to place her order.

The light of the coffee shop dimmed now with evening's approach. The setting sun ignited the busy Friday nightlife of the city and had me yawning simultaneously at the thought of it.

"Tessa?" Tessa looked up at me, coffee cup in hand. "Do you think I should go out more? You know I put myself out there. It's just hard with school all day, Alf is already such a handful, and my heart condition doesn't help… I can't help but feel like a bag of excuses when it comes to dating."

"Are you kidding, Brooke?" She lowered her head and gave a slight roll of the eyes. "Really, if any of us has a good excuse, it's definitely you. Your body just needs things a little… slower paced. Don't worry about 'going out' all the time." She looked off to Julie over at the counter and I followed suit. "Frankly, I don't know how Julie keeps up anyway. It's like the girl doesn't require a lick of sleep—just runs off of attention—but that's another story," Tessa said with a laugh. She looked back at me with optimistic eyes. "Don't forget, if you ever want to double-date, Lowell has some great coworkers and…"

"No thanks, Tessa," I abruptly cut her off, shaking my head at the idea of Lowell's coworkers. "I appreciate the thought, but I've met some of his friends, and we both know that's not happening."

"Alright, then, duly noted." She dropped the topic and took a sip of coffee.

Julie sauntered back a few minutes later, chai latte in hand. I momentarily deliberated that perhaps that's how she did it; lived on caffeine to make it out until all hours of the night, and then drank more caffeine in the morning to make it through the workday. Being that my condition had surfaced in my late teen years, before the coffee-crazed college days most young adults encounter, I opted for the decaf stuff or tea instead, so there went the hope of thriving on a caffeine buzz—ever.

The girls and I discussed our days the rest of that evening at Impresso Espresso. Tessa talked about her students and a trip she and Lowell planned to take sometime over the summer. Apparently, he'd gotten into scuba diving, so they would probably go somewhere tropical. Julie gossiped, of course, about the world of marketing and her co-workers, followed by her most recent date's faux pas. I spent the time dreamily living vicariously through Tessa's settled ways and Julie's vivacious social life.

After the passing of an hour's time, the clock rolled to eight, and instinctively, the desire to be at home in bed consumed me. I rose from the couch, turning to both girls, indicating my willingness to make an exit.

"Alright, ladies, I'm vacating; off to bed. You both enjoy the rest of your night."

"Alright, I'll call you." Tessa grinned.

"Get some Z's for me." Julie raised her third cup in the air and smiled.

"I can absolutely do that. It's my best talent," I laughed then gathered my Chanel purse and turned to leave.

I stopped near the entrance, intending to chuck my empty cup into the garbage on the way out, but spun back around to offer one last wave to the girls first. They were immersed in conversation so I didn't bother and turned back around as someone plowed into me. As I sensed my body tipping backwards, hands gripped one of my shoulders and the opposite forearm, saving me the misery of an embarrassing fall. I watched as the remainder of my tea splashed over a nice gray shirt. When the initial shock had fizzled, I peered up. Heated brown eyes met mine and set an unexpected flutter off in my stomach. I struggled to say something and make a quick escape out the door, but he spoke before that was an option.

"Hey, wanna try looking where you're going next time?" His eyes still exuded anger but I was distracted by his handsome stature - tall and robust, with muscle half-showing through his now wet shirt. His hands released me, but his intense stare did not. I tried not to stare idly back at him any longer, attempting to think of something quick-witted to smooth out the increasingly awkward situation instead. Unfortunately, I was momentarily paralyzed in both thought and speech until he spoke again.

"Are you just going to stand there, or what? I mean, you ran into *me*." I'd never been berated by someone who I'd initially found so attractive.

"I'm so—"

"Sorry? Well, good. Some of us have jobs and can't show up a filthy mess to them. Sure hope your purse didn't get ruined." My mouth dropped. At first I'd wanted to be nice and apologetic, but after that response, I was not about to let my beautiful white Chanel purse bear the brunt of this repulsive being.

"It's more like excuse *you*. Sorry for even *trying* to apolog—"

"Whatever." What the hell was his problem? It had been an accident.

"Maybe if you stopped interrupting me, I could get a word in."

"No, maybe you should look where you're going!" Backing away, I looked to see if Julie or Tessa were coming to my rescue, but, alas, they appeared to take no notice of my situation.

"Fine, I'll remember that." I glowered at him. "Now, if you'll excuse me, I have better things to do than deal with a middle-aged child." He was acting like a juvenile, and I was over his rude antics. Before escaping, I noticed a guitar case on the ground next to him.

"Wow. Hope you have a *great* night." His sarcastic tone stung, but I continued out of the coffee shop without another word. After hearing the door click shut, I took a deeply-needed breath to clear my head and walked past the coffee house window towards the parking lot, but my eye caught sight of a blackboard housed in the window. In chalk, was written the music talent scheduled to play. The name displayed on it was Riley Proctor. I shook my head and rolled my eyes. If I'd just met Riley Proctor, then I could confidently say he was an asshole. That asshole's intense brown eyes surprised me, staring at me through the window, seeming to follow my every move like a beast about to jump its prey. He gazed intensely at me. I was starting to believe it was the only look he had. I caught myself staring back and gave him one last sneer before hastily turning and continuing to my car. It was a relief to see the red Acura and plop into the driver's seat. I searched for the set of keys in my purse and, after locating them, stuck them in the ignition and started for home.

The city lights of downtown, now springing to life, faded in the distance as I crossed the bridge over Lady Bird Lake. The bridge divided the hectic downtown nightlife on the north shore from the calm artsy district of the city nestled on the other side. After the fifteen-minute drive, I turned into my apartment entrance gate and parked in a spot in front of my building. Based on the car clock, several minutes had passed before I realized I'd just been staring into space as the car idled. I thought about those dark, intense eyes and the strange flutter inside my stomach they'd set off, along with the disgust I'd felt for a perfect stranger. It was an enigmatic response, for sure. Shaking my head back and forth, I forced my way back to reality.

"Snap out of it, Brooke, you'll hopefully never see him again anyway."

Climbing the stairs to the second floor, I could hear Alf in the apartment, squealing with eager readiness to be let out. I'd always remember the first time I saw the mutt puppy at the pound, just after graduating college. Little did I know that mutt would grow into an enormous mammoth, with layers of fluffy hair like a shaggy dog I'd seen on TV as a kid. I entered the doorway, and his squeals turned to barks.

"Hey, Alf. How's my buddy?" He pawed at my legs, eager for attention, which I was more than happy to give. Finally, a pleasant interaction! Although typically covered in layer upon layer of snow-white and gray fur, Alf was currently shaved so close a stranger might consider him a closely-shaven bear. There was no way he'd survive the Texas heat if I didn't keep it that way.

"You ready to go outside?" The barks turned to constant woofing, and I quickly tried to calm him, not wanting to wake the entire floor. He darted out the apartment door but halted, as was his routine, waiting for me to go down the stairs.

About ten minutes later, we returned to the apartment, and Alf set a path for the food bowl, drool building in his jowls. I followed him and filled the bowl in the snug kitchen.

I headed for my bedroom and felt for the light switch in the darkness. After flipping it on, my sanctuary lit up; it was just what I desired after a long day. Having had the itch to paint one random weekend, I'd drenched the walls in a rich, golden, butter tone, and had completed it with blues and purples that accented pillows and knick-knacks. The bed was an enormous abyss, complete with a large, pristine white duvet comforter that always made me feel like I was being swallowed up by a giant marshmallow. *Heavenly.*

I slipped off my tan Yves Saint Laurent pumps at the foot of the bed and hopped onto it, falling backward without hesitation. I stared at the ceiling for a while. It was nice to sit in silence, reflecting on the day of students eager for the vacation, teaching plans, and conversations with Tessa and Julie. Then my thoughts drifted off-course, and I homed in on the beats of my heart. I felt the palpitations, and thoughts of my condition took over, flooding my mind.

The doctors could never really tell me how my life could play out. All things considered, I was pretty healthy for a person with cardiomyopathy. I could be fine for decades, or things could turn downhill randomly one day. Although so far, it didn't look like it would go that route. The device implanted in my chest just before college helped regulate my enlarged heart, and ever since then everything had been pretty good. Tracing a line across my left collarbone where it was implanted, I tried to refocus and just turn off the world. Finally about to doze, I forced my eyes open, needing to slip into some pajamas and remembering to take my meds before calling it a night. Moving to the edge of the bed, I slid off, my feet hitting the carpet below. My legs moved the short distance to the bathroom lazily. I looked at the counter top, my medications lined up in front of the mirror. Popping open the bottles one at a time, I collected the pills in my hand then swallowed them together, chased with a few swigs of water. I stared at my reflection in the mirror. Bags had formed under my gray eyes, a near replica of my father's. My curled caramel locks had lost their body from the morning's hairspray. My hair was one thing that usually cooperated with me, and I'd spent good money and time making it that way. My skin, on the other hand, was not quite my favorite thing: pale and pasty, definitely a byproduct of my mother's Irish decent. It made summers in a swimsuit feel foreign and uncomfortable in Texas, the land of suntans and bleached-blonde babes.

As I stared at myself, thoughts of Dad flooded my memory. The day he'd suddenly died of a heart attack felt fresh, no matter how many years had passed. It wasn't long after his death that I discovered I also had a heart condition. I was only sixteen when he died. He'd worked for a high-stress, fast-paced law firm in Houston. I believe his career proved to be too much for his body to keep up with, especially not knowing that he had a form of cardiomyopathy. He went to sleep that weeknight and never woke up. Mom and I were utterly devastated. He was so young, just forty-four. Mom and I tried to pick up the pieces, but it was definitely never the same again; it always felt like being incomplete. My father was the backbone, the humor, and, above all, just a good person. Without him, my mom sort of broke away from the world. It became hard for us to really talk for a while; we were both broken and on edge, especially when my condition was diagnosed.

Mom had been left with a good sum of money. No doubt my father, "the planner", always wanted to make sure we'd be more than okay if something catastrophic ever happened. Money, however, never made up for the fact that he was gone. She never remarried. He was her soul mate. I could only hope to ever know half the love she felt for him and felt even still. I sighed at my reflection one more time and picked up my toothbrush. Even after nearly a decade since his passing, it was not any easier without him. I have recurring dreams about him standing at the end of a bridge over some river in a peaceful place. He stands, waiting on the other side for me, looking as happy and healthy as I remember him, his salt and pepper hair, tall stature, and gray eyes the same. I think it was my way of knowing he'd be waiting for me if I should ever leave this world, which gave me a little sense of peace in the reality of my heart condition and dealing with the concept of death.

After I finished up in the bathroom and changed into my favorite satin pajamas, Alf waited in his spot at the foot of the bed. I patted him on the head a few times and then laid down again, this time to get some serious shut-eye. But it didn't happen. Not five minutes after re-settling on a comfy spot in a small sea of pillows, my cell phone rang from somewhere across the apartment, and I remembered I'd left it on the table by the entry door.

"Are you kidding me?" I shimmied my way off the mattress for the second time and rushed for the front of the apartment. I reached for the Chanel purse and shuffled through it. Just before I was sure the call would go to voicemail, I pulled it out and answered seeing 'Mom' lit up on the caller ID. *Here we go.*

"Hello, are you there, Brooke? Brooke?"

"Hi, Mom. It's okay, sorry, it just took me a second to get to the phone. What's going on?"

"I'm just calling to check on you, sweetie, that's all."

"I'm doing great, Mom, just tired. I was about to go to bed."

"Oh, baby, I'm sorry. I just wanted to make sure we were still on for your visit in a few weeks. I wanted to go with you to this appointment, remember?"

"Yes, Mom, I remember. I will definitely be there. You know I never miss my checkups, and, *of course,* you can come." I visited my specialist in Houston about once every three months, just to make sure everything was up to snuff with my heart. Mom felt it her duty to stay on top of these things, despite my diligent attention to the matter. Really, I believed she was terrified of losing me, too, which I could understand, but still felt she was a bit overbearing sometimes.

"Everything is fine, Mom. I feel great, and I am sure the doctor will say the same thing."

"I'm sure you're right. I'm just doing the mom thing, ya know. Have to make sure my only child is okay."

"I know, Mom," I exhaled, releasing some of the inevitably building waves of annoyance. *Brooke, chill, she means well.* "I know. I love you."

"When you come, why don't we do some serious retail therapy? My treat."

"You know I won't turn that down, Mom." She always found little ways to spoil me, and fashion was a huge weakness of mine. I think she felt she needed to make up for the times when conversation was more or less forced between us, as well as get me the things I couldn't afford on my teacher's salary. In her eyes, the money wasn't comfortable enough for what her child deserved, but I never minded the money. My father had left me a small trust fund that I could access in a few years, so I knew some monetary stability would come eventually. I was fortunate enough to be able to pay my rent and bills and

16

keep shopping the way I liked while never veering from my main focus: my students. I loved them wholeheartedly, and even more, I loved to watch them learn and grow into the next stages of life.

"I'll call you back soon, Mom, okay?"

"Alright. I love you, sweetie. Bye."

"Bye, Mom."

I took the phone with me to the bedroom this time. You never know, she may have forgotten to tell me something and call back, and I was not about to get out of bed again or get the lecture from her for not answering the phone. Crawling back to the most comfortable spot I could find, I closed my eyes when the rings started again. "I knew it!" I answered the phone without even looking. "Mom, what is it now?"

"*Mom?*" the caller questioned, annoyed.

"Oh, Julie." I would have recognized the sarcasm in Julie's voice anywhere. "I'm sorry, I just got off the phone with my mom and was convinced she was calling me right back. You know how she is."

"I get it. No biggie. So you left before Tessa and I decided to try to get all of us together tomorrow night. We're headed to Carters. You know, that little Irish-type pub off Eighth?"

"Yeah, I remember it." It had been a while—no, make that a few years—because the last time I'd been there was when Tessa had tried to set me up on a date after a football game in college. It didn't end well. His name was Mark, and he'd belched...a lot, and without any consideration for those around him or care for anything beyond himself. I'd left without giving him my real phone number and luckily never heard from him again.

"So, are you up for it? You don't have to stay out real late. We'll probably be there around seven-ish, so you can leave whenever."

I reminded myself life still existed outside the confines of my occasionally habitual schedule. I needed to live a little. What would it hurt? "Okay, okay. I'll call you when I'm on my way tomorrow. Cool?"

"Alright, Brooke. That's the kind of answer I like to hear. So, I'll see you tomorrow, then?"

"Sounds like a plan. See you tomorrow." At that, I turned off the phone. Alf gave a last doggy sigh and settled his head on his paws. "Good night, Alf." I turned off the lamp and faded off into Never-Never Land.

Chapter Two

The weekend began with laundry and grading the kids' math tests, followed by yoga prior to lunch, and then a long walk with Alf. After that, a power nap was long overdue and I nestled into my burgundy sofa to the hum of sportscasters, who had me asleep in minutes. I awoke as the sun started its descent for the day and glittered through the window sheers, deciding it was time for a shower. After a long while just letting the stream of steam-filled moisture run over me, I completed my typical female ritual: shampoo, condition, exfoliate, shave... Lord, sometimes it seemed like ten thousand steps to accomplish a decent beauty routine.

Alf waited at the tub's edge as I stepped onto the bath mat. I reached for the freshly laundered towel, wrapping it around my slender torso. Looking down at Alf, his expression meant serious business.

"It's dinner time, isn't it? We wouldn't want to miss that, would we?"

His paws pattered against the floor as he followed on my heels to the kitchen and scrambled to the bowl before

I'd even finished filling it. Strolling back to the bedroom, my hair dripped water drops on the floor, leaving a small trail. I grabbed another towel, wrapped up my hair, and rummaged for the stereo remote. I found it hidden under last week's *People* magazine on the bedside table and clicked the stereo on, giving a much-needed peppier atmosphere to the quiet apartment. With the towel still on my head, I did a little Chiquita Bananaesque dance to the Shakira song now filling my entire apartment. I needed to get my energy up and blood flowing before going out, and doing a little dance always helped with that. Remembering the list of numerous tasks at hand, I settled in front of the tall mahogany floor mirror and went to work putting on makeup, followed by styling my hair now forming into damp waves. Afterwards, I scavenged the closet for the BCBG black cocktail dress I'd splurged on last spring and a pair of red heels for extra oomph. With a final spritz of my favorite going-out perfume, I was out the door. This was a night I knew I'd needed for a while, time away from the mundane routine of work, Alf, home, bed, repeat. I did a little dance outside my door as I locked it before getting serious again and confidently sauntering to my car. I put one foot after the other with my hips moving accordingly, laughing at how well Shakira had prepared me for my night so far. I knew I looked great and was filled with giddy anticipation for a good long night out—no matter how tired

I knew I would be tomorrow. Once in my car, I turned on the music again and started towards Carters.

***

I managed to find a parking spot close by the club, avoiding the valet. "Yeah, that's five bucks *still* in my account." Grabbing my purse from the passenger seat, I skillfully shimmied out of the car in the fitted dress. Approaching the club door, it emulated a rustic Irish pub vibe tucked in between two bars. It was sprinkled with neon signs and music rumbled the outer walls. Having been well over a hundred years old, but obviously renovated a half dozen times, new steel doors and furnishings amidst the century-old brick displayed an obvious overlap of eras. The bouncer glanced briefly down at me, and I put the ten-dollar cover charge in his large, commanding grip. "Have a great night," he smirked, cash in hand.

Like a Marine on a mission, I intently scoured the room for a trace of Julie or Tessa. At first glance, I failed to locate them. It was dark and noisy. Loud music blared from speakers scattered around, making it difficult to concentrate. Glasses clinked, and nearly every square inch of space was full with groups of four or more clamored together around tables, like tightly packed sardines. The overall atmosphere was very lively and happy. It felt like most were embracing the freedom of the weekend. I made out the faint call of my name and turned in all directions to locate its source. Far beyond the bar, planted directly in the center of the noisy room, I heard it again. "Over here!" I now made out Tessa's voice. Eventually, I spotted her standing on a chair at a table to catch my attention.

"Be there in a sec!" I yelled and waved back, beginning the task of meandering through the crowds of people with a dozen "excuse me's". Finally weaving my way to Tessa, we greeted each other with a hug.

"What a crowd! It's a little early for this many people, right? Or have I missed a memo?" I asked in what felt like a scream, trying to be heard over the blaring noise.

"Yeah, I'd say so, but some band is playing tonight. That's the big deal, I guess."

"Hmm, guess we'll see if they're any good." I tucked my purse near Tessa's in a chair at the back of the table. "Where's Lowell?"

"He's coming later tonight. He stopped to have a few beers with some of his old baseball buddies." I pictured Lowell's old pals and him all drinking and laughed to myself. They never seemed to get any older.

"Did he have a good business trip?"

"Aw, you know, typical business with a little fun. That is if you consider golf fun. But you know me, I'm not a golf enthusiast," Tessa chuckled. She hated golf; always saying how boring it was to watch, let alone play. But she knew it was just part of the Lowell package.

"It will be nice to see him. It's been a while," I happily chided and settled myself into a chair.

"I guess Julie isn't here?"

"No," Tessa replied. "She texted me a few minutes before you arrived and said she was trying to get out of a date with a guy from the office then she'd be on her way."

"Guess she doesn't want to mix business with pleasure," I laughed.

"I wouldn't if I were her." Tessa smiled.

"Well, I guess it's just you and me for a while. Want a drink?"

"You're drinking tonight?" Immediately, Tessa's eyebrow lifted in surprise.

"Maybe a glass of wine. I won't overdo it. You won't be carrying me out of here or anything, but I'm not making any promises." I smiled mischievously. Tessa and Julie knew I hardly drank alcohol, not being the best thing to do for my heart, but a little didn't hurt, and I was feeling unusually social and rowdy.

"So… what do you want?"

"I'll take a vodka tonic!" Tessa hollered over the noise.

"Be right back." Grabbing my wallet, I began the trek to the bar. After another round of "excuse me's" through what felt like an endless sea of tipsy people, I claimed a space at the bar and waited to catch a bartender's attention. Nearly five minutes and several attempts later to wave one down, a twenty-something, brown-haired bartender placed the red wine and vodka tonic in front of me at unprecedented speed; obviously having mastered the art of drink making.

"Here you go."

"Thanks." I placed cash on the bar and made my way back to the table.

"Here you go, Miss Tessa." She was still sitting in her chair as I handed her the short glass.

"Thanks, Brooke." She took a sip and motioned with her glass to the stage. "I think the band is getting ready to go on. I actually heard someone walking by saying they're called Waiting to Win."

"Never heard of them, but I'd probably be the last to know local bands since I apparently live at school. Hey, I wonder if the kids really think we do live there." Tessa and I laughed together, agreeing that our students did, in fact, think teachers lived at school.

"Well, we sometimes escape! This band, though, they must have a following 'cause this place is packed." Tessa scoured the bar.

"No lie," I said, sitting back down in the chair next to Tessa, sipping my glass of wine as I got comfortable. Music was something I liked a lot but didn't really keep up with, which I realized was a shame since Austin had such a big live-music scene.

Four guys about my age, dressed in jeans and plain or slogan t-shirts emerged on stage a short while later. Their backs faced us as they performed a quick tuning of various instruments. There were two guitar players, one bass player, and a drummer—at least I knew the basics of band setup. After a few minutes of warming up, the music streaming through the loudspeakers finally ceased, and a bar employee stepped on stage to introduce them. He was a large man; he looked like a giant linebacker and sported a short beard.

"Good evening, everybody! I know you've all been waiting for this act, and we finally got them here. Ladies and gentleman... Waiting to Win!" He handed the microphone off to one of the band members and stepped off stage. All at once, the sound of live music filled up every corner of the club with rock alternative, a cross between John Mayer and maybe even a hint of Pearl Jam, lively and energetic with snazzy little guitar riffs. As I inventoried each band member, the lead singer instantly had me fixated on his face. He looked eerily familiar... Oh, God, was it the face that had been staring back through the window after that awful scene at the coffee shop yesterday? I could barely recognize him from this distance and with a more cordial expression exhibited on his face, but I thought it might be. The bar was so low-lit and we were so far back, it took me a long while to work out even the most basic details of his features. His height was just less than six feet and seemed to fit the bill of what I could recall. Other than that, I'd hardly paid attention to anything but his eyes, his deep, chocolate-brown eyes that I was inevitably developing a love/hate feeling towards. If he were up close, I'd know for certain. I began cataloging other features I didn't recall. His hair was dark, nearly black, with hints of copper. It had a slight curl to it and was just long enough to be tucked behind his ears. I observed a slight muscular tone to his arms displayed through his fitted black shirt.

"Hey, Brooke?" Tessa interrupted my focused gaze, and I felt my eyes flutter as I moved my eyes to her.

"Yes?"

"I think I've seen that guy. The lead singer, I mean. I'm not totally sure, but he might be the guy who sang at Impresso Espresso last night after you left. His voice sounds pretty much the same. The only difference is that it was just him and a guitar. Actually, I think you bumped into him yesterday when you were leaving." I looked at Tessa and felt my cheeks blush.

"You saw that, huh? You don't have to lie. It was more like I slammed into him and he bit my head off."

"Yeah, okay, you really couldn't miss it, you two looked like trucks colliding in a game of chicken—except no one swerved. Wait, he yelled at you after those shenanigans? Julie was in the middle of one of her stories so I didn't notice. What a jerk! I don't know if it's him, but maybe we'll get a closer glimpse of him later."

"I can't believe I don't know if it's him. I mean, I ran smack into the guy, but I just wanted to get out of there—it was awkward! I would remember his eyes, though. I caught him staring at me through the window before heading to my car. He still looked pissed and crazed, but those eyes had me stumbling."

"Oh, really?" A smile erupted across Tessa's face. "Maybe he saw something that he liked."

"Oh, please, Tessa. I seriously doubt that. He was probably just still boiling with anger. I didn't even care to apologize after arguing with him, which I can guess didn't make him like me any better. Besides, if someone had just run into me, I might give them a stare-down, too. But I'd never get crazy bipolar on them like he did!"

"Come on, you've got to admit, Brooke, at least from this distance, he's pretty darn easy on the eyes." She squinted at him on stage as if trying to more clearly make out her assumption.

"Whatever, Tessa. Maybe I just need to drink this wine faster to see that!" I fought back a smile because I was still too scarred from my first interaction with this guy to be certain if he was even sane or not. Yet, I couldn't help feeling this weird physical pull to him that I'd never experienced before.

Tessa's expression still displayed the urge to keep on the topic, but she hesitated, biting her lip. All I knew was I didn't need a guy in my life, even if he was incredibly handsome. Especially if he had anger issues. Before I dwelt on it a second longer, my cell rang—thankfully breaking me away from my thoughts that were easily consumed by this stranger. Leaning over and grabbing it from my purse, Julie's name appeared on the screen and I answered it.

"Hey, Julie, almost here?"

"I'm here, at the door. Where are you guys?"

"We're near the back. I'll stand on the chair so you can see me." I set the phone on the table and hopped onto the chair in search of Julie. After spotting her in a smoldering red, strapless cocktail dress, I waved my hands, getting her attention, and she began the journey through the crowd over to us.

"Holy crap, can you believe this place? I've been here tons of times but I've never seen it this packed. Oh, and I've heard a lot about this band from some people at work." Julie suddenly did a double take at the lead singer, just as Tessa and I had earlier. "Hey, isn't that the guy…"

"Yeah, we both think it's the guy from the coffee place yesterday," Tessa cut in.

"Guess you two already had this conversation." Julie glanced back and forth between us a few times, reading the curious expressions on both of our faces.

"Yeah, and apparently he was a real douchebag to Miss Brooke when they collided on her way out the door last night." Tessa pointed towards me, her drink now empty in the other hand.

"What?! Him?" Julie said in disbelief.

"He might be the guy from yesterday. I don't know anything about him, except, if it is him, from firsthand experience I can tell you that he tends to go ballistic on people who bump into him!"

"Brooke, you *smashed* into him. I don't know, maybe he was having a bad day. At least if he comes around, you two will have something to talk about." Julie grinned from ear to ear.

"What am I hearing right now? I don't know what I'm going to do with you girls. I hope he doesn't see me here at all, I don't think I could handle another stare-down from him anyway... Uh oh, I seem to be out of wine. Do you want a drink, Julie?" I asked to derail the topic.

"Yeah, I'll be right back."

"No, I'll get it for you. Tessa, let me grab you another." By this point, I was ready to separate myself from the current conversation. There are hundreds of bars in Austin, and we end up going to the one bar *this* guy is playing at. I couldn't help but shake my head at the thought of it.

"You're a doll, Brooke. It's so nice to have you out with us." Julie gave me a quick side hug. "I'll take a Crown and Coke."

"Alright, be back in a minute." Just as before for Tessa, I grabbed my wallet, tucked it under my arm, and set course for the bar. Compared to just a short while before, it was an even tighter squeeze. I felt like the only fish swimming upstream. I didn't know how I'd accomplish the task of getting a bartender's attention amidst the chaos.

Although it was crazy to me, it seemed like nothing to the bartenders as they sinuously weaved back and forth, making each drink with amazing speed. I was fortunate enough to have a random guy notice me attempting to get a bartender's attention, and he, in turn, did the job for me. "Excuse me, sir, this little lady needs some drinks." He pointed towards me.

"Thanks," I smiled. "I would have been waiting here all night."

"Not a problem. Have a good night." I was appreciative to the stranger who'd picked up his own drink order and scurried off. The same bartender who had served me earlier promptly served up Julie's and Tessa's orders, and I also grabbed a glass of water to go with my new glass of wine while I was there. No sense in coming back for one in this craziness.

With the drinks in hand and my wallet tucked under my arm once again, a balancing act ensued as I made my way back through the crowd. I cut my way back near the stage, with all other routes seemingly sealed off. I almost made it past with the drinks untouched when a guy rocking out to a song the band played knocked my water glass, catapulting it to the ground. It didn't seem like much of an attention-grabber, with all the noise and people entranced in music or conversation, yet it appeared to be enough of a distraction that the lead singer turned and looked at me. We locked eyes for a brief second, affirming what I already knew: he was the guy from Impresso Espresso. His double take was enough for me to realize that we privately recognized each other. Keeping what little was left of my dignity after the guy from yesterday's collision had seen me collide with someone else, I rebalanced the remaining drinks in one arm, moved the downed glass of water to a table, and resituated my wallet under my arm. I flushed with embarrassment. *Damn, I've got to start paying more attention to what I'm doing,*

I was about to continue to the table, when the guy who'd knocked the glass from my hand apologized relentlessly. I repeated to him over and over that he shouldn't feel bad; it was just a glass of water, for heaven's sake. He attempted to redeem himself by offering me another drink, but I again refused and affirmed there was really no need. I peered over my shoulder at the stage one last time, catching the lead singer gaping at me yet again. I couldn't tell if his look was pity or kindness, though he probably thought I was a real idiot with an undeniable ability to run into things at this point. Turning away before his gaze had a chance to turn sour, I resumed my way back to our table, not even bothering to excuse myself this time through the throng of people. I didn't care anymore; I just wanted to be back with my friends and out of the sweaty, packed mass.

Approaching the table, I noticed that Lowell had arrived. Tessa was all smiles. Lowell's sandy-blond hair was cut short and tidy, his skin was slightly tan—no doubt from a round or two of golf—and he still carried the physique of the baseball player he'd been during his college days; his tall stature in direct opposition to how tiny Tessa was—they really were an adorable pair.

"Hey, guys. I actually made it back can you believe it? Here's your drink, Julie."

"Are you alright, Brooke? You look disheveled," Julie asked as I handed her the Crown and Coke.

"I'm fine. Just seem to be destined for human fender-benders lately. I just ran into, I mean a guy just ran into *me* on my way back and knocked the water I was carrying straight out of my hand. No big deal, though. Anyway, how are you doing, Lowell?" I leaned in to give Lowell a friendly hug. "It's been a while."

"I'm doing great. It's good to see you." The deep tone of Lowell's voice was warm and friendly.

After our hello, I sat next to Julie while Tessa and Lowell stood together, Lowell's arm draped across her shoulder. They were the closest example in my life, other than my parents, of what real love should be.

The four of us enjoyed the next hour of each other's company and listened to the band. Lowell filled us in on work, Julie talked about how relieved she was she'd managed to get out of her date tonight, and Tessa mentioned the lesson plans she needed to do over the rest of spring break. It was refreshing to simply be with people who meant so much to me. Life was good, and the music was actually really good, too.

The band eventually took a break, and the members scattered to the bar for a drink or conversed with the crowd. I'd finished my second glass of wine just as they dispersed, and Julie popped up to grab herself another drink. Lowell went to snag abandoned chairs from another table as soon as its occupants vacated the area, but as he set the last chair down, his eyes caught someone staring straight at our group. "Ladies, any of you know that guy?"

"What guy?" I questioned.

"The guy headed this way."

I looked up, and, sure enough, there he was. This mysteriously devilish man whose name I could only assume was Riley based on the coffee shop's entertainment board the previous night. I didn't have much time to think, he was just suddenly there.

"Hi, guys. I'm sorry to interrupt your evening, but I think this young lady and I met yesterday under some negative circumstances. I just wanted to apologize and finally make appropriate introductions."

The words rolled off of his tongue in a soft but determined tone. His eyes locked on me, apologetic and, for the first time, endearing. My lips felt like they were glued together and, to my dismay, again, no words surfaced—I was too caught up in this unexpected introduction and perhaps the wine, as well. And, to be honest, I was still on the fence about whether I cared to give him the time of day. After a few awkward seconds, Tessa finally saved me from the uncomfortable silence.

"Well, it's a pleasure to meet you. I'm guessing you're the guy who's been the topic of conversation tonight," she announced.

"Really? Well, that's debatably good and bad. My name is Riley, by the way."

"Proctor," I said, awkwardly breaking my silence.

"Yeah... how'd you know that?" He looked at me, surprised.

"I, um, saw it on a sign at the coffee shop yesterday."

"Good observation."

"So, wait a minute," Lowell cut in. "How is it you two have already been introduced?"

"Well, this pretty little lady and I literally ran into each other when I was coming and she was going yesterday. I was rushing and late for my show, and I admit, I should have been kinder to her. Anyway, it was an even bigger surprise to see her here tonight. I felt I owed her an apology." He turned again to look into my eyes and I tried to look away but failed to peel my eyes away from his tempting gaze. I hadn't spoken aloud since referencing his last name and realized I was in a state of shock at the unusual reunion. I mean, how could this amazingly attractive and cordial guy before me now be the same jerk from yesterday?

34

"Well, it's nice to meet you, Riley, I'm Lowell," Lowell initiated and moved to shake Riley's hand, the greeting breaking Riley's eyes from mine.

"Hey, good to meet you, too, man." Riley smiled at all of us, awaiting more introductions. "And who else do I have the pleasure of meeting?"

"I'm Tessa," Tessa exclaimed in a bright bubbly voice and then continued, "This is Brooke." Tessa, sensing my frozen state, saved me by completing introductions.

"It's really nice to meet both of you, and I'm glad I can finally put a name with a face, Brooke." He smiled widely at me, like a boy opening a gift on Christmas morning, and that smile had me feeling all types of ways. My heart thudded uncontrollably, and for a moment, I only heard it beat. I couldn't think or move, just sat statue-like—still in shock, absorbed in my wino thoughts. When again I had no response, I believed he'd certainly make his exit, but he didn't and caught me totally off guard with his next request.

"So, can I grab a seat here for a few minutes? We have a little while before the band goes back on." I felt my face projecting a painful look at the thought of him sitting with us because this current episode of shock and social awkwardness was starting to drain me.

"Of course," Lowell rebounded into the conversation quickly. I guess Riley had passed some informal guy test I was unaware of, but I was barely grasping onto reality at that point. Riley found another vacant chair from a table that had emptied at the band's break. He swung it around backwards and sat with his stomach pressed against the chair's back. He and Lowell started a casual conversation, and my mind melted away into oblivion. Their voices seemed muffled, like a weird out-of-body experience. I needed to say something, anything, to replant myself on earth again.

"Excuse me, but I need to use the ladies' room." *Dear Lord, did I really just say that?* I didn't even grab my purse, just sprang from the chair and darted in the direction I assumed the restroom might be before the red flush of my cheeks displayed my inner embarrassment. I didn't look back. Luckily, I'd guessed right and the restroom was right where I'd presumed. Pushing open a heavy black door, I was immediately halted by a long line of bodies waiting for the bathroom stalls. I didn't really care, and honestly, was a little relieved that it would give me time to clear my fogged brain.

"Seriously, Brooke, snap out of it," I whispered under my breath.

Gradually, I felt like myself again, although definitely tipsy. Still, it made no sense. To begin with, I rarely had a problem talking to anyone. What the hell was my problem now? At any rate, I figured by the time I made my reappearance, this Riley guy would have fled. I would. I had been rude, or at least thought I'd been rude, but still was nowhere near as foul as he was the previous night. I used the fifteen minutes that went by according to my watch as a time to regroup, then retreated back to the table.

After filing through the now re-filled crowd of people, I was utterly astonished to see Riley still at the table talking to my friends. From where I stood, you'd have thought they'd known each other forever. Julie had also returned and was obviously absorbed in conversation with Riley. I thought for sure she would be after this guy; he was too good-looking to pass up. Yet, I could tell from her expression that she was being more informative than flirtatious. I made the approach cautiously.

"Hi, guys," I cut in.

"Hey, Brooke, glad to see you finally met your new acquaintance from yesterday," Julie laughed.

"Yeah, isn't it a crazy coincidence?" My voice was a little shaky, but better than before and I was even able to follow that up with a laugh.

"I'm sorry we didn't get the chance to talk. Hopefully, I'll get that opportunity later." Riley's eyes homed in on me. "I've gotta get back to the stage. Will you be here after the show?"

Glancing hastily at everyone at the table playing third wheel to this awkward turn of events, I knew I was the center of attention at the moment and loathed it. "Uh, maybe? I mean, I'll try."

"I can live with a maybe," he answered, too sure of himself, his eyes only on me. It was uncomfortable yet welcomed.

"Well, guys, it was a pleasure meeting all of you. Tessa, Lowell, Julie, and… Brooke."

I couldn't believe the ease and fluidity with which he repeated everyone's names. "Also, thank you, Julie, for the info. I look forward to our *maybe* meeting later, Brooke."

He exited our little corner of the bar, and after he was out of earshot, everyone's voices ensued with an endless onslaught questions and comments.

Lowell started, "Nice guy."

Tessa followed, "He seems really down to earth and definitely date-worthy, Brooke."

"Date-worthy? Why the hell would you think that? Surely he's completely uninterested, what with his whole charade yesterday at Impresso. Furthermore, I'm curious, what did he mean by 'thanks for the info, Julie'?"

"Wow, Brooke," Julie went on the defense. "First of all, he couldn't take his infatuated eyes off of you, he's totally interested, and secondly, to answer your question, I gave him your number."

"What!" Irritation blasted through my veins.

"Brooke, the guy's interested—maybe he just had a bad day yesterday." Lowell offered a buzzed smile. "And I'd never steer you wrong. You're my girlfriend's best friend. You know I practically look at ya like a sister.

While you were gone, all he did was ask us stuff about you."

"Like what?" I felt the flutter in my stomach from the previous night return. The girls I could brush off, Lowell, on the other hand, would only speak up on an issue like this for a damn good reason.

Tessa went on, "Well, for starters, he wants to know where you're from, what you do, if he's your type..."

"Did you happen to tell him what kind of underwear I wear, too, while you were at it? Good grief. I still think he's an asshole!" I couldn't help but laugh.

"No," Tessa laughed back. "We didn't tell him *everything*, but he assured us he's a down-to-earth guy who just feels really badly about the other night." She paused until I looked at her. "He likes you, Brooke."

"I don't really know what to say. Thank you, I guess. I'm not usually in this position."

Julie turned to me, a serious look on her face. "Brooke, he's a nice guy, super-hot, obviously talented, and completely the opposite of anyone you've ever even had a remote interest in. Give the guy a chance. If he calls, one date isn't the end of the world. I wouldn't give your number to just anyone, you know."

"Fine, alright, we'll see," I sarcastically remarked. Everyone glared at me like I was a three-year-old who'd just thrown a tantrum.

"Fine with me," Julie said.

"Alright," Tessa reluctantly finished.

The night lingered on, and my second glass of wine left me feeling drowsy. The crowd remained continually upbeat with the band's tunes, and I would catch Riley looking back through the hoard of people at me from time to time. I didn't really know how to think or feel about it all, liking and loathing the idea of being distracted by a guy just when I was accepting the predictability of my life. We all enjoyed the music and I couldn't deny the band was talented.

By the time midnight neared, Julie, Tessa, Lowell, and I were all either tipsy or full on drunk. We laughed at each other, finding humor in the most mundane things, no doubt the effects of the alcohol. Regardless, it was nice to kick up my heels. I could feel myself getting sluggish, and my eyelids grew heavy. If I was going to make it home without falling asleep, it was time to leave. I wasn't used to late nights, let alone two glasses of wine that left my heart feeling slightly funny, and furthermore, I wasn't sure how to process the flirtatious advances put upon me tonight by someone I'd wished to never see again only a day ago. If this Riley guy were truly interested, he'd call. Right? Again, I couldn't believe I was even pondering the whole scenario, but the thought of him calling produced knots in my stomach from anticipation.

"Well, guys, I am going to head home."

"Really?" Tessa frowned, sticking out her bottom lip.

"Oh, stay, Brooke!" Julie followed, swaying a little, her words slightly slurred. "You're not going to wait for Mister Riley to finish up?"

"I'm thinking no." I cocked my head. "He'll call if he's interested."

"Alright then, Brooke, play hard to get, adds a fun element," Tessa chided and then gave me a hug. Lowell followed. After I picked up my purse, I gave Julie a hug, too. Before I could pull away, she whispered in her tipsy stupor, "Brooke, don't be afraid to let someone in. You never know. Oh, and he's a cutie," she giggled.

"Okay, Julie," I whispered back, knowing she had sincerely meant it, tipsy or not. I made one last goodbye and headed for the exit, the band in-between songs. What happened next sent shock waves through my already rocked world.

"Brooke?" My name blared through a microphone in front of a room of strangers. I turned immediately to the stage, already knowing whose voice it had been. After obviously getting my attention, Riley continued. "You'll be hearing from me."

Random whistles and chatter rang through the swarm of bystanders. I felt a smile on my face, and Riley followed the comment with a wink. It took all my might to turn back around and attempt to seductively saunter out of the bar, but I managed, fighting the smile on the outside while glowing on the inside. I didn't know if I was ready for anything like this, but, boy, did it leave me feeling breathless.

Chapter Three

The rest of the week moved at a snail's pace so I filled the time cleaning and organizing, a byproduct of being slightly obsessive-compulsive. I filled in the rest of the hours grading papers and creating lesson plans, prepping for the end of spring break, which was now merely a few days away. Mom called, wondering if I'd planned on coming home at all during the break, but I'd decided I'd rather lay low in Austin. She was disappointed, but I'd see her soon enough to meet with the heart doctor in Houston, so I didn't dwell on disappointing her too much. It was better to have her a little disappointed than to have me act mean or annoyed with her micro-mothering me in Houston. It inevitably happened whenever I was with her for too long.

Alf was getting restless, pacing the apartment, dragging his toys all over the place, indicating it was time to get out. I'd hardly left since getting home Saturday night from the bar; the night that had seemed to turn my weekend and my mind upside down. Would this guy Riley actually call? It was Thursday already. Five days had passed, and having not gotten his number, the ball was completely in his court. I tried to not think about him or his potential call, but something in me couldn't resist. I clearly needed to get out of the apartment, not just for Alf, but to use the fresh air to help make some sort of sense of it all. I decided to take Alf somewhere he loved: the park downtown by the lake.

I pulled myself from the bed and turned off the TV, the sky outside looked bright and inviting, the sun shining through the half-opened blinds. Rummaging through my large dresser and an assortment of loungewear and workout clothes, I yanked out some black yoga pants and a gray tank top. When Alf noticed me lacing up a pair of tennis shoes, his inner dog beacon alerted him that a temporary escape of the apartment was approaching and he leapt to attention in anticipation. By the time I went for his leash, hanging from a hook at the front of the apartment, he was barking up a storm, tail wagging with eager readiness as he pawed at the door.

"Calm down, Alf. We'll leave in just a sec, bud." I went to pick up my keys and phone from the entry table and then clipped the leash to Alf's collar.

"Okay, Alf, let's get out of here." I opened the door and he darted out with such force that I nearly tripped over my own feet. By the time I got to the car, his barks had thankfully diminished, but he'd pulled me the whole way. Walking him could really be a workout. I opened the passenger door of the Acura and he hopped right in, knowing his spot well from trips to the park or visits to Mom's.

After he was situated, we made the short trip. Several people were out jogging or walking when I pulled into an empty space. Alf leapt out of the seat when I opened the door, and we headed to the trail. I was careful to pace myself, knowing the doctor wanted me to stay fit but by no means run marathons. A ways into the walk, I decided to stop and rest at a wooded park bench that overlooked the lake and the city skyline. Alf's leash hung loosely at my side, and he took advantage of the moment to lie down on the blanket of grass next to the bench. I stared at the sky. It was beautiful, clear and radiantly blue. The breeze felt relaxing against my cheeks. I lowered my eyes from the sky to the people running and walking along the trail. There were many runners intermingled with couples, young and old, on leisurely strolls. Some held hands and others carried on conversations. I wondered what they might be talking about, imagining varying dialogues in my head. The moment's serenity broke when my cell rang. Alf's head popped up from its resting place on his front paws. I pulled the phone out of my pocket and glanced at the screen, displaying a number I didn't recognize.

"Hello?"

"Hey, pretty lady."

"Hi?"

"It's me, Riley."

"Oh, hi, Riley."

"You wouldn't happen to be wearing black pants and a gray shirt, would you?" he questioned.

"What, are you following me now?" I responded obnoxiously, hoping to continue playing hard to get.

"Well, let's just say it appears we're destined to run into each other."

"You're here?" I replied in surprise.

"Yup, I'm across the lake from you right now. I was jogging and noticed you sitting on the other side. If you look across the lake, I'm waving at you."

Sure enough, there he was, as handsome as I'd remembered him—olive skin, dark hair. This time he was dressed in a white t-shirt with blue shorts that reached his knees—hot, in an athletic sort of way.

"I guess we can't seem to find somewhere the other isn't, can we?" I spoke into the phone while waving back at him.

"Guess not, but I'm glad you and I keep having this problem. I've been meaning to call you all week, but was playing gigs with the band around town. I took off work this week, being spring break, so we squeezed in a few more shows than normal. What are you doing tonight?" Riley asked.

"You know, I haven't decided yet." My voice was cool and collected. I wasn't about to admit my plans were zilch, and I damn sure wasn't about to sound overly interested. The memory of the man-baby I'd met a few days prior was quickly being replaced by this new Riley I couldn't help but admit *was* "date-worthy".

"Feel like getting out?" he asked. It felt like an eternity since my last date.

"Hm?" I said hesitantly, to put him on edge before offering an answer. "Sure."

"Can I pick you up at your place?"

I didn't know this guy from Adam and wasn't sure if I wanted to tell him where I lived. Yet something inside of me pushed me forward. Maybe it had been Julie's conversation at the bar persuading me to relax? I took a breath into the phone before answering. "Alright, do you know where Vine Oaks apartments are, just on the other side of the river? It's just down South Congress a little ways."

Riley didn't waste a minute. "Yeah, I've passed by it a few times. What number is your building?"

"I'm in building ten, apartment 1012."

"Alright, Miss Brooke, I'll pick you up about six-thirty if that's okay."

He seemed to have a knack for being straightforward and polite all at the same time. This new, more attractive Riley was growing on me, setting off a sea of butterflies in my stomach like I'd never experienced before.

"Okay. I'll see you at six-thirty," I answered, then realized he didn't say where we were going, giving me no clue how to dress, and I had every intention of knocking it out of the park. "Wait!" I said. "Where are we going, if you don't mind me asking?"

"Let's just say dinner and then a surprise. I would just put on something you would wear to a casual dinner, but you've look stunning each time I've seen you, so I don't think I even needed to say that." He obviously knew why I'd asked him where we'd be going.

"Nice play, Riley. Are you this debonair with all the girls?" A guy this handsome definitely gets girls all the time; might as well make him realize I wasn't a girl to be played so easily.

"Maybe. I'll see you in a few hours then," he replied without a definitive answer.

"Alright, bye."

I set the phone down on the bench and casually glanced back at him across the lake. He appeared to be all smiles. He waved one last time, and I returned the gesture. He got back to his jog as I slipped the phone back into my pocket.

"Alright, Alf." His head spun obediently around to wait for my next command. "Well, I guess we'll see what this Riley guy is all about. If you don't like him, I guess he won't last long." Alf got to all fours and walked over, setting his head on my lap. I knew it was his way of saying he loved me. "I know, Alf, I love you, too," I looked back into his sweet puppy eyes. "Let's get going, sounds like I need to get ready."

After moving to get up from the bench, Alf followed, and we completed the walk we'd set out on before returning to the apartment.

After Alf had been fed and was settled, I finished the afternoon getting ready for my unexpected dinner date. Feeling my inner fashionista dying to look smoldering-hot, I fumbled through my packed closet and stopped counting after trying on the tenth outfit. I was massively over analyzing this, but then again, it felt a little different, like it wasn't just any date. Eventually deciding on a harlot-red skin-tight sweater that teased by showing my navel, and snug Seven jeans, I finished it off with a pair of black heeled boots, happy with the completed masterpiece before me in the mirror. I made one last trip to the bathroom to take my meds and tousled my hair, followed with a final spritz of perfume on my wrist. Now it was just a matter of waiting for Riley to arrive. I glanced at the clock. It was nearing six-fifteen, and I wondered if he was the early, on-time, or late type. Guess I was about to find out. I rummaged through issues of gossip magazines lined in a perfect row on the coffee table and glanced at the clock with the flip of every page. At six-thirty on the money, there was a knock at the door. Alf huffed small barks and sprung from his nap on the floor beneath my feet.

"It's okay, Alf. I need you to be a good boy for me, alright?"

He stayed right at my side all the way to the door. I suddenly realized that opening this door was either about to open many new things or provide proof after tonight's ending that it had never been anything at all. My heart pounded as my head flipped through a multitude of questions. I pulled myself together, smoothing my hair and outfit, hoping to appear calm and casual. My nerves were out of control.

"Here we go," I said softly to Alf then turned the doorknob.

I took a last deep breath as Riley's figure came into view, devilishly handsome, a head taller than me, dark hair a bit wild. *Boy, did I want to run my fingers through it.* The scent of his cologne was undeniably hypnotic, and I slowly breathed him in. His olive skin glowed, and his dark eyes were entrancing—too entrancing. He wore dark denim jeans and a long-sleeved black sweater with stylish black shoes. For a guy living on an aspiring musician's budget, he dressed exceptionally well.

"Hi," I smiled. "You'll have to pardon me for a second, I think my dog is intent on meeting you before he lets me leave this apartment," I laughed. "His name is Alf."

"I can't blame him. I'd be protective of you, too," Riley chuckled back. I held Alf's collar with one hand as I fully opened the door with the other so that Riley could step inside. Riley immediately ducked down to Alf's level.

"Hey there, buddy. You look just like the shaggy dog but…" He paused briefly, slightly laughing, then continued, "But the shaved version."

"You've seen that movie, too, huh?" I asked.

"Yeah, I remember it from when I was a kid."

"Alf's my baby, and, as for his hair, well, the poor guy would die of heat stroke if I didn't keep it short." Riley squatted and scratched the top of Alf's head. I got down next to him. I was relieved when Alf sat in front of Riley. He'd never really seen a guy around me before, but he seemed to sense that Riley wasn't a threat. Alf took the opportunity to sniff all around Riley's face and torso, and then surprised us both by pawing his hand and creating a priceless moment.

"Good to meet you, too, Alf," Riley responded to Alf's pawing gesture. Riley furthered by asking jokingly, "So, do I get the seal of approval?" Alf just continued pawing at Riley's hand again for attention.

"Yeah, I'd say so," I said coyly.

Riley and I stood back up in the entryway, staring at each other until Riley broke the awkward silence that had built from our locked gaze. "Well, would you like to go to dinner?"

"Oh, right." I'd almost forgotten about dinner altogether, something about Riley overwhelmed my senses. "Of course, let's go."

"You look phenomenal, by the way," he added.

"Thanks, you look phenomenal, too—I mean..." I felt my cheeks blush as intense heat rushed through my face. Why couldn't I keep it cool?

"I'm glad you think so," he said as he cocked his head back with a little grin at me before turning to Alf. "Alright, Alf, hopefully I'll see you again soon." With a final pat on Alf's head, we both stepped for the door and Riley let me lead the way.

I turned back to Alf after we'd both exited the doorway. "Be good for me. I'll be back in a little while, Alf baby." He let out a whimper and sat watching me as I closed the door and locked it.

Riley and I walked down the wide steps of the apartment building to his car side by side. It was a black Chevy Tahoe and sparkled from every crevice. He was obviously clean-cut, both in dress and his vehicle.

"Nice car, Riley."

"Oh, it's just something I've had since college. I finally paid it off."

"Very impressive; it looks brand new."

"I try to keep it that way. My parents always tried to teach me to take care of my things. I guess it stuck."

We neared the passenger door and he opened it for me, closing it after I'd settled into the seat. A minute later, he was situated in the driver's side and we headed off. As he drove, the basic get-to-know-you conversation ensued. It reminded me how little I actually knew about him, and a flash of our first encounter came to mind.

"So, are you from here originally, Brooke?"

"Sort of, I'm from Houston, actually. I decided to stay here after I graduated from the University of Texas a few years back. I love Austin, so after I found a teaching job I decided to call it home. What about you?"

"I'm originally from Chicago. I came down here to get a music degree from Texas, Austin being a growing music mecca and all. I fell in love with the city and, like you, didn't leave after school. Sounds like we may have been there about the same time. How old are you?

"Twenty-six."

"Then, yes, we were probably there around the same time. I'm twenty-eight. Too bad I didn't meet you then."

"It's such a huge school, it's very possible to never meet a fraction of the students who actually go there," I grinned.

"Very true." He smiled back.

"Do you miss your family, living so far away?"

"I'd be lying if I said no. I'm the middle of three kids. I was the only sibling who aspired to chase a crazy pipe dream and attempted to make it in the music business. I think my parents always knew I'd travel whatever distance necessary to give it a real chance. No one else in my family plays music or anything, but they're very supportive. I've got a great group of friends down here, too. I guess I just made my roots here." He focused on the road as we crossed the bridge over the river, and ceased his questioning momentarily until reaching a stoplight. "So, is your family still in Houston?"

"Yeah, well, my mom is. My dad passed away when I was a teenager." Riley's face turned pale, clearly sensing he may have brought up a touchy subject.

"I'm so sorry, Brooke. Were you close?"

I searched his face and offered a smile to lighten the mood and hopefully reassure him that he shouldn't feel bad. "He was the perfect dad to me, and I don't mind talking about him. I have a lot of great memories of him. Please don't feel bad for bringing it up."

Riley glanced over at me, the color returning to his face. "Okay. I wouldn't mind if you talked about him now, or the next time we go out." My heart warmed at the thought that he was already thinking of a next time.

"Of course." I stared out the window a moment then continued. "No one has really asked me to before, besides my mom and my therapist."

"Your therapist?"

"I was kidding. Relax, I don't have a shrink."

I'd gotten used to the way conversations would go once the death of my father was brought up. I dealt with it by immediately putting people at ease. I had people feeling bad enough for me once they figured out I had a heart condition.

Daylight glittered between the buildings and through the window as Riley turned down the busy streets. A few moments passed in silence.

"Do you like sushi?"

"Um…yeah." I cringed slightly, giving away my real answer.

"So, what you're really saying is not no—but, hell no." Riley laughed.

"Sort of—yes." I bit my lip.

Riley laughed again, "Good because I was only kidding. Barbecue's more of what I had in mind."

"Now that's definitely my style. I'm always in the mood for it."

"In the mood, huh? Me, too," Riley kidded. I caught his naughty joke and laughed out loud.

"You know, I have to admit, so far you're completely surprising me, Riley."

"Good surprise or bad surprise?" He winked at me.

"What do you think?" I laughed to make sure he knew it was a good thing—a very good thing.

"Well, I told your friends I was a decent guy, and I'd like to live up to that."

"A decent guy, huh? Then, what was with the angry guy act at the coffeehouse?" I couldn't help but bring it up. The disconnect between that Riley and the one next to me was too perplexing not to. I suppose subtleties weren't a specialty of mine either.

Riley's posture tightened and he looked anywhere but my direction. "I'm sorry about that. I really overreacted. It was, uh… it was a bad day."

"I know I didn't help the situation. You just got a rise out of me, threatening my precious Chanel purse." I laughed again, thinking back to the whole thing. "I guess we can look back and laugh at it now." I suspected a lot more to it all but didn't push Riley further.

He looked over to me and chuckled; however, his eyes seemed vacant. I realized immediately this was a sore subject.

"You won't ever see me like that again, Brooke. I promise."

"I hope not, for your sake," I giggled. In time, I speculated I'd find out why he was so off the day we met.

After pulling into the barbecue joint, the conversation was never-ending, from the moment we sat down at the picnic table nestled under the enormous oaks, to the moment we left after Riley had paid the bill. After a bottle of beer, I'd loosened up a little more and a nonchalant game of footsie was going on underneath the table. The sun was setting and we had talked about our time at U.T., as

well as our past failings in the dating world. I was more
surprised than anything that he didn't admit to dating more.
As handsome as he was, he struck me as the kind of guy
who could get almost any girl he wanted. He did allude to a
long-term ex but didn't offer much else, which was fine
because ex-talk could be a bad move on a first date
anyway. I was getting a better idea of whom Riley was and
was enjoying his company much more than I had expected.
Later, after getting into the Tahoe to leave, he'd let the car
idle for a moment, appearing as if he were debating his
options.

"Are you up for something else?"

"What were you thinking?" A part of me wished he
were referring to something inappropriate. The chemistry
between us was building by the minute. I wanted to close
the gap between us, but I'd leave the first move to him.

Riley playfully continued, "Want to be surprised?"

"Yes."

"Okay, I hope you like it."

"Guess we'll find out. I haven't been disappointed so
far."

***

My lusty thoughts simmered down as we entered the
heart of downtown. The streets teemed with life. I knew
downtown pretty well, but I didn't know what we would be
doing down here, other than going to a bar at this time of
the evening. We turned down a few more streets and then

parked in a small, low-lit parking lot next to an old building.

"Okay, we're here."

"Here, where?" I asked, confused.

"It's an art gallery," he explained.

"Oh. I would have never expected one here. I haven't been to one in years."

A part of me had envisioned him as a schmooze musician who took a girl to a fancy restaurant and then had his way with her after a few drinks at a bar. Thus far, he'd been sincere and interested in getting to know me. He again got the door for me, and we walked side by side to the entrance of the small art gallery. One person was stationed directly inside the old building and took the admittance fee from Riley. As we walked a little further, the room suddenly opened into a very large, brightly lit, ironically modern-designed space. It was stark white, but where the artwork hung, color spoke vibrantly from the walls.

"It's amazing! How did you know about this place?" I asked.

"One of my friends in college was an art major and had a lot of his stuff shown here. I still come here a lot; it's sort of a break from reality. I think we all need that from time to time. When I can't think of any new music to write or it's been a bad week, I come here and indulge in someone else's creativity. Sounds a little corny, I know. You're actually the only other person I've ever brought here."

"It's really great. I'm glad we came. Thank you, Riley."

We started at one end, walking from one piece to the next. The particular artist we were admiring portrayed the local landscapes of the rolling Texas hill country. We stopped midway through the gallery and sat on a bench centered in the room, the light intensely bright and the colorful artwork circling us.

"I'd like to ask you something, Brooke, but I don't expect you to answer. It's really probably too soon for me to ask anyway."

"What?" My heart started double-timing.

"The other night, when you left for a few minutes, your friends said something to me. They said, 'Call Brooke, but only if you are really serious. Brooke is very special.' I got the feeling they were getting at something more. Can I ask what they meant?"

Oh. Of course, Julie and Tessa had said something. It was only our first date and I'd already revealed the baggage of my dead father. I didn't want him to think I was a downer. "They are just really protective of me. We have known each other for years. Besides, do I *not* seem special?" *He can find out another time…*

"I never said that!" Riley exclaimed. "You are. You are very special. I hope I got your friends' approval."

"Well, I'm here now, aren't I?"

"I'm happy you are."

"Me, too." We looked intensely at each other. My body was screaming for his touch and attention. I loved how he looked at me and didn't want him to stop.

"I am hoping you'll let me take you out again."

"I'd like that a lot."

"Then that's settled. Let me concoct something else to entertain you."

"Concoct something? Oh, so this isn't just a natural gift, knowing what will magically keep me enthralled?" I half-laughed.

"Believe it or not, no. Outside of work, I'm a music workaholic. This is very much outside of the scope of my everyday life, but I'm not minding it one bit." Riley's grin and flirtatious eyes reassured me.

"A musician's world is something I'm clueless about. I imagine it's really hectic but rewarding."

"For me, it's a lot of hard work mixed with a lot of hope. Meaning, hope that the band or the music I write will get noticed or in the hands of the right people. I have a day job, believe it or not. I teach music at a local music store to pay the bills, and then play or write music every chance I get. When I'm playing or singing, I feel like I'm truly doing what I was put on this earth for. You definitely meet a lot of women in the music scene, but I am really serious about what I do. I'm not into dating a new girl every night or one-night stands. I think you probably pegged me for the guy who picks up every girl he meets, and while I'd be lying if I said I have never tried, I hardly ever do and haven't for a while now. There was something about you that drew me to you, something that enticed me to pursue this, especially when we randomly saw each other again."

"I feel the same way," I interjected. "I've had the best time tonight, and you're making a cultured woman out of me here. But, do you think we should get out of here? It's nearly ten. Surely this place is going to be closing soon."

"Yes," Riley replied. "It'll close soon. Are you ready for me to take you home?"

"No, not really. My mind says I'm totally up for something else, but my body is begging for some sleep."

"I think we'd better call it a night then. Let's get you home." Riley frowned and then grinned.

We both stood and walked the remainder of the gallery before leaving. This time, his arm was draped across my shoulders as we made the short walk back to his car. His touch set my body aflame. I was angry with myself for not pushing the idea of staying out with him later, but I was very tired. We talked about light things on the way home, like Riley's bandmates and my second-graders. Riley pulled his Tahoe up to my building. We talked for a few more minutes and I wondered what the next few moments would bring.

"Are you ready for me to walk you to your apartment?"

"You don't have to do that," I paused, "but it's not every day I get a man like you at my door."

"Oh, really?" He laughed then got out of the car and opened my door. "It's not every day I get the attention of a woman like you." I couldn't help but blush.

We made the final leg of the night up the steps to my door. Anticipation grew inside me. I fumbled to get my keys in the door but, before unlocking it, turned to find Riley standing directly behind me.

"Can I call you tomorrow?" His face was inches from mine. My heart pounded and I felt a little faint.

"Yes. Definitely." I had to cut the conversation short because I really wasn't sure how much more I could resist him if he didn't make a move.

"I'll talk to you then. It was a pleasure." This was the moment I was so unsure of. Would he turn and leave, or go for a goodnight kiss? I could feel physical heat growing between us and it took everything I had to not jump and close the taunting space with my lips. Riley looked intensely into my eyes. Without breaking eye contact, he gently put his right hand to my face, cupping the side while rubbing my bottom lip lightly with his thumb. Like a ragdoll in his grasp, I was completely at his will. Swiftly, hc took my right hand in both of his, held it to his lips, and kissed it softly and slowly—never rushing the moment. The gesture said more than anything else could have at that moment. After one final look into my longing eyes, he turned to leave, and I watched him disappear down the stairs.

<u>Chapter Four</u>

I never really fell asleep, unable to stop thinking about that night or calm my body's unexpected want for a man, how much I wish it hadn't ended, and how much I looked forward to the next date. Sunlight snuck its way in between the blue curtains and reminded me of the bright light at the gallery where we'd shared an intimate conversation. Alf was still in dog dreamland, huffing little muffled barks in his sleep. Typically, he'd be the one waking me up, but not this morning. I stared at the clock. 7:15 a.m. showed in bright red numbers. So much for sleeping in.

I spent time trying to do anything but think about Riley—all attempts failed. Hours felt like days, wondering what would come next from this guy who'd suddenly appeared in my generic life. I'd always thought I wanted simplicity, but a big wrench had just been thrown into the mix. As uncomfortable as it made me feel, deep down somewhere inside, a part of me was budding to life.

The day crept by until my cell jingled and I leapt from my bed to search for it eagerly beneath a stack of folded laundry on the living room sofa.

"Hello?"

"Brooke, it's Riley." My heart thudded. "How are you?"

"I'm great, just getting caught up on some things. You?"

"Good, just working, but at least it's Friday, right? You have the day off, don't you? No school for spring break?"

"Yeah."

"I wondered if you had plans Sunday." *Sunday?* Two whole days from now. Instant disappointment penetrated my spirit. I'd barely made it a day, and now I had to wait two more? *Act cool, Brooke, play the super-busy card too even if it's a lie. Think, think—yoga, TV...*

"Oh, Sunday. No big plans."

"Good, because I have the day all planned. Breakfast and dinner."

"Alright, I guess I'll see you Sunday morning."

"Probably about ten. I wanted to do something sooner, but the band and I are headed to Dallas tonight after work. We're playing a show there tomorrow and then plan on heading back afterwards."

"Oh, alright, I'll plan on seeing you Sunday then." My confidence slowly regained its footing knowing he had other obligations, but I still couldn't help feeling discouraged.

"Can't wait to see you on Sunday, Brooke."

"You, too. Bye." I hung up and fell on top of the neatly folded laundry on the couch. Alf appeared a few minutes later to join me.er

"Sunday sure feels like a long way off, Alf. This guy is really doing something to me." He looked at me as if recognizing the difference in me, too. I wanted to spend time with Riley; to get to know him. We'd only been on one measly date, yet he consumed my every thought. I was in for a long weekend. On the verge of accepting the idea that the weekend would have me on a combination of pins and needles and bored out of my mind, the phone rang yet again. But this time, it wasn't Riley. Tessa's number and sunny face were displayed on the screen.

"Hi, Tessa," I answered.

"Hi, Brooke. Just thought I'd check to see how your week was going and see if you wanna grab lunch tomorrow at Baker's?"

"It's been really good, actually. I went out with Riley last night. That guy from the bar last weekend."

"Brooke, how could I forget him? That's so great! You have to tell me everything!" she nearly shouted with enthusiasm into the phone.

"I thought you would say that. Yeah, let's do lunch. I'll tell you everything then. But I will say that I was more than pleasantly surprised." It was a nice change to be the one with juicy news. I'd always been the one listening. The thought of dishing about my date to my friends filled me with a girly giddiness that I hadn't felt since high school. It only added to my growing anticipation for Sunday.

"I can't wait to hear everything. I'll meet you tomorrow at one."

"I'll be there. Bye, Tess."

"Bye."

***

After tackling a trip to the grocery store, I read a steamy romance—fitting for the mood I was in but only amplifying my already lusty thoughts about the next time I'd see Riley. When the sun began to fade, relief came over me. There was only one more day until I'd see his perfect face, and at least on Saturday I had plans with Tessa to help pass the time.

I spent the day's final hours tackling needed tasks for class Monday, when I remembered I'd forgotten a bag of groceries in the car. "Shit, the milk!"

After bolting downstairs to the car, I climbed back up the steps, carrying the half-gallon container. When I had almost reached the door, the feeling of faintness I'd learned to dread made my body feel abruptly weak. My heart wouldn't slow down, and a sharp pain seared through my chest. I instantly dropped, crouching just outside the apartment. I forced slow, deep breaths, as I often did when

67

my heart had these episodes, and felt the adrenaline-filled anticipatory energy of seeing Riley that I'd carried throughout the day leave my body. *Yoga breathing, Brooke. In through the nose, out through the mouth.* Slowly pushing myself up against the door after the palpitations had slowed, I maneuvered to the bathroom, straight for my medicine, then fell on the bed. Alf appeared at my side, sensing that something wasn't right as he often seemed to do during these episodes. It reminded me how thankful I was for him.

"I'm okay, Alf," I groaned in response to another bout of heart pain. Alf sat, ears perked at attention as I rested my hand on his head.

***

Eventually succumbing to sleep, the same dream I'd often had about Dad on a bridge flooded my slumber.

"Daddy!" I sat straight up in my bed and wiped an accumulated layer of sweat from my forehead. I took one deep breath, Dad's face still fresh in my mind. I was comforted by the soft morning light in my room, relieved it was daytime. As silly as it seemed, I knew I'd be okay when I went to bed the night before, but the idea always lingered of the "what if". What if I didn't wake up? I spent the morning soaking in the tub, my mind and body exhausted from the night before. It was only then that I realized I actually hadn't thought about Riley since forgetting the damn milk, which was probably for the best because he had been consuming my every thought.

***

Tessa was already at a table on the patio at Baker's overlooking the lake when I arrived, her hair in a perfectly placed ponytail. She sported shorts and a cute, fitted, powder-pink tee.

"Brooke!" Tessa sprung from the table and hugged me.

"Hi, Tessa. How have you been?"

"Girl, I'm great. Sort of bummed our time off work is almost over, but Lowell and I have been making the most of it. We're headed to San Antonio tonight for a little last minute get away. God, I love time off. "

"Sounds like fun. Eat some Mexican food for me."

"Ha, I will." She smiled, paused a minute, and then she couldn't help herself.

"So, Brooke, let's get down to business. You have to tell me everything. Is this Riley guy really as amazing as he seemed at the bar or was it all an act? Oh, and was it a take me to bed date, or just the nice getting to know you kind?"

"Whoa! Wow. I think you're more excited about this than I am." I giggled.

"Heck, yeah, I am. This is a major new development in the world of Brooke. Aren't you ecstatic? He's a hunk."

"Ecstatic, yes, but I still hardly know the guy. All signs point to good things though, I think. I feel something there, something words can't really describe. To answer your

69

question, Tessa, he is, he's... well, he's so the last thing I ever expected."

"I can't believe it. It's like everything is changing for you, literally, in the span of a week. There is a new light to your eyes, like you opened a door you never knew existed."

"Actually, I think that's putting it pretty close to perfect, Tessa."

The waiter came to the table, breaking the conversation. We ordered the usual; our favorite fried chicken salads and fell back into intense conversation about Riley and the date. She listened with wide eyes and, by the end of lunch, they'd nearly popped out of their sockets with intrigue.

"He sounds like a heck of a catch, Brooke. When will you see him again?"

"He said he had something up his sleeve for tomorrow but he had to go out of town this weekend first. His band is playing in Dallas. As stupid as it sounds, I've been like a corny lovesick teenager, anxious for tomorrow to finally get here."

"That's not stupid," Tessa cut in. "I can totally remember those first days with Lowell. All I wanted was to spend every possible second with him. I knew he was the one when I never wanted that feeling—or need, whatever you want to call it—to stop. I still don't. That's how I know Lowell and I are meant to be. I think Julie thinks we overdo things a bit, but I hope someday, when she finds that special person too, she'll lay off and understand. I'm thrilled for you. You deserve this."

Tessa's words meant so much and definitely cast influence on my decisions. Not having any siblings of my own, she was the closest thing to a sister I had. She wouldn't steer me wrong.

"Thanks, Tessa."

After finishing our second glass of iced tea, we wrapped up lunch and each headed our separate ways.

With Sunday so near, enthusiasm budded in me on the way home, and nearly sent me through the roof with delight when I walked up to the apartment steps to find an enormous bundle of brilliant roses carefully wrapped in colored paper. Clipped to them was a note.

Brooke,
Couldn't help myself. See you very soon.
Riley

Chapter Five

The next morning, after dressing in *very* fitted skinny jeans I knew accented my slim curves just right, I paired them with a cream, long-sleeved shirt with lace accents around the neckline and wrists. I sipped a cup of Earl Grey tea at the kitchen table, staring at the amazingly beautiful roses starting to bloom. Their scent lingered throughout the apartment, reminding me of Riley every second. This weekend had been better than I had initially bargained for, allowing me the opportunity to sit back and reflect on everything. The final verdict: I couldn't deny how ready I was to see him again. Tessa's words rang in my ears. She'd said the eagerness to be with Lowell never went away and that's how she'd known he was the one. Was it possible that person for me was entering my life now, after never thinking it was in the cards?

A knock at the door broke my trance. The weekend wait was over, and I briskly walked to open it without hesitation. There he stood, all six feet of scrumptiousness, and the immediate scent of his cologne consumed me.

"Riley. Hi."

"Hi, Brooke. How are you?" He immediately went to hug me, and my knees nearly gave out during the embrace. I managed to stay upright, holding onto his perfectly toned back and shoulder muscles.

"Good so far. Did your band's stuff go well?" I asked, somehow bringing myself to pull away from his chest. I looked up at him and was instantly pulled into his gaze. It seemed, in one way or another, when I was with him, the physical connection was unbreakable and our emotional connection rapidly followed suit.

"Wasn't too bad. We had a great turnout, but I was definitely ready to get back. I've been looking forward to this all weekend."

"Me, too." The readiness in my voice couldn't be overlooked. Alf rushed to the door after hearing Riley and me in conversation. He barked his way from my bedroom to the door and upon seeing Riley, became even more excited at the return of his newfound friend.

"Alf, buddy, how are you?" Riley knelt down to scratch both his ears.

"Well, I guess that makes two of us happy to see you," I joked. "But I'm eager to figure out this breakfast surprise you have in mind. Are you ready?"

"Yes, I'm ready. Let's get out of here and get you some breakfast." Riley gave Alf a final pat on the head. "Later, buddy. Don't worry, I'll take great care of her." He stood back up and turned towards me, again looking intently into my eyes, igniting my body in a way I had never felt before. His face was tantalizingly close to mine. His lips. His hands. My dazed stupor was broken as his left hand made its way to the small of my back while the other opened the door for me. I wanted to melt into his arms, close the door and take him to my bedroom then and there. Then reality intruded and I remembered it was an early Sunday morning and he was still basically a stranger to my world.

After hitting the road in Riley's Tahoe, I couldn't help but ask, "Where are we headed?"

"Have you ever heard of The Donut Hut?" he replied.

"Actually, I have. It's a little donut shop north of town, right?"

"Yup. Have you been there?"

"No. But I've heard they're world-famous and crazy good."

"I can't lie, they're damn good." Riley's voice was upbeat, and had me looking forward not only to the supposedly amazing donuts, but our day together, too. We continued on the car ride north and I took advantage of the opportunity to ask as many questions as possible, mostly about his music.

"So, Riley, tell me more about the band. You talked a lot about music and stuff the other night, but I didn't get to talk to you much about the actual band." Riley's face was easy to read; he was obviously happy I was interested in his world.

"Well, we started together midway through college. Two of us were music majors, and the others were local musicians we'd run into. We just sort of meshed musically. We named the band Waiting to Win and then started playing anywhere around town that would let us. We'd all dreamt of making it big. I had bigger aspirations than just pursuing a music degree and working in a music store teaching lessons. I want to reach people with our music."

"So, what made the band decide on the name, 'Waiting to Win'?" I swiped a piece of loose hair behind my ear and spied Riley eyeing my legs. *So happy I chose these jeans.*

"We decided on the name because the name itself is a goal. We're all waiting to win in this industry, to truly make it."

"I think that's awesome. When did you start playing music?" I asked then bit my lip to hide the smile I felt from his obvious ogling of my legs.

"I started when I was twelve. I don't really know what possessed me, but I convinced my parents to get me a guitar for my birthday, and then began lessons shortly after. I was hooked from day one, haven't put my guitar down since. I started writing music in high school and found that I loved that even more than just playing."

"I wish I had a gift as great as that," I complained, but continued, "Of all the millions and billions of people on earth, there are really only a few who can do extraordinary things, people who really seek out more than just the norm. I envy your gift."

"You don't think you have a gift?" Riley questioned.

"Not really. No real God-given, recognizable talents like you've been blessed with.

"Brooke, you have to admit teaching is a huge gift. Hardly anyone I know would have the patience for what you do. You change lives, shape minds. Didn't you ever see it that way?"

"No. There isn't much I have patience for, actually, but my kids are an exception. Maybe teaching is my gift. Huh, that's funny." I wrinkled my nose.

"What's funny?"

"I never thought about teaching like that. It was always something I enjoyed and didn't royally suck at."

"Well, it's a gift, I promise." His eyes met mine for only a second but for the first time I made out small specks of hazel in them. "On another note, want to come out to a show or two sometime?"

"Of course. You didn't even have to ask."

"I'd love it if you could. It's not glamorous by any means. I have to warn you of that."

I decided to be brave. "As long as you're there, I don't think I'd care one way or the other about the glamorous stuff."

For the first time, I actually caught Riley blush through his olive skin. "I have to tell you ahead of time, though; I'm notorious for being a wimp at staying up late. It's never really been my forte after my whole heart thing happened. I get tired easily."

"What?" Riley asked seriously.

"Huh?" *Shit.*

"You're whole heart thing?"

Oh, damn, Brooke, you haven't told him yet! "Yeah, my whole heart thing... It's nothing. I just get tired if I overexert myself, that's all." Riley's face looked like a girl had just told him she was pregnant. "Don't look at me like that; it's nothing bad!" Riley finally relaxed a few awkward moments later. I hesitated to look at him, and he picked up on the vibe that I didn't want to talk about it. He didn't pry further.

"Brooke, you don't have to prove anything to me, including staying out 'til all hours. Five minutes looking at those baby blues would make my day."

I was warmed from head to toe by his words, and falling fast, not really caring about anything else.

***

We drove so far north that the landscape changed from city to rural. It was kind of nice to have a change from the city skyline. When we reached the bakery, it was packed. A line extended beyond the doorway with a dozen or more bodies stacked one after the other. Riley parked and we walked to wait in line, the morning air still cool and the sky foreshadowing a beautiful day ahead.

"These have to be some crazy-good donuts with this line." I smiled up at Riley.

"I'm telling you, you'll wonder why you've never had one sooner after you try one."

While we waited, Riley stood behind me and rested his hands on my shoulders, rubbing my arms in a gentle motion that gave me goose bumps. I felt as if his hands already knew me, even though they'd never really touched me before.

After the long wait, Riley bought a small box of donuts and we found an empty table. After the first bite, I was in sugar heaven.

"Holy cow! No lie, these are so good!"

"Told you." Riley grinned, his own mouth half full of donut.

"We'll have to do this more often."

"I don't have any problem with that," Riley assured me.

I gobbled down a donut, my mouth full when he asked, "Brooke, would you mind telling me more about your father?"

"Oh." My face clenched a bit. It wasn't at all what I'd expected to talk about with the lighthearted spirit of the day, but I'd already opened the door about Dad on our last date.

"Is... that okay? I mean, we don't have to."

"Yeah, no, it's okay. It's not bad. I'm just not used to telling many people about him." I wiped sugary glaze from my fingers with a napkin and licked my lips. "Hmm... what should I say about him? Well, his name was Tom, Tom Denton. He was an exceedingly loving father. Always there, never missed anything I was ever a part of, sports, school functions, you name it. He was very tall; a handsome man. We have the same eyes and dark hair."

I looked down at the ground for a moment, and then back up at Riley, realizing this wasn't as difficult to talk about as I'd feared.

"The way he loved my mom is how I want to be loved. Always supportive, always there, loving her beyond all words. The last day I had with him, he told me how proud he was of me. I'd just gotten my grades at school, all A's. Before bed, he'd kissed my forehead and said he loved me. It was the last time I saw him alive. I am thankful for our last moment together. It made a horrible situation a tad easier. But it was anything but easy." I took a deep breath of morning air until my lungs were full. Riley lightly touched the top of my hand with his. I felt my eyes glaze a little.

"I'm sorry. I probably shouldn't have asked."

"No, I'm glad you did, Riley. I sometimes feel like I'm starting to forget him. I don't want to do that. Talking about him makes him real again." I batted my eyelashes to keep a tear from escaping and shook back any residual forming tears. Remembering Riley had said he'd made dinner plans; I took the opportunity to change the topic.

"So, you also said you had dinner plans for us. What have you been scheming?" I questioned and raised my perfectly plucked eyebrows.

"Actually, I am beginning to like surprising you, so I'm not telling. Let's just say the more comfortable the attire, the better."

"I have to say, so far, your surprises have been five-star, so I won't attempt to pull this one out of you." Riley snickered at my response and delightedly gazed at me with his enticing eyes.

***

The drive home went by too fast for my liking. It seemed like there wasn't enough time when I was with Riley, and too much time in between our moments together. After arriving back at the complex, Riley walked me back to the apartment and I asked him one last time about tonight.

"So, when you said wear something comfortable, does that mean jeans? A dress?" *Lingerie.*

Riley leaned over me, a hand on either side of the wall behind me, and peered into my eyes, "I'll leave it up to you. Either one works."

"You know you're not helping me here," I joked as my pulse quickened.

"I know, that's the point." He offered a mischievous smile. "I'll pick you up at five. I know you have school starting up tomorrow. I won't keep you out too late. You trust me, don't you?"

"Yeah, I do." He pushed back from the wall and pulled me with him into a hug then released me and cradled my face in his hands. He finished with a kiss to my forehead, sending shivers down my shoulders.

"I'll see you soon, Brooke."

My heart was on fire. I could find no flaws in him, at least nothing I had a problem overlooking because those flaws made him who he was, and I didn't want to change a single thing about him. He had me. Yes, he did.

<u>Chapter Six</u>

What was in the cards next? Scenarios rushed through my mind that I hadn't contemplated before now. Was Riley someone I could trust with my heart? What would happen if it ended badly? Could my heart take it—literally? I'd never given it to anyone and I was terrified of what hadn't even started. If I didn't try, I'd never know, and I'd rather risk the consequences versus never discovering what this could be.

Alf followed me all day, from the very second I'd arrived home. It amazed me the intuition my dog had, as if he were totally in tune with my emotions, like he could sense things. Alf finally crashed on his doggy bed after hours of following me non-stop.

I paced back and forth in my closet, wondering what to wear based on Riley's hints. I was going casual for sure. Twirling my hair with my fingers, I scoured the closet for ideas, finally deciding on my favorite pair of dark denim Levi's and a brand new white silk top with strategically chosen matching bra and panties underneath. Satisfied I looked as hot as casual would allow, I reflected on the conversation we'd had that morning about Dad. I thought about my father often, but actually discussing Dad with someone else reminded me of him even more. I'd expected it to hurt, but, on the contrary, it had been nice. Dad would've really liked this guy, reassuring me even further that it all seemed so perfectly right for a reason.

As five rolled across the clock, I inventoried my purse, making sure I hadn't forgotten anything; phone, keys, lip gloss; it was all there. I set the small, vintage leopard-print purse on the table by the door and completed the nightly routine for Alf. Filling Alf's food bowl, I heard a knock at the door. Riley's arrivals were becoming habit, and I opened it with the giddiness of a schoolgirl. Riley appeared as excited as me, judging by his marvelously handsome grin.

"Your outfit's perfect for what I have planned," he winked.

As he looked me over with eager eyes, I took the moment to do the same. It was now obvious the guy could be good-looking in anything, making jeans and a brown pullover hooded sweatshirt look hot. Not only that, but the brown in his sweatshirt made his dark eyes even richer.

"Is that so? What do you have up your sleeve?" I asked.

"You'll see," he assured me. "Ready to go to my place?"

"Your place? You bet. I'm ready when you are."

***

The car ride was short. We pulled into a garage below a building I'd seen a hundred times in the years I'd lived in Austin. It was a warehouse-style apartment building on the outer rim of downtown. He pulled into a parking spot located near an elevator in the garage. After getting out, we entered the elevator and he hit the button for the twelfth floor. Riley stood on one side and I was on the other. We stared at each other with such vigor, creating undeniable physical tension in the air. He casually looked me up and down and, for a split second, had the hungriest look on his face; hunger for me. I was glowing on the inside. I wanted him to want me. After reaching his floor, we strolled down a short white hallway to a door located at the end.

"This is me," Riley said, opening the door.

Immediately upon entering, an enormous room came into view, full of large bay windows and old hardwood floors, the ceilings nearly two stories tall.

"This is great, Riley. What a place."

"I won't lie, it's been pretty nice. I wouldn't be able to afford a place like this on my own, though. I have a roommate. His name's Troy, but he's out for most of the night. He's in a band, too."

"I must say, you boys didn't do too shabby finding this apartment." I continued to scan my surroundings, walking next to Riley. I noticed guitars resting on stands, a piano,

84

and other miscellaneous musical equipment organized with great care in an open area next to two black leather sofas. The entire apartment was one large space, only dissected by a small kitchen and the strategic arrangement of the furniture. The décor was simple, but the view was phenomenal and enough decoration in and of itself. The downtown skyline could be seen from the large windows on the back wall. "I can't believe your view. Wow," I continued in awe.

"You like it?" Riley smiled. "I've seen better," he said, looking down at me.

"Oh, stop." I lightly pushed his shoulder and smiled.

The sun was beginning to set and the range of colors flowed through the windows and onto us. It was indescribable against the skyline. I wanted to take it all in. This was all starting to feel like a dream, almost too good to be true.

"Are you ready for dinner, Brooke?" Riley moved behind me like he had while in line this morning, resting his hands on my shoulders. I wanted to turn around and embrace him but withheld the desire—secretly enjoying the chase of it all.

"Yeah, I am," I said.

"We're going to head upstairs, to the roof."

"The roof?" I felt my brow rise.

"Yes," Riley replied and pointed upward. "This apartment's on the top floor. If you like the view in here, wait until to see it from up there."

He let his hands slide slowly down my shoulders and set his right hand in mine to guide me up a set of small stairs that spiraled up to a narrow hallway overlooking the main area of the apartment. There were two white doors that led to what must have been bedrooms in the hallway, and beyond them another large, heavy, industrial gray door that revealed more steps upward, out of the apartment area. We traveled the stairs up to the roof with my hand still in Riley's. It felt more natural than I could have ever anticipated. When we reached the top of the steps, what awaited me was a scene I'd never forget. A TV and couch, which had seen better days, were out in the open air of the rooftop. There was a box of pizza and bottle of red wine on a blanket laid in front of the couch, with a few candles scattered about. *Oh, boy, he knows what he's doing.*

"Surprised?" Riley asked.

"Oh, gosh, yes. This is more than I ever imagined. Thank you."

"I wasn't sure which wine you'd like, so I guessed red but I grabbed some water, too."

"I love red! This is really so sweet, Riley."

"I hoped you'd like this. Ready to see the view?" Riley continued.

I nodded my head yes and he proceeded to guide me to the edge of the rooftop. There were no words for how beautiful the city buildings were in the setting sun. I stared at the twinkling lights starting to show from the buildings as the sun lowered in the sky.

"Wow. I'm speechless."

"I'm glad it makes you happy," Riley said, smiling. We both stood staring at the city. It was a surreal moment, and we both seemed to take it in with great prospect of what the night could bring. The urge to kiss him was irrefutable and I was beginning to desperately want it more and more with every passing moment. After a few minutes had passed, we moved to the worn couch and spent an hour eating pizza, drinking wine, and laughing. I couldn't remember the last time I'd felt this happy. Truly, truly happy. As dinner wrapped up, I asked,

"So, what movie are we watching tonight?"

"Do you like *Uncle Buck*?"

"Are you kidding? I love that movie. It's hilarious."

"You know, Brooke, I'm finding out more and more that you're pretty easy to please."

"Really? I guess when you are not a very exciting person, the littlest things can seem perfect."

"You need to give yourself more credit."

"Okay, okay, maybe it's the wine, but it's true. I've always seen myself as fairly plain, except for my impeccable fashion sense," I giggled.

"I don't think you're plain. I think you're beautiful," he said with sincerity.

"Of all the beautiful women in this city, you think *I'm* beautiful?"

"More than you know."

My knees were tucked against my body, facing Riley on the couch a mere foot away. I had a glass of red wine in one hand and my opposite arm against the back of the sofa, using it as a rest for my head. We stared at each other silently for a moment before Riley picked up the conversation again.

"You're the first person I've ever met who's so amazing in every aspect, and I want to know you more...." He paused a moment as if debating his next words then finished, "More than I've ever wanted to know anyone else."

I gave him a disbelieving look and he shook his head. "Don't give me that look, it's not the wine talking."

My cheeks were inevitably ablaze from the wine and the raw emotion being thrown at me. It was true, though, everything he'd said. "I know what you mean, I feel the same way about you." Not knowing how to properly follow up on what I'd just said or deal with the vulnerability of voicing my feelings, I quickly changed the topic. "Well, we'd better get to watching this movie, don't you think?"

"Sounds good to me. Ready if you are," Riley hopped up to turn on the TV and hit 'Play'. He sat back down on the old couch, this time a little closer than before and reached for my hand. Every time he inched closer to me, my heart beat faster. Waiting for him to make a move was killing me, but I was truly enjoying the sweet ride, knowing that when our lips finally did meet it would be well worth it. The first half of the movie passed, and, to be honest, I didn't pay attention to it. All I could think about was what I prayed came next, the kiss. His lips on mine. His body on mine. A moment when I could experience Riley in a whole other way, knowing it could only be better than the feelings that came simply from his hands touching mine. I couldn't believe I was really here, now, wanting this so intently. I glanced over at Riley—his gaze was locked on me.

"Everything okay?" I said awkwardly. *What was I thinking? Is everything okay?*

"More than okay. I'm not really watching the movie."

"Hm," I somewhat laughed under my breath. "Me neither."

"You want me to take you home? I know you have work early tomorrow. I'd hate to keep you out too late."

"No, I don't want to go," I affirmed. I didn't intend to waste one moment of the night.

"I was hoping you'd say that," Riley replied and then shifted to face me. What happened next didn't leave me much time to contemplate. Inches from his handsome face, it required him little effort to pull me in, gently wrapping both his hands around my waist. His lips met mine and I felt weightless. It was more than I'd hoped for. His lips were gentle but intense, and kissing him felt so right. After a few moments, he pulled away, and our eyes opened to find each other awaiting the other's response. I didn't waste a second, moving my hands to his warm cheeks and leaning in for another kiss, but this time he followed my lead. The second kiss, less hesitant than the first, was even better and lasted longer. My hunger for him became insatiable. I lost all sense of reality and felt tingles run up my spine before it finally ended. I knew in that very second, this was it. He was more than just some guy whose path had crossed mine on a random day in a random coffee shop, but rather a person whose entire being connected with mine.

As our kissing continued, passion took control. Without breaking our embrace, Riley slowly laid me down on the couch. We kissed deeper and deeper—at times gasping for air, neither one of us wanting to stop the growing need for one another's bodies. I wrapped my legs around his torso to bring him in closer to me. As close as he was to me already, I needed him closer. I wanted to be engulfed by him. My hands moved under his shirt, revealing his perfectly toned and muscular back to me.

"Brooke."

"Yes, Riley," I said playfully.

"It's nearly ten, I should take you home." He pulled back and got up from the couch.

"Oh, you should?" I couldn't believe that he was getting up. I felt a little embarrassed that I clearly had less self-control than he did. I sat back up, letting reality set back in. I did have work in the morning and, if I didn't leave now, I knew what would happen. "Yeah, I guess it's time to go."

We walked hand and hand to his car. It all seemed like a blur. The car ride back was spent joking about the movie, what our upcoming weeks were looking like, and Riley's love of Bob Dylan. Once home, he walked me to my door in true gentlemanly fashion.

"I can't tell you how great this night was, Riley."

"It couldn't have been better," Riley assured me. "I'll call you tomorrow."

"You'd better," I laughed. Riley lifted my chin gently and we ended the night with one last kiss.

Chapter Seven

Going back to work was a hard, fast dose of reality. It was great to be back teaching, but it made the previous week seem somewhat distant and dreamlike. Riley was true to his word and called as soon as he got off work Monday afternoon. I learned that Riley practiced with his band two nights a week, which didn't leave as much time as I'd hoped to spend together. We settled on Thursday night to meet up again, making my week feel never-ending. The kids were as restless as I was as the days following spring break crept along. I pondered how these kinds of feelings towards Riley could suddenly fall out of the sky and change me so quickly; the desire to see him again growing within my heart.

Thursday afternoon, I wrapped up grading papers and preparing for my substitute teacher so I could make my appointment in Houston on Friday, and watched the clock the entire time, minute by minute. At five-thirty, I flew out the door, only to hit Austin rush-hour traffic, all the while on a single mission to get home and fit a shower in before

Riley came by. Yet, with each passing minute, my available window of opportunity diminished. Finally arriving at the apartment, I darted for the bathroom, showering quickly and throwing on a pair of old jeans and a fitted black shirt.

"Oh, yeah—medicine," I reminded myself aloud and scrambled for the bathroom. I popped open the pill bottles and threw my head back, swallowing hard without a glass of water. The bottles jingled with only a few pills left, reminding me that they would soon need to be refilled. But I could get more after my regular checkup tomorrow in Houston. It was just another reminder that I would miss an entire weekend with Riley, and even worse, that I would have to take another dose of reality and deal with an update about my heart. Sometimes I felt like an eighty-year-old woman, with all the pills and appointments. But what choice did I have?

Alf let out back-to-back barks at a knock from the door, breaking my self-loathing thoughts. By the time I reached the door, Alf's massive body was jumping up and down.

"Alf, calm down… sit." He halted at my command, sitting but continuing to bark. Shimmying my way between Alf and the door, I smiled at the sight of Riley.

"Hi," I greeted him and continued, "Come on in." Alf's barks stopped when he realized it was his now-familiar friend. He paced around Riley, smelling his legs and feet. Riley acknowledged him immediately, patting

93

him on the head before he walked over to me, now leaning against the back of my living room sofa.

"Hey, you." Riley picked me up at the waist, twirling me once and kissing my lips. They were just as I'd remembered them, and I realized how much I'd missed his kiss. "Mmm," Riley sighed. "It's good to see your smile, Brooke."

"You, too. I've been looking forward to this all day." It was so good to know we enjoyed each other so much, and after our newfound lip-locking enjoyment had ensued, Alf pawed at our legs, breaking the embrace. "What do you say we go to dinner?" Riley asked, sneaking in one last kiss.

"I'm absolutely starved. What did you have in mind?"

"There's a little Italian place on Fifth. Does that sound good?"

"I'm always up for Italian." I laced my fingers with his at my agreement for our dinner plans.

"I have an idea," Riley spoke while twisting a ringlet of my hair with his free hand. "Why don't we come back and take Alf for a walk together after dinner tonight? We can head down to the lake if you want."

"I think we'd both like that a lot," I answered. With all plans for the evening finalized, we hit the town. The restaurant was quaint, with a family-oriented vibe. The typical red and white-checkered tablecloths donned the tables, with candles and a single flower in a vase. It was simple but romantic just the same. From an outsider's view, we must have looked bitten by the love bug, without the ability to unglue our gazes from one another.

For once, I understood Tessa's words about Lowell. How she couldn't wait for every moment she'd ever had with him. It seemed premature to think of such things, yet I felt like Riley was someone I'd known all along, like a piece of a puzzle that was waiting to be filled. During the middle of dinner, Riley mentioned he had a gig the upcoming weekend.

"The show Saturday is going to be a little packed, but tomorrow night, Friday, it should be pretty low-key. I'd love for you to come to either or both, but I'm not going to get greedy," he said.

"Well, I'd be there for sure, except…" I hesitated for a moment. "I have the day off work tomorrow and I'm headed to Houston for my appointment, just my regular checkup with my… uh, heart doctor."

"What? A heart doctor?" In an instant, his hand was on mine, his face worried. "I thought you said you just get tired. That's not the whole story, is it?" Luckily, his tone was more cautious than mad. I don't think I could handle him being mad at me for not telling him.

"I usually always go up on a Friday and then make a girls' weekend of it with my mom. I hesitated to tell you. It's something I don't want you to dwell on. I don't want it to change how you feel or act towards me."

"Brooke, I promise that won't happen. You can tell me anything. I want you to."

"It's a long story."

"Please?"

I looked down at the table, getting my thoughts together before beginning to tell Riley my vibe-killing medical history. "Okay, basically, not long after my father died, things started happening to me. My breathing would get rapid for no reason, I felt weak at times, and other things I'd just brushed off as going through grief over the loss of my dad. Then one day I actually passed out during a volleyball practice in high school. After the doctors had run a bunch of tests, they told me I had a heart condition called cardiomyopathy, or, in normal terms, an enlarged heart. They assured me it was caught in the early stages and controllable, so they prescribed me medicine and then I had an ICD implanted in my chest just before college, which definitely helps, too. If more intense and invasive surgeries are needed, it seems right now it would be many years off, but they also warned that the condition could worsen at any time."

"Wow, that's pretty intense, Brooke. Are you scared?"

"No. I mean… I was at first, but not now. I've been pretty healthy so far. I go to Houston every three months for checkups. On top of it all I have a dre—…" I paused, wondering if it would seem far-fetched, but bit my lip briefly and continued, "I have this recurring dream every

96

time I have an episode with my heart. I dream the same thing and know I'll be okay."

"What happens in the dream?" Riley questioned, staring deeply into my eyes.

"They started happening shortly after my dad's passing. My dad is waiting for me at the other side of a bridge. He's vibrant and very much alive there. It's a beautiful place, and I know he's okay. I feel like he's waiting for me if it's ever my time to leave this world. I have peace knowing he'll be waiting for me in whatever is beyond this life." I stared off into the dining room of the restaurant, not wanting to see Riley's reaction. My words were deep and my condition more serious than I'd let on. He might be totally freaked out or not want to get involved with someone like me now. I looked away because I was afraid to lose him.

"Brooke, look at me." I didn't. "Okay, your friends are right then, you are special." He looked intently into my eyes. "If you think I'm going to bolt, which I get the impression you do, I'm not."

I sat speechless. "I'm sorry I didn't tell you sooner. You probably weren't expecting all of this. I promise there aren't any other sob stories tucked away anywhere. If I were here this weekend, I'd be at your show—both of them."

"I'm bummed you won't be here this weekend, but your heart should definitely come first. I'm glad you told me though." Riley paused for several seconds and then looked straight at me. "Hey, would you mind if maybe… sometime down the road, I…" Riley paused mid-sentence, in obvious deliberation.

"What?" I couldn't help but ask, hoping he'd continue.

"This is definitely hasty and all, I realize, but down the road, maybe I could go to an appointment with you so that I can learn more about it."

I couldn't believe the words coming out of his mouth. No one had ever asked anything like that before, not even Tessa or Julie. They were always concerned, but never to that degree. I was shocked, but not in a bad way. I stretched my hand across the table to his resting on the edge and gave it a squeeze while looking as deep into his eyes as possible.

"No one has ever asked me that before. I mean, other than my mother. That would mean a lot to me, more than I can say."

Riley gave a gentle squeeze in return.

"Getting to know you means getting to know all of you, and I think that's a crucial part of who you are. I know it's not by choice, but I don't think it's something to just be overlooked. I won't bring it up all the time, I promise, but I don't want to ignore it either. Does that make any sense at all?"

"Yes, perfect sense."

***

After dinner, as promised, we picked up Alf, who went into instant leaps and yelps at the realization he was going to get to go for a walk, and after dark, which nearly never happened unless it was just to go out for the bathroom. Making our way downstairs, I assumed we would take my car to the lake for the walk. Riley's car was too immaculate to fathom Alf in it. But he surprised me by taking out his keys and aiming for his Tahoe. "Are you sure you want to take your car? I don't want him to shed all over it, as clean as it is."

"Are you kidding? I don't care. It's absolutely no problem." Alf hesitated at first but jumped into the backseat when I patted it for him to get in. After arriving at the park and a few minutes into the walk, I inquired for more information about Riley, specifically his music.

"So, have you ever had any times you thought the band would actually get signed or anything?"

"No, not really." Riley had one hand in his pocket and the other holding mine while I held Alf's leash with my other hand. "I've noticed a few music label guys occasionally at shows, but it's usually for people we're opening for. The guys and I have sent out some of our demos to several labels, but no luck. Yet, that is." He seemed to hint that it could happen eventually.

"I'm not really a music aficionado—at all, but from what I heard a few weeks ago, you guys are really good, and seem to have quite a following."

"I appreciate that. I guess we've built a bit of a local reputation. Maybe someday it will extend beyond that. Never know." Riley glanced over at Alf then back to me, and questioned, "Are you okay with the music scene? It sounds like it's a totally new scene from your world. I never even asked how you felt about it."

"It's definitely different, but I don't think I've really been around it enough yet to have anything negative to say. I've never really known anyone like you before, but I'm not worried if that says anything."

Riley chuckled at my response. "Well, in that case, I hope you'll come to some of the shows so we can see each other more."

His words made me feel warm and wanted. I leaned up and answered him with a good long kiss. It appeared to catch him off guard, but it didn't take long for him to go along with it. We must have been lip-locked for a while because Alf resorted to lying down on the trail. His leash dangled loosely around my wrist. I wanted Riley more and more, and felt like putty in his hands. We finally surfaced from the moment, our lips parting, and he reached for my hand as we continued the walk. There weren't many other people on the trail at this hour so it was nice, peaceful. After walking the trail of the park twice, learning more and more about each other, a yawn escaped me.

"I think it's time to get you home." Riley squeezed my hand.

"I really don't want to leave. What time is it anyway?"

Riley looked down at his watch. "Ten."

"Alright," I sighed. "I guess we can call it a night."

"You know I'd keep you out if I could, Brooke."

I laughed then yawned once more. "Ditto."

After returning home, I let Alf inside and turned to invite Riley in. "Want to come in for a while?"

"Would love to, but I think I've stolen you enough for one night. You'd make me happiest if you'd get some rest. Call me whenever you can this weekend, especially when you get back into town."

I swept a piece of dark hair from his forehead then rested my hand on his cheek.

"You know, you've got me wrapped around your finger and could probably get away with just about anything." *And I mean anything.*

"Really?" Riley bit his lip. "I'll have to remember that. I'll be thinking about you this weekend."

"Me too."

Riley kissed me goodnight, lifting me so high my feet left the ground, his tongue parting my lips. He tasted divine and I dug my nails lightly into his neck. He only drew me closer in response. It was a kiss that would leave me with endless yearning all weekend.

Chapter Eight

I awoke bright and early to set out for Houston. My appointment with the cardiologist wouldn't be until one, giving me just enough time to reach Mom's, grab lunch, and head over to the doctor. I stuffed the items needed for the weekend into my Louis Vuitton suitcase, stuffed another bag with some of Alf's food, and was on my way.

The highways were easy going, especially traveling during the middle of the workday. As I drummed my fingers on the steering wheel, I re-ran the lesson plans I'd left for the substitute teacher through my head, afraid I had forgotten something. Finally, I decided even if I had it wouldn't matter now anyway as I reached the outskirts of Houston. I knew the city like the back of my hand and thought I'd miss it after leaving for college. But, to the contrary, I never really had, that is, except for Mom. I wished she'd move to Austin, feeling she'd worry less about me if she were closer, but she'd said Houston was her life, and her friends and best memories were there. It was and would always be her home even if I weren't there.

I exited the highway at Memorial Park. The suburbs became thicker and thicker as cookie-cutter houses grew into larger estates and trees arched over the streets. Reaching my old street, Statesman Lane, always felt like a step back to childhood, and a lifetime of memories flooded my thoughts every time I returned. The hardest thing about returning was the bittersweet combination of being home with the lifeblood of dad's presence there. I pulled into the driveway that stretched several yards back from the street to the familiar enormous home with black plantation shutters and tall, cream-colored columns.

After finding my usual parking spot opposite Mom's Mercedes SUV, I juggled my purse, suitcase, and bag with Alf's food, hoping to manage it all in one trip to the house. Managing to free a few fingers to free Alf from the car, he leapt out and sniffed for a spot to pee. Mom was already stepping out the back door of the house, which had always been used more than the front door, to greet me.

"Hi, honey. Let me take something in for you."

"That would be great, thanks." Mom swooped in and took the Louis Vuitton from me in her small hands. She sported a perfectly styled blonde bob and donned a multi-colored fitted sweater with capris and cream ballet flats.

"How was the drive?"

"Not bad; smooth sailing."

"Well, I have to tell you, you're looking great, Brooke. From the looks of it, I'm hopeful Doctor Carlson will have a good update for you. You look fabulous. Have you been doing anything differently?"

"Um, sort of, I guess. Just trying to stay, you know, healthy." I wasn't sure if I was prepared to jump into the "Riley" subject quite so early into the visit, so I hesitated. A little relaxation time after the drive was all I felt like doing.

"Well, whatever it is, it shows." Mom moved to set my bag down in the gargantuan living room that displayed vaulted ceilings and an enormous brick fireplace. I set my purse down with Alf's things next to the suitcase. A picture of Mom and Dad graced the mantle from one of the many world travels they'd taken, and several pictures from my childhood all the way to college graduation filled the rest of the space. The picture of Dad reminded me how handsome he'd been, his blue eyes standing out from anything else in the pictures he graced. I tried to look at anything else in the room, to dismiss the sadness that washed over me. A shiver ran down my spine. The house suddenly felt so cold and empty. Hollow. How did my Mom live with this display of memories every day? *Snap out of it.* I pulled my eyes from the mantle and my stare fell upon a new piece of artwork in Mom's collection that filled the house. Strangely enough, it looked very familiar.

"Mom, is that a new painting over there?" I pointed over to it.

"Actually, yes, I just ordered it from an artist in Austin. Beautiful, isn't it?"

I knew it looked all too familiar; it was the same artist's work that had been in the gallery Riley had taken me to on our first date. It was breathtaking and had me instantly thinking of Riley. I felt my eyebrows furrow.

"Don't you like it, Brooke?" she asked.

"I've seen this artist's work before." I felt the surprise fade from my face. "I think it's amazing."

"Really, where did you see the artist's work?"

"Oh, I went to a gallery not long ago."

"Really? I know you appreciate art and all, but I guess I didn't know you frequented galleries."

"I like art, but no, you're right, Mom. I typically wouldn't go to a gallery, but I've sort of expanded my horizons you might say." I still hesitated to mention Riley, knowing Mom would pelt me with a zillion questions.

"Look at that, I don't see you for nearly three months and you come back like a new woman. You'll have to tell me everything that's been going on with you. I feel like I'm missing something."

I knew at that moment Mom was totally zeroing in on something. The change in me was obviously more visible than I'd grasped. We spent an hour eating sandwiches together on the back porch in large Adirondack lawn chairs, chit-chatting under the shade of the pine trees. She was bubbly and jovial, which made me happy, even though she could be a bit much with her aspirations and desires for me. Soon after eating we hopped in Mom's Mercedes for the physician's office. I preferred Mom driving and hated navigating the maze of downtown Houston, not to mention her car was so comfortable; like sitting in a beautiful black leather lap of luxury. The ride was filled with talk about Mom's hobbies, from the ladies' guild to bunko, and assisting with the upcoming country club charity auction. She could master just about anything she put her mind to with impeccable perfection. Mom also asked how Tessa and Julie were doing, and I filled her in on my hunch that Tessa would probably soon be engaged, and that Julie was working her way up the corporate ladder. Then Mom stunned me, "So, who's the guy?"

"How did you—?"

"You think I was born yesterday?" Mom's intuition could be scary, almost psychic.

"What gave it away?"

"Honey, you could see the look of love all over you. I remember what that looks like, you know."

"I was going to tell you about him after the appointment, but I guess there's no better time than the present."

"So, tell me about him." Mom smiled. Her perfectly-manicured hands reached to lower the radio.

My face hurt from smiling at the mere thought of him.

"Well, he's a Texas Alum, first of all, and a musician. His name is Riley."

"Wow, a musician. Wasn't expecting that at all," she said a little skeptically. I was expecting that kind of response since she'd always been the hard to impress kind, except with my dad. It didn't bother me because she was also very easy to win over in the end.

"You're telling me. I never in a million years would have even considered dating a musician, but I don't know, he's kind of..." I paused and Mom questioned my hesitation with an edge of concern.

"Kind of what, Brooke?"

"He's different, Mom, special. I can't really explain it, it's all still so new. I mean, literally, only a few weeks."

"From personal experience, Brooke, it doesn't have to take very long if it's someone special. I was ready to tell your father I loved him within the first week I met him back in college."

"I didn't say *love*, Mom, but I won't say I don't wish I was with him all the time either. It's all still too new and intense. I feel out of control sometimes, except, I like it. I love how I feel when I'm with him. Is that a bad thing?"

My mom glanced at me briefly and her face relaxed.

"No, honey, I don't think it is."

"I like him a lot," I admitted.

"You ought to bring him with you next time."

"I think that's a great idea. I'd like that very much." The nervous tension I'd held from concern over telling her lifted, and my shoulders loosened with relief.

We pulled into the medical center and walked together to the elevator that took us up to Dr. Carlson's floor. His office was intermixed with other physicians in the group. A slew of nurses in scrubs walked in and out of rooms, carrying clipboards and wearing stethoscopes around their necks. The office was informal, with light gray-colored walls, warmed slightly with a few strategically placed plants and a coffee table full of random, heavily looked at magazines. I checked myself in at the front desk and returned to the waiting area with Mom. Almost in sync, we each pulled out a book, attempting to pass the time. I'd brought Wuthering Heights, and Mom was paging through some sort of self-help book. Before completing the first sentence, Mom's interrogation ensued with back-to-back questions about Riley. What did he look like? Where was he from? She was stunned that he wasn't a "Texas boy", but appeared to overlook it when I told her he was a Texas grad like me. I conveyed that he didn't want to leave Austin after graduating. That is, of course, if he didn't get signed by a record label.

A nurse my age emerged in the waiting area.

"Brooke Denton?"

"That's me." I gathered my purse and proceeded to follow her back with Mom. The nurse guided us into one of

the patient rooms in a short hallway lined with gray
linoleum tiles. I went through all the motions of a typical
visit: was weighed, and asked a series of questions about
any changes or worries I had since my last visit. I confessed
I'd had a few small episodes, but not more than I could
count on one hand. My blood pressure was taken, which I
loathed because of the cuff's super tight squeezing
sensation on my small arms.

"110 over 70. Not bad." The plump brunette nurse
placed the cuff back on a counter. "Alright, Brooke, Dr.
Carlson will be right in to see you." She gathered up a
clipboard in her hands and left, shutting the door behind
her.

Before I could even get a good stretch of my arm
where the cuff had been, there was a light tap on the door
and Doctor Carlson stepped in. Through all the years, he
never seemed to age in my eyes. Not short, not really tall,
average. His chest was squared and slightly sculpted as if
he worked out. His salt and pepper hair was neatly
trimmed, and a jovial expression was always on his kind
face.

"Hello, Brooke. How are you?" He smiled.

"Not too bad, Doctor Carlson."

"Well, I'm glancing through the nurse's notes and
noticed you've had a few small episodes with heart racing
and shortness of breath. How often has that been
occurring?"

"Um, not much. Maybe four times since my last visit. They're not nearly as bad as the ones I experienced before."

"Well, I'm glad they're not severe, but keep an eye on that and call the office and let us know if they progress and happen more often. Have you felt like your defibrillator has been working quickly when you have noticeable episodes?"

"Yes, I feel like it's working. I typically recover within a few minutes."

My last episode had been a bit on the worrisome side, but I'd felt so good since then, I didn't want to worry anyone. The medication appeared to regulate most of the issues associated with my cardiomyopathy, apart from my ICD.

"Let's listen to your heart. Depending on that, we'll determine if we need to run any additional tests this visit."

"Okay," I sighed and felt the cold of the stethoscope through my blouse.

Doctor Carlson listened to my chest and back. I couldn't interpret his expression as to whether his news would be in the green or the red.

"Well, everything sounds good this time. No tests this go-around, but, stay on your medications and keep doing what you're doing. Remember to call us if anything changes…"

I finished for him, "Yes, sir, I'll call the office," I said dryly. It was the same spiel every visit. Doctor Carlson smiled, shook my hand, and continued,

"We'll see you in a few months. Take care of yourself."

The man had dealt with me going through some of the worst times in my life. He saw how my diagnosis had changed and destroyed some of the innocent, carefree parts of me. And as childish as it sounded, I couldn't bring myself to like him fully. For years, my heart checkups caused me great anxiety and stress. Soon after I was diagnosed, I'd thought I'd die instantly if my heart beat too fast. It was terrifying as a teenager. I felt like the condition defined me to a certain extent, and, as a result, I hated nothing more than focusing on my condition, which was all these appointments were for.

The doctor exited the room, and after the door had clicked shut, Mom and I smiled at each other, more relaxed than when we'd arrived.

"That's good news, Brooke," Mom exclaimed, appearing to relax her shoulders for the first time all day. I'm sure my checkups stressed her out, my being her only child.

"Yeah. I still hate having to do these visits. But what choice do I have?"

"You know there's no way I'd let you miss one, Brooke. I've got to take care of my baby, even if you're grown."

"I know, Mom, I know," I said unenthusiastically and hopped off the examination table.

"How about we get out of here and do some shopping?" Mom asked, knowing it would lighten my mood.

"Sounds great."

Mom and I walked back to the front desk and I scheduled the next appointment. Then we headed for the shopping district in the most expensive part of town for the rest of the afternoon. Mom spent nearly the entire shopping trip quizzing me about Riley, obviously intent on knowing nearly everything short of his blood type. I answered everything with clear admiration for the new man in my life and some disdain towards my mom's endless questions. *Would she ever let up? I'd just met the man, I wasn't marrying him.*

***

We managed to fill the entire weekend talking about Riley, and ironically, she brought up Dad a lot more than I recalled her doing in recent years. I suppose our conversations reignited her memories. It felt so good to hear her talk about Dad. Riley called on Saturday night and we talked until I couldn't keep my eyes open any longer. The call only made me miss him more. He mentioned that

112

he had something for me this upcoming week and that we'd talk more about it when I got back to town, leaving me anxious. On Sunday, Mom and I hugged goodbye, and Alf and I piled into the car, making the trip back to Austin. What could Riley surprise me with now?

Chapter Nine

Rushing back to Austin, I eagerly phoned Riley, letting him know I'd returned. He said he'd be over shortly, and, true to his word, he was at my apartment before I'd finished unpacking. As soon as I opened the door, he swooped in, taking me in his arms and greeting me with a deep kiss. No verbal greetings, just embraces. I was in heaven. Riley pulled away and looked down at me, his eyes as dark and enticing as I'd remembered.

"I missed you."

"I missed you, too," I said, running my fingers through his sable hair. "Would you like some dinner?" I ran my thumb across his bottom lip.

"Love some. What did you have in mind?"

"Well, I can cook a mean chicken Marsala. Sound okay?"

"Are you sure you want to cook after just getting back into town? I'll take you out."

"Yes, *I* want to cook. It's easy to make," I snapped, slightly irritated because after being at my Mom's all weekend I needed a break from all the pampering. I shouldn't have been so short with him, but he was one of the few people in my life thus far who didn't treat me like I might break. I felt normal with him and didn't want it any differently.

"Okay, okay, only on the condition that I can come over tomorrow and cook you dinner. And it's not a request." He kissed my forehead.

"Hmmm… okay." My attitude cooled at his gesture. "It's a deal." I offered a grin, looking back up to him.

Riley settled into the couch, looking back at me while I worked on dinner.

"I know we talked on the phone yesterday, but you only briefly mentioned your appointment. I figured you probably didn't really want to talk about it—but really, did it go okay?"

"Yeah, it was fine, promise. It's not the highlight of my life, but I have to do it. They're like clockwork now. The doctor said I'm doing fine. I didn't have anything different than normal really come up. I mean, other than a few episodes."

"What sort of episodes?" Riley's face crinkled in concern. I could've kicked myself for letting that slip out. *Think before you speak, Brooke.*

"Nothing new to me. I just have these random moments where it's like I suddenly can't catch my breath, my heart starts racing, and I have to sit down for a while. It's sort of like feeling like you're about to faint. I'm sure there will be a time when it happens around you, but I'm really not looking forward to that."

"Brooke, I promise you never have to be embarrassed about stuff like that."

"I know, I just hate being different." I rolled my eyes and turned back to turn the burner off. Riley surprised me, slipping behind me. I caught my breath at the unexpected move.

"Brooke, if I have to tell you this a hundred times, I will." He gently turned me and pulled my hips to his. "I don't care that you have this heart condition. I care about you." His eyes were serious but gentle. He brushed his hand from the nape of my neck to my cheek.

"I believe you, I just didn't expect someone to ever understand." I laid my hand over his on my face, rubbing it softly, letting my body do all the talking. I leaned in and kissed him, biting his top lip playfully as his hands made their way up and down my back. After the kiss, I looked at him with half a smile, "I need to finish dinner, you know."

Riley laughed.

"Alright, alright, I'll leave you alone." He moved back to his spot on the couch. I felt the moment was finally right for me to ask him about his newest surprise for me.

"So, you mentioned having something for me last night. What do you have brewing this time?"

"Well," Riley chuckled. "Are you okay with me coming up to your class tomorrow?"

Boy, I was completely unprepared for that one. I wanted to say yes instantly but hesitated, not knowing if I truly felt ready for him to come to my place of work and see my class and kids. I ran every possible scenario, positive and negative, through my head at lightning speed to consider the best answer, but was stumped.

"What exactly did you have in mind?"

"Well, I don't want to ruin the plan, per-say, but I was going to play some music with the kids."

"Do you even like kids?"

"I love kids. I do have two siblings, remember?"

This was something new about Riley that I hadn't even thought to ask, but I was relieved now that I knew he liked kids, or at least he'd said he did. I finally decided it couldn't hurt if he came, and supplied him my answer.

"Alright, what time do you want to come by? I'll have to squeeze you in," I said jokingly.

"How is one? That's usually when I go to lunch at work."

"One is perfect. The kids are usually pretty restless by then. I think it may help us all through that last leg of the day."

"I'll be there tomorrow then."

***

After dinner, Riley filled me on the weekend's gigs. He even mentioned that they'd tried some newer song material they'd worked on. He seemed content when he

117

talked about music. Like me and my condition, Riley and his music were inseparable. The evening was perfect. And, for the first time in my life, I realized I wanted to tell a man I loved him. I wouldn't be the first one to say it though, not yet anyway, and maybe I was feeling too much too fast. We'd only known each other a few weeks, but it didn't seem to matter.

Sitting together on the couch, Riley received a call. He got up abruptly and huddled in the hallway. What didn't he want me to hear? *Relax, Brooke, you're not even his girlfriend—yet.* I did, however, hear a few bits of his conversation and it appeared whomever he was talking to rubbed him the wrong way.

"I told you no. No," he said in a maddened tone. "How did you get this number anyway? I told you not to contact me... I don't care... don't bring that up..." His aggression toward whoever he was on the phone with reminded me of the first time we'd met. What side of him was this? I decided to stop eavesdropping and turned the TV up; it wasn't my business anyway.

Suddenly, Riley was back in the living room, "I'm sorry, Brooke. I have to leave. Something's come up. Nothing bad, just something I have to deal with."

A surge of contradicting emotions rushed through me. "Is everything alright?" I was concerned. I wanted to make sure he was okay, but he didn't give me the opportunity.

"I wish I could stay. I'll see you tomorrow." He gave me a quick kiss on the cheek before departing, leaving me feeling empty and unsatisfied.

"Okay… see you tomorrow."

I lay awake in bed most of the night, pondering his abrupt departure, mysterious phone call, and visit to my class. Thoughts circled loudly in my head until it felt like the room was spinning. Was this a reality check? Would Riley's nasty side appear more and more? I wasn't sure how to make sense of what had occurred, and I wished he'd stayed the night. I finally forced myself to get up for a glass of water and watched a little TV to clear my head. Eventually, I fell asleep at some random hour of the morning.

The alarm buzzed at five-thirty and I dragged myself out of bed, making it to work at my usual time. The day of teaching started with the kids in good spirits, making it flow by with greater ease. I was already on pins and needles about Riley's disconnectedness from last night and his arrival at my class. Shortly after the class had finished lunch, I informed them that a visitor would be coming soon to see them. They were even more interested when I let them know he was a musician. Excitement emanated from their little faces, easing my own tension about the idea of Riley's visit. If they were happy at the end of the visit, it would be worth it.

Before Riley arrived, I got them started on their math assignments and then retreated to my desk. Sitting back in my chair, I let out a quiet sigh, the night of wonder and lack of sleep taking its toll on me. I glanced up from my desk and caught Tessa peering through the glass window of the classroom door. When she realized I saw her, she waved me to the door. The kids were distracted with their work, so I stepped outside the door and immediately noticed Riley standing just behind Tessa with a giant grin plastered on his face. *Was this really the same person from last night? I don't get it.*

"Would you look who I found in the hallway?" Tessa beamed. "I was taking one of my kids up to the nurse's office and saw Mister Riley here come into the building. I thought I'd show him to your room."

"It was a relief to see Tessa when I walked in the door." Riley winked at her. Handsome as always in dark denim jeans, black designer boots, and a dark long-sleeved shirt, he carried his guitar case in his right hand and a light jacket in the other. He swept a piece of his dark hair back from his forehead.

"If you don't mind me asking, Riley, why are you here?" Tessa's curiosity radiated with a mischievous smile.

"Oh, Tessa," I answered for Riley to cut out any uneasiness. "He's just here to play some music for the kids. Why don't you bring your class over, too? Is that okay with you, Riley?"

I hoped he wouldn't mind, being that I'd asked Tessa before I'd even thought to ask him first, but I was a little edgy with Riley here.

"Why not? The more, the merrier," he said.

He seemed sincere and back to his normal self again, temporarily blocking my confusion with his moods. He entered the room and Tessa set off for her classroom. By the time she returned with her students, I'd already situated all of mine on the floor at the front of the room. Tessa positioned hers on the floor with mine while Riley took out his guitar and made his way to the front, standing next to me in front of the class full of kids. Finally, all of the little bodies were settled, and I made introductions.

"Alright, guys, I've got a special treat for you today." The kid's faces glowed with excitement and anticipation. "This is my friend, Riley. Can you all tell him hello?"

The kids shouted "Hello" in unison, already eyeing his guitar. "He's here to play some music for you today."

Again, the kids showed excitement.

"They're all yours, Riley." I retreated to the back of the room to meet Tessa sitting on the edge of my desk and she whispered,

"Brooke, he's got the hots for you. To come here like this..."

"I have no idea why he's here. He sprung it on me last night."

Riley was standing at the front of the room, already strumming his guitar strings and interacting with the kids, not noticing my conversation with Tessa.

"Alright, guys….how many of you like music?" Several "me's" leapt from their mouths.

"That's awesome," Riley replied to their animated answers.

"Well, what songs do you all like? We'll sing them together."

I was in absolute shock. He was sincerely laughing and enjoying the kids, not minding their young tendencies to want to talk over him or get easily distracted. In fact, I'd say he commanded the room, with all eyes glued to him. One of the kids shouted over the others for Riley's attention.

"Oh, oh, Mr. Riley, can you play, 'If you're happy and you know it'?"

"You bet, good choice!" Riley began to play his guitar.

This must have been the stuff of his earliest days learning guitar, but no matter; with his extreme ease of the song, you could tell he enjoyed it. What was more impressive was how he managed to get the kids to sing along with him. They were having loads of fun with such a plain and simple song.

After completing the first request, Riley took five other song requests. It was a sight to see. I couldn't remember the last time I'd seen the kids have so much fun. When Riley wrapped up the sixth song, he looked squarely at me, still sitting half-crouched on the desk next to Tessa.

"Alright, kids, I have a question for you." He looked back down at the kids and then back at me. "I have something I'd like to do for Miss Denton." I'd never heard him call me that before. It was sort of funny. "Can I sing a special song for Miss Denton?" he continued.

The children looked very curious, and I was feeling lightheaded when he asked the question, but all shouted 'yes!'

"Great, everyone, let's have Miss Denton come sit up here, okay?" He looked back up for me, still sitting at the back of the classroom with Tessa.

My nervous eyes met his. "Okay."

I made what seemed like a long journey to the front of the room, my heart racing. I struggled to hide my anticipation. I sat on the edge of one of the desks near Riley as he began to strum his guitar, but not with the typical children's songs that had filled the past half hour. He looked up at me as he played, and before beginning any lyrics, we locked eyes. Everything else in the room disappeared. It was as if it were only Riley and me in the room. Then he sang, lyrics I instinctively knew were meant for me. At that moment, all I wanted was him, all of him.

The lyrics wooed me and melted my heart at the thought of him taking the time to write this. *When would he have had the time? We hadn't known each other long.* At the completion of the moving lyrics, he gently strummed the strings of his guitar one last time. It was the most beautiful thing anyone had ever done for me. I was awestruck, staring at him, trying to withhold my emotions in front of the children, and was afraid I was about to lose my composure when I heard Tessa doing the boohooing for me at the back of the room. I fought back tears as my eyes filled, but took a long breath to force them back. Riley got up from the chair he'd been sitting in and unclipped his guitar strap. He looked at me with such intensity he could've said let's go the parking lot right now and I would have let him take me any way he wanted me. But reality returned when Riley broke the height of emotion by continuing conversation with the kids. *Planet Earth, calling Brooke. Don't forget you're in a room full of kids.*

"Thank you for letting me come sing with all of you today. Can I come back sometime?" All of the kids were elated and their requests for him to come back boomeranged around the room. When the children's initial excitement quieted, Riley waved to all the kids, "Alright then, if it's okay with Miss Denton, that's a promise." He moved next to me, gently put his mouth to my ear and whispered, "I'm sorry about last night. See you after work?"

I answered with a discreet nod back.

He followed by pulling away to give me one final look. His eyes spoke to me when words didn't. I knew what I saw there and I was in love.

Tessa's soft sobs had subsided. I turned to her and giggled. Tessa's mushy emotional side could be cute. Right now, it just made me laugh. I loved her for it though. I needed it right then. She smiled back at me through tears and then helped me get my class back in order before returning to her classroom. Riley said a final goodbye to my kids and I walked him out the classroom door. I couldn't find the words I wanted to say. Instead, I hugged him harder than I ever thought possible and whispered against his neck, "Thank you, from the bottom of my heart, thank you."

He took my hand in his and kissed my knuckles. "I know you need to get back to your class so I won't keep you. When can I come over later? I've got another surprise for you."

This was all happening so fast. Maybe he was ready to say what I felt. But what was the dark, unsettling side of him I'd encountered again yesterday? Did I really know him enough? I was worrying too much, and feeling the out of control feeling I had been describing to Mom. Regardless, I wanted Riley tonight.

"I'll be home five-ish, so you can come over any time after that."

"I'll be there at five-thirty then."

"See you in a few hours." I gave him a final gentle kiss.

Riley spoke against my lips, "You know, I'd give you one hell of a kiss if we weren't here right now."

"Believe me, I'd be fine with that... and more," I whispered mischievously back to him.

"Don't tempt me."

With a final smile, he turned to leave with his jacket, guitar, and my heart in his hands.

<u>Chapter Ten</u>

Nothing else mattered for those few, but seemingly eternal, remaining hours. After getting home, I rushed Alf outside and changed into something sultry, hoping the black satin slip would do the trick. The knock at the door came earlier than I expected, but I didn't care. I just wanted Riley here with me, and the sooner, the better. Alf's head had been going back and forth the past half hour, trying to keep up with me in my frenzied straightening of the apartment and lighting candles to set the mood. He shifted from his laying position on the floor when I loudly yelled, "Alf, stay!" He obeyed, though clearly fighting the inherent urge to cling to my side. When I opened the door, Riley rushed in, lifting me off the floor. I wrapped my arms and legs around his muscular body, needing to be as close to him as possible. His insatiable kisses moved from my mouth to my neck. I wanted him in every possible way, my body eagerly awaiting his next move.

"Riley, I—" He pushed his lips to mine hard before I could finish, and slid his hands up the back of my slip. My

libido ignited with a fury of passion. He pulled back just
enough for our lips to separate, finishing what I'd started.

"I know, Brooke, I love you, too."

I said it back again and again, in between passionate
kisses. With my arms and legs still wrapped around him,
we moved to my bedroom. I undressed him, eagerly pulling
his pants and boxers down and tugging his shirt over his
head. As I did, he pulled the satin frock over my head,
revealing everything beneath it. The kisses, embraces, and
emotions built like a lit firecracker. I wanted him and he
wanted me and for a while the world disappeared. He flung
me onto the bed and jumped on top, straddling me, then
pinned my hands above my head. Riley kept the perfect
pace, kissing me on my neck, moving slowly down to my
still-clothed breasts, then abruptly stopped and moved back
to my neck where he nibbled on my ear. Riley was toying
with me, so I grabbed his hair at the back of his head and
pushed him down my body. He kissed every inch of my
love trail, not missing a beat. After feeling myself build
with a desire that would soon combust if he didn't stop
with the foreplay, I reached for his chiseled, strong arms,
pulling him up to me.

"I need you, Riley. Now."

I heard him reach for something in his pants on the
floor, followed by the tear of a wrapper. He pushed himself
inside me and we became a blur of body parts and passion

for hours, the weeks of tension leading up to this moment finally released.

***

I awoke to an already-dark sky outside my bedroom window. Riley lay next to me, his arms grasped me tightly with no intention of letting go. I turned over in the bed and glanced into his tired eyes. He pulled me closer.

"I love you, Riley."

"I love you, too," he managed with a rugged voice and heavy lids.

"I wasn't really expecting all of this when I got out of bed this morning," I giggled and kissed his nose.

"You're telling me," he huffed. "By the way, I never got you that dinner I promised you. Are you still up for it?"

"Absolutely, except I'm worn out. I don't think I'd make it past the front door."

"Hmm, me neither, but you've got to eat." Riley slowly pulled away, moving to the edge of the bed and slipping into his boxers.

"You really don't have to cook anything."

"Of course, I do; don't be silly."

"Can I help?"

"Ummmmm… no," he laughed and raised his finger sarcastically, pointing it at me. "Why don't you rest and I'll bring it to you in bed when it's ready?" He rose and headed for the doorway.

"Fine," I brusquely remarked as I pushed myself up in the bed and pulled the sheets over me. I leaned over to flip the lamp on and the extent of our sexual exertion hit me like a ton of bricks. I felt exhausted physically but rejuvenated in so many more ways. On the sex side, my experiences had been minimal, just a guy at U.T. I'd dated sophomore year. But it was nothing—not even close—to what I'd just experienced. It had been incredible. I'd never wanted anything so badly in my entire life. I slid out of the bed, grabbed a blue nighty set from my dresser, slipped it on, and went to take my meds. Afterwards, I went back to bed and crawled under the plush comforter, hungry for dinner and starving for another round of lovemaking with Riley.

Riley returned a half hour later with dinner in hand. It smelled divine. Not only did this guy have musical talent and could make love like a Greek god, but it was apparent he could cook, too. A pasta dish in some sort of wonderful, yummy-looking sauce appeared on a plate in front of me.

"It smells wonderful. Did I have all the stuff to make this? And where exactly did you learn to cook?"

"Yup. I *am* pretty good about working with whatever's available. I've had to eat out a lot when we've played, and you get tired of it really quick. I just sort of figured it out." He rested the plate of food on the nightstand.

"Are you going to eat, too?"

"Yes, I'll be right back." He stepped out of the bedroom again then returned a moment later with his own plate, balancing two drinks in the other hand. He nestled into the spot he'd left beside me in bed, and we ate the first dinner he'd cooked for me, on a night of many significant firsts. After dinner, Riley returned to the kitchen and I could hear water running as he cleaned up everything he'd used for dinner. It was nearly nine when he made it back to the bedroom, and my lids felt heavy.

"Are you tired?" Riley thumbed my cheek after getting back to my room.

"No," I fibbed.

"I think you're lying." He cocked his head to the side and raised his brow. My body hadn't been worked like it had been tonight in far too long.

"Oh, God, Brooke. Are you okay?" He dropped next to me on the bed and pulled me to him firmly. "I mean, I never even asked you about your heart before we…" The thought of my condition and what we'd done appeared to suddenly hit him with the force of a sledgehammer.

"Riley!" I cut him off. "I'm fine. I'm fine." I placed both hands on his warm face. "Don't worry. I feel, well, great! The doctor never said no sex, ya know?" I chuckled.

"That's a relief," he said in a serious tone, his face slightly relaxing. "Are you okay with all of this? I mean, this was a lot to happen so soon."

"I'm more than okay with this. I love you, Riley." I leaned in, kissing his forehead and cheeks.

"I love you, too, Brooke." He kissed me on the lips, long and hard, reinforcing the words he'd just spoken.

"Before we do this again, I mean, if you *want* to do this again, Brooke, is there anything you or we need to do?"

"Riley, don't. If I were concerned, I promise I'd tell you. I don't feel any different than I normally would. The doctors only ever told me it wouldn't be safe to consider having kids."

"As long as you're okay, that's the most important thing to me, and I promise..." Riley paused for a split second. "No babies."

"Well, now that that's settled." I grinned, but deep down wondered if the revelation of no kids would ever be an issue. "With everything that's happened, does this mean we're...?"

"Yes." Riley finished my sentence. "We're definitely together... exclusively." He seemed just as eager as I was to be on the same page. "On another note, should I think about heading home? I don't really want to leave, but with us both having work tomorrow and all, I'm not sure what you want to do."

"I would love for you to stay, but wouldn't you have to leave pretty early to make it to work tomorrow?"

"Yes, but I don't care. I wanna stay if it's okay with you?"

"You bet. Who needs sleep anyway?" My eyes locked on his and more kisses followed. His hands gently caressed my skin and our embrace intensified. Before long, his real objective surfaced as his commanding hand journeyed down my stomach.

"Should we? Again, I mean," Riley whispered in my ear then nibbled at the lobe, while slowly taking off my nighty once more—tantalizingly slow.

"Yes," I whispered, unable to hide my want for him, but this time I'd make sure it was all about him. I climbed on top of Riley's hard, flexed body and the whirl of sweat, need, and limbs began again.

***

The next morning when I woke to my alarm, Riley had already left. But he'd left a note on the bedside table for me to find. On it read,

Brooke,

I left pretty early and didn't want to wake you. I have to meet with the band tonight, but I'll call you afterwards and come by if I can.

Love you,
Riley

P.S. I took Alf out for you.

Going to work left me feeling like the night before was some sort of a dream. The feelings and events rushed through every bone in my body. I was in love, emotionally and physically, and for the first time in my life wanted nothing more than to be with that special someone every possible second.

As soon as I entered my classroom that morning, Tessa was waiting like a kid on Christmas morning. The eagerness to find out every juicy detail emitted from her aura.

"Brooke, you have to tell me everything! What on earth happened yesterday?"

"Well, Tessa, simply put, Riley and I are together, and spent the entire night physically exploring our new togetherness."

"Oh, my God, Brooke! Really? No wonder you're glowing. I am so happy for you—and exclusive?! What a day!" Tessa's arms wrapped around me and hugged me so tightly I lost my breath.

When she pulled back, I continued, "Actually, Tessa, it's more than that. I love him. Am I crazy? Are we moving too fast?"

"You can't put parameters on something like that. Every relationship moves differently, so as long as you're happy, Brooke, it doesn't really matter how long it's been," she assured me.

"It was amazing. Hours, Tessa. I don't know how I could be glowing because I'm exhausted."

"Wow! Brooke…" Tessa paused for a moment with the same look on her face that Riley had displayed when the thought of my cardiomyopathy after the deed last night had hit him. "Brooke, I'm not going to butt in on your business, but is everything okay on that front? I mean, are you okay to be doing that, with your heart?"

"Yes, of course. I'm perfectly fine, Tessa," I menaced. It's not every day you're in love, especially not for me, and I was tired of everyone bringing up my heart. I wasn't going to die from one night of passionate lovemaking. And I damn sure wanted it to happen again.

"Okay, *okay*. I'm sorry. So, what's next?" Tessa asked.

"One day at a time, I guess. I just know I love him, a lot. I've never felt more alive or healthy."

"So, I guess this means we can have some double date nights! Riley and Lowell really hit it off that one time," Tessa happily recollected. "Oh, and we'll have to go watch his band again with you sometime."

"You have no idea how much I'd love that. This is a whole new ball game for me. I'd love to have you all there with me. At least he already knows I'm not exactly a night owl," I laughed. "Though last night proved I could stay up extremely late, under the right circumstances."

"Definitely a useful bit of information for him to know," Tessa laughed back. After debriefing Tessa, everything about the day was normal except for the string of emotions that showed in my every move. Life was different and would be different for the foreseeable future. Every cell in my body felt alive. It was clear to me that, for the first time, I was actually living.

<u>Chapter Eleven</u>

Months passed swiftly, and the summer arrived, bringing with it the conclusion of teaching until the next year. Julie, Tessa, and I spent a lot of time together at Riley's gigs around town, and I loved being able to be with them even more than I had been before Riley.

The transition to his world was not all that complicated, and a heap more fun than I'd ever predicted. No doubt the lifestyle he led was different from mine, and he had women hitting on him right and left, but I never worried. He made it clear his affections were only for me. I had become another person entirely, on the outside, but still harbored the same heart and soul. Life had changed me. Riley had changed me. For once, I welcomed more than just an everyday ritual existence. What bigger gift can a person give you than a refreshed view of life and constant love?

Riley showed no qualms about spending time with my friends. In fact, we'd often spend time out at the lake or just go out for dinner with them. He fit into the small puzzle of my life perfectly. Lowell had become good friends with

Riley, and they acted more like brothers, with their humor and quick wit. All in all, I couldn't have been happier.

After the first few months together had passed, the reality of my condition resurfaced one late summer afternoon when Riley and I returned from walking Alf, something that had now become somewhat of a normal routine. I noticed the light flashing on my answering machine. When I reviewed the message, it was just loud enough that I knew Riley could hear it from across the living room in the kitchen, where he was getting a drink from the fridge.

"Brooke, this is just a reminder that you have an appointment scheduled with Doctor Carlson, next Friday at two. Call us if you have any questions. Thanks."

The message ended and Riley trailed into the room. "You have an appointment next week?"

"Guess so. I'd forgotten all about it."

"Well, I guess we'll finally be making that trip to Houston then," Riley decidedly stated.

"We? You don't *really* want to go, do you?" It was suddenly sort of weird to imagine him being with me at Doctor Carlson's.

It was such a serious and depressing topic, quite a deviation from what had become our everyday fun relationship. We didn't talk much about my heart. I preferred it that way.

"Of course, I mean *we*. Remember, a while ago I told you I wanted to. Are you still okay with it?"

"Yeah, I guess so." I dropped my gaze to the floor, feeling defeated.

"It won't be that bad, I promise. I really want to go, and besides, it will give me a chance to finally meet your mom." He raised my chin with his hand and searched my eyes. I didn't know if I was really ready for their meeting. I mean Mom and I had talked over the phone about Riley a lot since we'd become an item, and I'd visited with Mom alone a few weekends when Riley had some out of town gigs, but there had been no formal opportunity for them to meet. I sort of liked it that way. I knew without a doubt Mom would try to intimidate him a little to break him in. She'd never thought her only daughter would fall for the musician type. His lifestyle was unstable. I laughed at the idea of her acting harsh and tough but knew she'd turn sweeter than sugar after she actually got to know Riley. She was unable to play mean for long. She just didn't have it in her. What was there to be afraid of? Like him or not, Riley was a part of my life now, and if she didn't like him at first she'd learn to love him. Or else.

"You're right," I replied but still tried to play a way out of it. "Wait, aren't you playing next weekend?" I questioned.

"Yes, but not until Saturday night. As long as I'm back early in the day Saturday, it'll be just fine. I can take a second car if you want to come back later."

"No, that's silly. Think about the environment, Riley," I said with mock seriousness, feeling a giant grin on my face. He laughed back at me. "Let's just plan on riding together. Can you get off work Friday?"

"Shouldn't be a problem."

"Alright, it's a plan then."

I moved to the couch and plopped down. Riley followed. I curled up in his arms and ran my fingers through his thick head of hair. He pulled my face gently to his and our lips touched. He followed my lead, running his fingers through my long caramel locks. Our perfectly molded mouths felt as if our lips were made for each other. He lightly bit my bottom lip, which he knew drove me crazy. I bit back, and a kissing tug of war ensued, resulting in advances to other areas. Riley suddenly pulled back and gave me a curious look, as if he'd had an unexpected thought flash through his mind.

"What?" I said, wondering if I'd done something wrong.

"Just curious. Where is the thing you were telling me about for your heart? I can't remember what it's called." He fumbled over his words and it was cute. He was trying so hard to be sincere and not seem like an idiot. I knew exactly what he was asking about.

"Oh, you mean my ICD. Here." I took his large hand and laid it on my left collarbone. He rested his fingers gently on the area and I traced the short length down to my heart with his hand in mine. "You will feel some of it sticking up a little bit, here," I pushed his hand a little more firmly in the area where the tiny generator underneath my skin protruded slightly. "Do you feel it?"

"I do," Riley whispered. His fingers grazed my skin lightly, as if he was afraid he'd hurt me. "I wouldn't have noticed unless you'd showed me. Does it hurt or anything?"

"No... well, at first, a little bit... it felt a little funny having something where there was nothing before, but now I hardly pay attention to it."

"What exactly does it do?" Riley asked, looking fixedly at the site.

"Basically, it keeps my heart beating at a normal pace when it wants to get out of line. And it acts sort of like a mini recorder of what my heart's been up to when I go to the doctor."

"I see." Riley moved his fingers from my heart to my face and stroked my cheek with his thumb.

Riley's deep brown eyes peered into mine with a look of fear. I quickly encouraged him to get whatever was eating at him off his chest.

"What?"

"It's the thought of losing you." He paused and then looked at me like a man who meant what he said. "I mean, really and truly losing you."

"That won't happen." I knew in reality I had little control over life, but I wasn't about to show Riley any weakness on my part. He was worth fighting to stay alive for if it came to it.

"That's why I want to know everything about your condition, Brooke. So that I feel like I understand and can help you if you ever need it." He placed his hand delicately over my ICD again.

"Thank you," was all I could say without a sea of tears welling up in my eyes.

I took a deep breath and swiftly moved to kiss Riley. He hugged me in his arms fast, very fast, holding me so tightly that I could physically feel the meaning of his words. To feel such love from someone when you didn't think it possible was more than I had prepared myself for. Instead of crying, I wrapped myself around Riley just as firmly as he held me. It was strange, sensing that we both wanted more, but I realized, in the candor of such a moment, love was all we really needed; being in each other's arms meant much more. The night went on, and Riley stayed the night, holding me in a strong embrace until we both drifted into a deep sleep.

***

The next day I called Mom about Riley making the trip with me. I couldn't gauge her reaction over the phone. She'd sounded neither thrilled nor unhappy about it, enhancing my suspicion she may give Riley a less-than-welcoming introduction. But, again, she'd given me the mother's inquiry of a lifetime about him and seemed excited to meet him last I had seen her. Early the following morning, I awoke to an empty space next to me in the bed and the clamoring of dishes in the kitchen. I pulled my phone from the nightstand. Six a.m. Forcing my body from bed, I smelled breakfast as I got closer to the kitchen.

"Well, good morning, sunshine." Riley grinned then bit into a peeled banana.

"How are you so chipper, Riley? It's freaking six in the morning." I rubbed my eyes.

"I have breakfast ready. Hope you're okay with fruit, toast, and eggs. And I already took Alf out." He grinned, seeing the disbelief in my face.

"Oh, I need your energy. I'm used to getting up early, but you clearly have me outdone."

"Come get your pretty butt over here, little lady, you need some loving." Riley set the banana down as I walked into his open arms. What started as a sweet gesture turned into an event when he flung me up over his shoulder and made his way into the living room. He plopped me on the sofa then tickled me so hard I lost my breath laughing uncontrollably.

"Now are you awake?" Riley leaned over and kissed me square on the lips before retreating to the kitchen. After we'd eaten, Alf moved to Riley for after-meal scraps, knowing his new favorite friend would always let him lick the plate or toss him leftovers. "Here you go, Alf." Riley lowered the plate to Alf and he licked up every tiny crumb.

Alf and Riley sat together on the couch after breakfast while I took a shower and finished packing my bag. Wrapping up, I meditated on the idea of having Riley with me at the doctor. If our relationship continued, and God I hoped it never ended, he'd have to see this side of things at some point, pleasant or not. After laying my hairdryer atop the neatly folded clothes in my suitcase, I zipped it up and carried it into the living room.

"Okay, let's do this."

"Alright. Mind if I drive?" Riley questioned and took the bag from me.

"Nope."

We made our way down the apartment stairs - Riley, Alf, and I. Alf made himself comfortable in the backseat of Riley's Tahoe as soon as Riley opened the door. Riley set my bag in the back with his and situated himself in the driver's seat.

"Our first road trip, how cute." I scrunched my nose as he fired the ignition.

"Houston bound." Riley squeezed my leg, sending beacons of desire for him off in my brain. *Can we do it at Mom's? I want him already and we haven't even left.*

***

Arriving in Houston, I directed Riley to the correct exit. As the houses and subdivisions grew thicker and the scent of pine trees became more pungent, I watched Riley's body language, which, thus far, had been pretty relaxed.

"Make a right turn at the next stop sign."

"Got it." Riley turned the wheel. "These homes remind me of back home."

"Really? I guess I thought houses up north would be, I don't know, different."

"Not really, except for basements."

"Awww, I guess that's what we would affectionately call a storm cellar; although Houston's more likely to get a hurricane."

"Definitely don't have those in Chicago."

"Make another right turn at the end of the street."

Alf began to whimper in the back seat, no doubt in need of a bathroom break. I reached back to scratch his head.

"We're almost there, Alf."

I turned back around and motioned to Riley with my finger, pointing through the windshield.

"It's the third house on the left."

"Wow! Nice house." Riley's mouth fell open.

"That's home." It definitely made a statement. I never felt like I acted as if I came from money, and I didn't like to brag about it. I'd always had a belief that it was important to make my own way on my teacher's salary. I hid that I came from financial comfort well, with the exception of some pieces in my closet, courtesy of Mom's shopping excursions. We pulled into the driveway and Riley put the car in park. Before I could say anything, Mom was already walking quickly from the back door of the house, grinning from ear-to-ear. *Thank God, she looks like she wants to play nice.* I exited the passenger door and promptly opened the back door for Alf, who rocketed out for the yard. I turned back around and Mom was face-to-face with me.

"Hi, honey." She hugged me tightly and then held one of my hands in hers. Riley made his way over to us.

"You must be Riley. I've heard so much about you. It's a pleasure to meet you." *Oh, please, let this not be a façade.*

"You, too, Mrs. Denton. I've been looking forward to it all week." Riley reached out to shake her hand, which instantly made her happy. She always liked a man with charisma and manners.

"You kids hungry? I made up some sandwiches and thought later tonight we could all go to dinner."

"Sounds wonderful, Mrs. Denton. I'm starving." Riley patted his stomach.

"Well, come on in. And please, call me Grace," she said, looking at the two of us together. "What a lovely pair you two make."

"Mom, don't act so surprised!" I responded quickly. "Let's go in, I'm deliriously hungry. You can look at us inside, Mom. *Go.*" Always after a long ride, I couldn't help but find my mom to be a bit too much. Now with Riley here, I feared it'd be more than I could handle.

Riley smiled, sensing my onset of irritability at Mom and then gathered our bags.

"Alf, let's go inside!" I yelled out to the yard for him once Riley had everything.

His collar jingled as he ran back towards us. After entering the house, a thought crossed my mind: sleeping arrangements. Kind of stupid to be thinking about that now, but I knew my mom was pretty old-fashioned.

"Why don't you take Riley upstairs to set your bags in your room and I'll get the rest of lunch ready."

"Oh, okay." I knew Mom could see I was a little flabbergasted.

"What is it, Brooke?"

"Nothing," I said, not wanting to bring it up.

"Brooke," Mom laughed, clearly enjoying herself. "You're a grown woman; don't be silly." I looked back at Riley and noticed a hint of a blush on his face.

"Alright then, I'll take you upstairs."

We trailed through the kitchen into the large living area. Riley looked at all of the family pictures placed about the room. We climbed the stairs to the second floor and walked a ways down the hallway, arriving at my old room. The door was half open. We entered, and it was as if I was letting Riley into a part of my youth.

"Just set the bags here." I pointed at the area in front of a large four-post bed covered with a cream comforter and purple pillows. The room was plastered with memories of my younger days. Pictures, ribbons, homecoming mums, and stuffed animals literally covered every inch of space.

"I guess my mom could never bring herself to take all this stuff down," I said, turning to look at Riley, and wondering what on earth was going through his head.

He walked over to my dresser and immediately noticed the picture of Dad and me after one of my volleyball games. I didn't have any pictures of Dad at the apartment. It was just easier for me that way.

"This is him?" He picked up the picture.

"Yeah, that's him."

"You both look so happy here."

"We were."

Riley set the picture back down.

"I've forgotten about being a teenager," Riley spoke.

"For me it's sometimes all I can think about, mainly because those are the clearest memories of my dad."

Riley pulled me to him in a gentle motion and kissed me. He then moved to kiss my forehead and hugged me tightly for a while.

"I really wish I could've met him."

"Me, too. You have no idea." The quiet of the moment broke as Riley's stomach rumbled. "Are you hungry? I think I just heard your stomach growl," I chuckled.

"Yes, ma'am."

"Let's go eat then."

We made our way back downstairs to the kitchen where Mom had a spread ready for us - sandwiches, fruit, iced tea, and chips. Eating lunch, Mom and Riley hit it off better than I'd hoped, chatting away. I hardly got a word in, feeling an anxiety growing inside me. Before long, I knew we had to get going to make it to the appointment, and interjected,

"Are ya'll ready to go?"

"Whenever you need to go, I'm ready." Riley smiled.

"You know, I think I'll stay back here."

"Really, Mom?" I was pretty astounded by her decision.

"I think it will be good for you to do this together. Without me. Besides, you know how tiny exam rooms can be. You two go, and when you get back we'll all get ready for dinner somewhere nice tonight."

"Okay, Mom, if you're sure." I raised a brow, not expecting this.

"Of course, honey. I'm sure."

"Alright." I got up from the table and picked up my purse off the kitchen counter. Riley followed, but as we reached the Tahoe he passed me the keys.

"You trust me to drive this tank?"

"You'll do fine," Riley laughed. "Besides, you know downtown Houston a lot better than I do."

"Say an extra prayer for me," I joked and clasped my hands in a prayer.

Chapter Twelve

Pulling into the hospital garage as I had a few months earlier with Mom, I felt a shiver climb up my spine. I was a little jumpy to begin with, driving the SUV in a sharp-angled, low-roofed, low-lit parking garage. It was gigantic compared to my tiny Acura. I cycled scenarios of the appointment in my head. Riley would either feel more in the loop about my condition or succumb to the potential reality of it. Thus far, he had shown nothing but support regarding it in our relationship and I prayed it would stay that way. Locating a parking spot on the end of the second level cast relief, as it was a bit wider that the rest of the spots so I wouldn't have to maneuver the giant thing in between cars. A little sweat had built on my forehead; Riley gave me a double take, finally realizing just how nervous I was while driving.

"Brooke, you did great, don't break a sweat over this big ol' thing. I'm impressed."

"Phew… I'm glad that's done. I've got to admit, driving this thing worries me to death."

"Ha, you've got bigger things on your plate to deal with. I'll drive back to your mom's if it makes you feel better, okay?"

"Thank you." Putting it into park, I removed the key and reached for my purse in the backseat. I opened the door, only slightly sandwiching myself between the small space of the door and the parking garage wall. After pulling the edges of my yellow Yves Saint Laurent blouse down slightly over my dark denim, low-rise skinny jeans, I was now thankful I'd opted for ballet flats instead of leopard heels for the visit—nothing more annoying than climbing in and out of a giant vehicle and meandering through a large parking garage in heels. Riley met me at the rear of the vehicle. His good looks radiated in his stone-washed jeans, gray tee, brown leather jacket and matching leather boots. We *were* a handsome pair, I thought to myself. Riley reached for my hand and I clasped his tightly.

"Lead the way, Brooke." Riley's words were light and airy, something I needed to try and lift my unease. After reaching Dr. Carlson's office, I finally let go of Riley's hand to approach the check-in desk. As always, the office was warm with bodies but cold in every other way a physician's office could be.

"Hi, I'm here for a two o'clock appointment."

"Yes, Brooke Denton, right?" She was one of the ladies I'd seen a few times already before. I guess names and faces stick after a while.

"That's right."

"Have a seat. They should be ready for you shortly."

"Alright, thanks."

I turned around and Riley followed closely to the waiting area. He fell softly into the seat next to me. There was a short table in front of us, covered with copies of medical journals and gossip magazines. I thought Riley would reach for one of them to kill time but instead he rested his arm behind my seat and met my gaze.

"You seem antsy."

"A little." A lot was more like it.

"I haven't seen this side of you before." He rubbed my shoulder with his hand and pulled me over slightly to kiss the top of my head. The gesture sent calm through me from head to toe. I took a deep breath and exhaled with a sigh.

"I'm starting to relax." I thought of anything to change the subject. "So, your boss didn't give you a hard time about getting today off?"

"Nope, told him I had an appointment. Not too far from the truth, wouldn't you say?"

"No… it's not." I smiled.

"Where's the band playing tomorrow night?"

"The Red Room off Fifth Street. It will probably be a late show, so if you want you can leave early and crash at my place. I'd love to have you there when I get home."

"You can plan on it." I loved spending any night with Riley. We'd been staying together at least three nights a week. In fact, he'd been at my apartment so much the scent of him lingered on my pillows and sheets when he wasn't there, reminding me of him constantly.

A nurse entered the waiting area.

"Brooke?"

I rose from the chair, indicating I was the patient.

"You ready to come back?"

"Yes. Can my boyfriend come with me?"

"Sure." She smiled at Riley and stared a half second, no doubt mesmerized by his striking face. After reaching the examination room, Riley maneuvered himself to the only open chair in the small space. A plant placed closely next to the chair annoyingly brushed his shoulder; he pushed it back slightly. I took a seat on the examination table and the nurse moved as always to place a blood pressure cuff on my lanky arm. After completing her task she spoke aloud the always seemingly random blood pressure reading,

"110 over 65."

"Is that normal?" Riley questioned.

"It's good," the nurse answered him. "So, Brooke," she continued. "Is there anything you'd like to discuss with Dr. Carlson or anything new going on?"

"Not really. Actually, I feel like everything has been going pretty well. I've hardly had any episodes with my heart, at least that I've noticed. Just hoping everything checks out well today."

"Okay, good. I'll let Dr. Carlson know you are ready to see him." She wrote a few final notes and made her way out the door. After she had left, I heard her lay the chart in the bin attached to the outside of the door.

"So far, so good," I told Riley.

"I don't think I've had my blood pressure taken in years," Riley remarked.

"Yeah, when I was little I used to stick my arm in those blood pressure machines in drug stores. Thought it was a fun game. Little did I know I'd be doing it for the rest of my life."

"I remember those. I did that, too," Riley grinned. "What next?"

"Well, Dr. Carlson will come in, listen to my heart, check my ICD and ask a bunch of questions to make sure nothing's a red flag for concern. That's the typical drill."

"Sounds pretty routine."

"Yup, like clockwork now. He usually doesn't take too—" I was abruptly cut off by a knock at the door. Dr. Carlson entered the room in his typical white jacket that made the salt-and-pepper in his hair stand out. He was cheerful yet professional and moved without delay to shake my hand.

"Brooke, how are you?"

"Hi, Dr. Carlson. I'm doing great." The pitch of my voice climbed slightly. He took notice of Riley right away, being very untypical of my visits to have anyone other than Mom there. He moved to greet Riley with a handshake.

"Hello, sir. Who might you be?"

Riley returned a firm but brief handshake. "Hi, Dr. Carlson, I'm Riley."

"This is my boyfriend, Dr. Carlson." I blushed.

"Oh, well it's a pleasure to meet you." A grin escaped from the corner of Dr. Carlson's mouth.

"He's been eager to see what happens at these appointments and to learn more about my heart. I hope you don't mind."

"Not one bit," Dr. Carlson assured me and then leaned back against a small cabinet that housed a sink and random medical supplies. He rested the medical chart he'd been holding in one hand on a small counter.

"So, I'll go through the appointment as normal and explain to Riley why we check certain things and about the condition from a medical perspective. Is that okay with you, Brooke?"

"That would be perfect." I was surprised by the relief I felt having Dr. Carlson open to explaining things to Riley. It never occurred to me that I might want Dr. Carlson's approval of Riley, as well. I guess over the years we had developed a closer relationship that I had thought. Dr. Carlson began the examination while he chatted back and forth with Riley throughout. They spoke as if they'd always been acquaintances and Dr. Carlson was quite thorough.

Riley must have gathered a list of questions in his head because they came one after the other after the other. He was much more interested than I'd grasped. After nearly forty minutes, the end of the appointment neared. Riley's face beamed, I assumed from a sense of greater assurance and understanding. I think I was the most eager of anyone for the appointment to be over, seeing as it had taken twice as long as normal. Surely Dr. Carlson had other patients waiting, but if that was the case he didn't show it in the slightest.

"Well, kids, I think we've covered all our bases today." He looked me in the eye and continued, "Everything is looking good, Brooke. I'll have the nurse call in your prescriptions as usual and anticipate just as good an appointment in a few months." He excused himself from the room, shaking first my hand and then Riley's.

"Well, Riley, what do ya think?" I asked playfully.

"I'm glad I came," he said, reaching for my hand.

"So, what do you say we get out of here and get some grub with my mom?"

"Sounds like a plan." Riley's hand left mine and I edged myself off the examination table. His hand returned to my waist and he stayed close to my side leaving the building. Riley drove back to Mom's house to my relief, and Mom took us to a wonderful steak house we'd frequented on special occasions when I was growing up. We got back to the house late in the evening and chatted for hours over coffee and tea. Eventually, I struggled to keep my eyes open and decided it was time to turn in.

"I'm headed off to bed, guys," I yawned.

"I'll be right up," Riley grinned.

"Alright, kids, I'll turn in, too." Mom rose from her chair as Riley cleared the table of the empty coffee mugs.

"You don't have to do that, Riley. I can get that in the morning," Mom said.

"I've got it. I'm not one to leave a mess. Besides, my own mother would skin my hide if I didn't clean up after myself."

"Well, your mother's got the right idea. Thank you." Mom smiled appreciatively. "Hope you both get some rest." Mom winked at me and headed in the direction of her room. *What was that about?*

"You, too, Mom," I answered, caught off guard by the wink. I ascended the stairs to my room, poked through my bag for pajamas, and then grabbed a small bag of beauty essentials. Once in the bathroom attached to the bedroom, I turned on the shower. Riley still hadn't made it upstairs. I reflected on his willingness to learn so much about my condition and I felt my cheeks hurt from the smile on my face. Steam filled the bathroom as I let my towel drop and stepped into the shower. I succumbed to my thoughts, closing my eyes and resting my face beneath the water of the showerhead. I was interrupted by arms around me from behind. Riley began kissing my neck. "What are you doing in here?" I giggled.

"Well, the obvious, I hope," Riley whispered in my ear. I turned to kiss him.

"I've never done this in the shower," I made sure my tone assured him it was something I wanted to try.

He picked up the body wash and started lathering it on my arms and stomach. "Let's take this slow then." The lather dripped slowly down my body and onto Riley's as things feverishly intensified beneath the water. Once finished in the shower, Riley toweled me off, then himself before moving to my bed. There, Riley caressed my damp body in his capable hands. Starting at my neck, he teased kisses to my ear and then lowered to places that had me grasping the bedpost. When I wasn't sure I could hold out any longer, Riley eased into me and we made love again, deeply and a little roughly. The physical yearning for each other was at times too much to contend with mildly. He had me in his control and I wanted nothing more than to give every part of myself to him.

***

The following morning we said our goodbyes after devouring Mom's famous waffles. Even Alf got a waffle, courtesy of Riley; he wouldn't deny Alf a treat, even at the slightest whimper. We packed our things, loaded up Alf in the backseat of the Tahoe, and made our way back to

Austin. Riley was unusually quiet, opposite his demeanor the day before.

"What's on your mind, Riley?"

"I was just thinking about our day yesterday; lots of firsts, meeting your mom and Dr. Carlson. I guess I didn't really know what I was in for."

"Should I be worried?" I didn't hesitate to ask as I glanced out the car window; my heart filling with cracks, ready to shatter. I wasn't sure I wanted to know the answer to my own question.

"No way, not for a second." My tensed shoulders eased instantly. It was crazy how certain phrases or topics sent my emotions into a tailspin. "I like your mother, and I feel like I can stay more in tune with you and how you manage your heart condition now that I know more. To be honest with you, Brooke, it's sort of like—feeling complete. I never thought I'd have those feelings for anyone." I slipped my hand into his as it rested on the center console and rubbed it lightly with the tips of my fingers. He leaned over while still watching the road and kissed my forehead.

"You're like home to me too, Riley." I lifted his hand housed underneath mine and touched it softly with my lips; knowing deep down I could be with this person forever. I wished that even the simplicity and quietness of our time together on the car ride home wouldn't end, aching for him every second we spent apart. In another hour, we'd be back to reality and he'd have a show at a bar until the wee hours of the morning. I usually wouldn't stay the whole time, but tonight I didn't want to be apart from him. I broke the brief silence that had built.

"Hey, I want to stay for the entire show tonight and just head up there with ya'll. That okay?"

"There's no way I'd say no to that. Why don't we swing by your place, get you unpacked and Alf settled, and then we can head back over to my place?" I gave a nod in assurance that I was on board with the evening plans. We reached my apartment by the early afternoon, where I unpacked, repacked, and walked Alf outside a good while; knowing I'd be gone the rest of the night. I went back upstairs where Riley had fallen asleep, napping on my sofa. I used the time to take a brief shower then dressed for the evening. It was secretly a little fun picking out outfits for his shows because it gave me a chance to reflect a fun, flirty, feminine side I couldn't show at work. I also felt Riley secretly liked seeing that side of me, too. I dressed in a fitted, black and white V-neck cocktail dress with black leather, mesh, and suede sling-back sandals, and a light, black mock leather jacket to go over the dress. I grabbed my repacked bag, went over to Riley, and stroked his hair to slowly wake him, but that abruptly ended when Alf saw me giving Riley attention and proceeded to run over and lick his face.

"Alf… stop!" I exclaimed, laughing.

"Whoa, what time is it?" Riley woke instantly from his catnap.

"Relax, you've only been asleep about thirty minutes; it's three." He stretched his arms over his head and let out a long yawn before noticing that I'd gotten ready.

"Wow, Brooke… you look hot."

"Why, thank you….just threw this on." I was beaming from the attention, hoping it would lead to other things later.

"Brooke, you can make a ratty t-shirt look good." I laughed at his comment, not sharing his opinion, but as long as he believed it I didn't really care.

"If you say so. Are you ready to get out of here?"

"Yeah, we better." He moved himself up from the sofa, taking one last stretch and we headed back to his place.

<u>Chapter Thirteen</u>

While Riley ran around endlessly, gathering his equipment, I called Tessa and Julie to let them know where we'd be, hoping to catch up with them. I was delighted when they both said they could make it out. I lounged on Riley's bed while he made his way in and out of the apartment, loading up his equipment, but made myself get up before too long so that I wouldn't be tempted to close my eyes. I decided now was a better time than later to take my nightly meds. I didn't want to forget later. Not that I worried anything would happen in a brief lapse without them, but I'd rather not find out. After venturing to the kitchen for a glass of water and swallowing the handful of pills, Troy, Riley's roommate, strolled through the apartment door carrying a guitar case over his shoulder. Like Riley, he was crazy into music, teaching guitar classes at the same music shop where Riley worked. His sandy hair was short and shabby, and he stood just a few inches taller than Riley. He wore ragged jeans with holes at the knees and a plaid button-down shirt; the polar opposite of Riley's savvy dress style.

"Hey, Brooke. How's it goin'? You look great." His Texas accent couldn't be disguised.

"Thanks, Troy. Not bad at all, how about you?" Troy moved to rest the guitar case in the music area they'd allotted next to the living room.

"Ah, you know, only working on a super nice Saturday. I'm not whinin' or anything." I knew behind the sarcasm he wasn't kidding. Teaching music classes versus playing music was not exactly a musician's dream, but I also knew, as Riley had told me with his day job, it paid the bills.

"Are you going to be able to make it out tonight?" I asked then sipped the glass of water still in my hand.

"I'd love to hang out with ya'll but I'm actually meeting up with my band tonight; last minute practice before a big gig we've got going on tomorrow."

"That's a bummer. Maybe next time."

"Yes, definitely." He turned for the stairs but not before giving me a too-flirty look. "You really do look amazing, Brooke." I quickly digested his advance and raised an eyebrow to let him know that his chance to check me out was over. Troy cleared his throat. "Well, I'm going to go jump in the shower. See you later."

"Bye, Troy," I said, shaking my head. He skipped every other step up the staircase with his long lanky legs until he disappeared out of sight upstairs. Riley re-entered the apartment a short moment later.

164

"Did you see Troy come in? I passed him in the parking garage."

"Yes, he just went upstairs." *Should I open the can of worms about his flirtatiousness? I think not.* "I asked him if he wanted to come out tonight but he mentioned he had practice with his band."

"I bet. They're playing at a place tomorrow night that's supposed to have some music execs in town from Tennessee. They'll want to be on top of their game. Never know, they could get signed."

"Why aren't you playing there then? Isn't that a perfect opportunity?"

"Yeah, but one of the guys in Troy's band knew someone, who knew someone, who pulled some major strings. Let's just say you don't want to ruin your chance trying to jam another band into the mix."

"I understand. I know your band has great things in store, too." I attempted to lift his spirits a little, although he didn't show the slightest hint of jealousy over Troy's chance.

"We can only hope and work hard."

"Well, you're amazing to me anyway." I grinned and moved towards him, placing my hands on his shoulders. He wrapped his arms around my waist.

"As long as I have you, Brooke, that's enough for me." I smiled at him.

"Oh stop. I know that's only half true."

"You got me. Okay, as long as I have you and a record deal, life would be pretty sweet." He slapped my bottom, both surprising and humoring me as I let out a squeal.

"That's better," I replied.

After everything had been loaded in his SUV, we headed off to dinner at a local burger joint before making our way to the bar. The other guys from the band were already setting up equipment when we arrived. The sun had set and the bar's neon lights lit up, setting the life of the bar into motion. There was hardly anyone at the bar yet; only being about eight, but that would change soon enough. While the guys were busy setting up, I saw Tessa make her way through the bar door. She had no trouble finding her way over to me in the half-empty place.

I tended to place myself as far away from the stage as possible; the noise level was just too much for my ears to take over and over. I was so excited to see Tessa as she motioned for a hug. She looked cute as always in a tight black skirt and bright blue halter-top; she had the best shoulders out of all of us. *I'm jealous*.

"How are you, Brooke?"

"Couldn't be better. We just drove in from Houston earlier. Had my appointment."

"Really? Riley went?" The look of surprise of her face was unmistakable.

"Yeah, said he wanted to."

"Well, how did it go?"

"I'm doing great, and on top of it all he hit it off great with my mom. I was shocked." I pulled a piece of hair behind my ear then wondered why Tessa was alone. "Is Lowell not coming out tonight?"

"He said no, he's really tired, had a long week, but it just means more girl time for me." Hardly five seconds after Tessa finished her sentence, Julie made her presence.

"Hi girls!" she shouted. She was, of course, dressed to the nines in a fitted white cocktail dress and spike heels. She moved to give each of us a small hug then sat beside us.

"I'm so happy to see you guys!" I exclaimed. "I love getting to spend time with my girls."

"Heck yeah! Work, guys, friends, and fun." Julie raised a drink in the air.

"Got that right. Now that I actually get out more with Riley in my life, I wonder what I missed out on before."

"Brooke," Tessa cut in, "you didn't seem this alive or happy before Riley. I mean to say, you were such a wonderful person before, but he's brought out a different side of you. I've never seen you glow like this." I thought about it a brief moment. She was totally right.

"You can thank Riley for that," I said with a bright smile on my face.

"Well, I'm ready to enjoy the evening if you ladies are," Julie chided. "Why don't we split a bottle of wine?"

"Great," I smiled.

"Sure," Tessa laughed.

Julie stopped the next waitress who walked by our table and ordered a bottle. My inhibitions were low tonight. Besides, I was under Riley's watchful eye, and my doctor had just given me a good bill of health. I wanted to have fun on one of the few times I'd actually stayed out to watch Riley an entire show and be with my friends.

As we chatted over our first glasses of wine, Riley made his way over to us, said hi to the girls and gave me a quick kiss before making his way to the stage to get started. An hour passed and the bar began to fill by the minute. A large crowd gathered around the stage and Riley made the intro for the band and then set the place to life with music.

After beginning my second glass of wine, I could feel a slight buzz developing. As far as I could tell, the busiest part of the night was in full swing. Tessa, Julie, and I laughed and laughed. I was elated; enjoying some of the people I cared for the most in my life being together.

Feeling tipsy and on top of the world, I scanned the bar, halting when my eye caught sight of something untypical across the bar. I did a double-take. There were two men sitting who looked oddly out of place. I couldn't quite explain it. It was almost as if they were in a deep conversation, but it seemed to be about the band the way they pointed over to them. One was dressed in designer jeans with a blazer, and the other in khakis and a starched button-down shirt with a young, hip haircut. I was a little slow to manage the words, but I asked the girls if they noticed them, pointing where the guys were sitting.

"Yeah, I see 'em," Tessa laughed at me, realizing I wasn't myself right now.

"Oh, they are totally music agents," Julie said with the utmost certainty.

"What?" My mouth fell open.

"Yeah, I've seen guys like them before. As much as I'm out, they pop up occasionally in town."

"It's sort of ironic. Riley's roommate is playing at a place tomorrow where some agents are supposed to be."

"Hm, well, if they are agents, that would be great for Riley's band, right?"

"Yeah, bu…" I paused mid-sentence. Deep down I realized I wasn't sure if everything he wanted was what *I* wanted. It would mean he may have to leave, and while I might be able to go, I felt tied here with my illness, doctors and health insurance from work. Not to mention, it would be really hard on my condition to travel all over.

"What is it, Brooke?" My worries must have been written all over my face but I decided to brush it off as if I were fine.

"Nothing, just the wine, I guess." My face felt doubly flushed now.

"Are you sure?" Tessa set her hand gently on my shoulder.

"Yeah, no, no, I'm fine." No need to spoil a perfectly good evening over it.

During the band's break, the two guys approached Riley and his bandmates. At that moment, something inside me knew what it was about. They spoke a few minutes; obviously a jovial conversation based on the laughter and gesturing of hands. Everyone was in good spirits over whatever the discussion was. When it ended, Riley came over, grinning ear-to-ear.

"What was that all about?" I inquired, pretending I had no idea, but the wine inhibited my ability to hide the obvious.

"Those are the guys going to see Troy's band tomorrow. They heard about this bar and the band and decided to pop in tonight."

"So, what did they say?" Tessa smiled. She appeared excited along with Riley at the idea of it all.

"Well, they liked us—said we should send them one of our demos. They'd like to have some other people back in Tennessee take a look at it."

"Wow, Tennessee." I forced a smile. I wanted to be fully supportive, but if Riley were to leave me I didn't know what I would do.

"Yeah, Tennessee. To be honest with you, I'm not going to dwell on it too much. Stuff like this isn't likely to come through, but it's great to know someone's at least taking an interest." I felt my shoulders slump slightly, but I gathered my composure and faked a smile.

"Well, I'm so happy for you."

"Thanks." He smiled back and placed himself in a spare seat at the table, then patted his leg for me to sit on his lap. I slid over from my seat to him and rested my head on his shoulder, feeling the wine.

"You okay, Brooke?" he whispered in my ear.

"I'm good, just a little, well, tipsy."

"Take it easy on yourself; don't overdo it. I won't tell you what to do, but I don't want you passing out on me or worse."

"I'm fine, promise." I caressed his cheek gently with my hand and then kissed him. He helped me up from his lap and made his way back to the stage with the band so they could continue on with the show. By two in the morning, we'd finished off two bottles of wine between the three of us and, while it may have hardly affected Tessa and Julie, I was a different story. From what I could tell, I was not an obnoxious intoxicated person; more like a very tired and slightly dizzy one. Julie insisted on taking me home, but I told her I was staying with Riley.

"Brooke, you need to get into a bed. It could be hours before they get packed up and home. Do you have a key to his apartment?"

"Yes… I do. It's in my purse." He'd asked me to keep it while he was playing.

Julie made a quick beeline to the stage in between songs and spoke into Riley's ear. She came back a few moments later.

"Alright, ladies, let's call it a night."

"Good idea," Tessa agreed.

"Fine," I added, perturbed.

"I already told Riley I was taking you to his apartment. Can you get me there?"

"Yes, I can get us there." Normally I'd have laughed at her for even asking, but she and I both knew I wasn't in the clearest state of mind. I hazily looked back at Riley to find him talking to a beautiful female whose body language screamed 'history'. It wasn't like she was coming on to him hard either. There was just clearly a past between them. "Wait. Wait," I said to stop Tessa and Julie. They looked over to where I was looking.

"Who *is* that?" asked Tessa.

"I have no idea," I slurred. Tessa and Julie obviously saw what I saw. Their bodies were too comfortable with each other, and the look on Riley's face was all too familiar. That spark, that twinkle in his eye. My world started spinning, actually spinning, and I ran for the door to go outside, collapsing on the nearest bench with my head between my legs, thoughts scattered. Julie and Tessa followed quickly after me with a bottle of water.

"Come on, Brooke. Let's go home. You're in no state to get into this right now," Julie sternly said, putting the water bottle in my hands.

"Who is she? *Who* is she? I'm not crazy, am I?" It felt like I had just run face-first into a wall. What was happening? Things were going so well and now… now I wasn't sure about anything. "I feel sick. I can't deal with this now. I need to go home."

Julie and Tessa were quiet, solidifying my concerns, each with a hand on one of my shoulders, comforting me. Comforting me because something was very wrong. "You want to go to your apartment instead?"

"Yes." Between the music agents and this mystery woman, seeing Riley later would be too much. I needed to clear my head from this dark heaviness and avoid unleashing my fury on him. I was too intoxicated to put up a good fight. It would only end badly.

"Here." I reached into my purse and pulled out Riley's key. "Will one of you make sure he get's this?" *Why did I even care?*

"I'll do it." Tessa offered and took it from me.

"Okay, I'll take you home. Ready?" Julie asked.

"Yes, definitely."

After walking from the bench to Julie's sporty little black Mercedes, she guided me to the passenger seat and I rested my head against the door after she'd shut it. Once at my apartment, Julie walked me inside.

"Alright, do you need anything, maybe some water?"

"No. Thank you, Julie. I just want to sleep." My words faded and then I didn't remember much. The mix of wine and emotions overpowered me. I must have fallen asleep after she'd let herself out because I didn't wake until I heard Alf barking loudly at hard knocking on my door. I tried to sit up but immediately realized that was a mistake; the room looked like it was spinning and my head throbbed. I forced myself up to answer the door and at least stop Alf's relentless barking. Deep within, I already knew who it was.

"One second!" I yelled to the door. *Lord, no more knocking or barking, please.*

"Brooke? Are you okay?" I heard Riley yell through the door.

I let out a sigh. *Here we go.* I opened the door. Riley looked drained but I'm sure I looked worse.

"Hey."

"Are you okay? Why didn't you go to my place? Tessa gave me the key but no explanation. I didn't get in until three in the morning and haven't been able to sleep wondering what's up." He sounded very concerned, which alleviated some of my rage. I moved so he could step inside but avoided his eyes. He had my things in one hand I'd left at his apartment and set them in the entryway.

"I really wasn't feeling well. That's all," I said passively. I didn't know if my stomach could handle bringing up why I'd actually gone home.

"Are you sure that's all? Listen, if it's about the music agents, seriously, don't worry."

"No, Riley. I'm happy for you, I promise." Unfortunately, acting was not a developed skill of mine and he looked at me with a frown.

"What is it, Brooke?" he said intensely.

"Nothing, Riley." But he wouldn't let up.

"Tell me."

"Nothing." I shook my head reproducing the throbs.

"Brooke."

"Ugh—fine. Who is she?" I snapped.

"What?"

"Don't *what* me. That girl from last night at the bar."

His face turned a shade whiter. "Oh, Brooke…"

"Don't. Don't, Riley." I walked away and into the living room. Riley followed.

"Brooke. It's nothing—"

"Don't lie to me, Riley! I know you. I know your body language. Who is she?" I turned around and his chest was in front of my face.

"It's my ex-fiancée." Another wall. I was smacked with another freaking blow. Breath left my body. I finally forced my eyes to his.

"Your *what*? There wasn't one time, one TIME you thought to bring her up?" I was shocked, my heart crumbling. "I told you everything. EVERYTHING, Riley!" I turned, stomping off back to my bedroom, sick from his confession.

"I know, Brooke—"

"You do? Well, thanks for being honest with me." I slammed the door in his face. Never had I been so angry with him, and even more, angry at myself about how vulnerable I'd allowed myself to be with him. "An ex-fiancée is a big deal, if you didn't know."

"Brooke, it's a long story. I should have told you. Look, will you let me in?" he pleaded.

"Are you still seeing her?" I blurted.

"What? No!"

"Then what was she doing putting her arms around you last night?" I was infuriated.

"Look, I'm so sorry you saw that. Yes, we were very serious, but that relationship was unhealthy. It wasn't a loving relationship, and damn well nothing like we have. It took a lot of time to recover from it."

"Recover?" I couldn't fathom where he was going with this. I finally relinquished and opened the door where he faced me.

"Yeah, it was a dark time. She had major co-dependency issues that I had to deal with. It's tough for me to talk about."

"Talk about… whoa," I whispered and suddenly felt my heart begin to thump a little harder than I knew it should. *Oh no.* I was going into an episode. I leaned against the wall next to the door and slid to the ground, struggling to get a deep breath in to help smooth things out and help it subside. Riley noticed right away that something was very wrong, dropping to his knees straight in front of me.

"Brooke."

"Hol… hold on a minute," I said, barely getting the words out while trying to keep my cool. I was just so angry that calming myself down was more difficult than usual.

"What do I need to do?" I shook my head side to side as to say "nothing". I closed my eyes, slowly forcing myself to manage my breaths as best I possibly could, feeling the pace of my heart's racing speed continue to worsen for a few seconds before slowly getting better. I counted in my head, 1, 2, 3, 4, 5, as I inhaled, sweat forming on my palms and on my forehead, and then exhaled slowly. It was scary to have very little control of my body during an episode. I was able to calm myself, but even during episodes that weren't as bad as this one, it was hard to keep a clear mind. My mind went into autopilot. I just needed to slow my breathing as best I could until my ICD could get things under control.

Finally, my heart's pace slowed and I felt my breathing sync better with its beats. The episode was passing. I hadn't looked up until that moment at Riley. When I did, his face was white, and I'm sure mine was no better.

"I don't really know what to say. I just want to know you're okay." His voice was shaky. Talk about bad timing.

"I'm okay, alright." This was the last thing I'd wanted him to see. "It could have been much worse."

"My God, Brooke, isn't that scary?"

"I've told you before, not anymore. It's just a part of life." Even after such an episode, I was not about to let Riley come to my rescue right now. I really wanted him to leave, to be honest. And I seriously needed to rest.

He moved from his knees in front of me to next to me against the wall. My body was screaming for him to hold me, take care of me, but my pride wouldn't let me look at him. My feelings were too raw.

I turned to him. "Riley, I don't want you here right now."

"Brooke, please let me stay with you." He wrapped his arms around me from behind, holding me as if terrified. For the first time, he'd seen the reality of something neither of us could control, but I wanted solitude.

"No. Please let me be. I want to be alone." I got up and broke our cold embrace. There was too much on my mind. I pointed to the front door to ensure that Riley knew I wasn't kidding.

"You know I love you. But I don't know what to think right now and I can't think straight with you around."

"Brooke…" I'd never seen Riley look the way he did. There was deep worry and sadness on his face. It didn't change my mind though.

"Riley," I said sternly. He rose from the floor and walked to the front door without touching me before leaving. Riley turned to face me.

"I'm not going to lose you, Brooke." And then he was gone.

Chapter Fourteen

It took Tessa a week and a half to convince me to even think about talking to Riley. Julie, on the other hand, did not try. She was very protective of me, and once someone lost her trust even a little, she didn't care for them at all. I understood where each of them was coming from. It wasn't like I planned on never talking to him again either, I just wanted to pull myself together. After he'd left on Sunday, I had cried for hours. I knew some of those tears were ones of basic exhaustion, but, in general, the entire situation had me down.

"So, you still haven't talked to him yet? Has he tried calling you?" Tessa asked at coffee the following week.

"She doesn't have to talk to him unless she wants to, Tessa," Julie gritted through her teeth.

"I realize that, Julie."

"I'm just *saying*."

"Okay. Okay, guys. I haven't talked to him yet, but I will," I said, interrupting them.

"Brooke, don't forget Riley said he had to recover from that relationship because his ex-fiancée had dependency issues. I think you should really hear him out. You know, when you are ready." Tessa had a valid point.

"Don't say his name!" The amount of disdain Julie had for Riley at that moment was almost humorous. My two best friends, being polar opposites, provided me with everything I needed to hear.

"What would I do without you two? I mean it," I said, breaking down a little. Throughout this entire week, I'd kept a callous, emotionally disconnected wall up—the result of feeling very hurt after opening up so much.

"Aww, Brooke. We love you," Julie and Tessa said simultaneously.

"I really love you guys, too. I think I'm going to head home though. I have to take Alf out." I started to gather up my things, humming along to the song softly playing over the PA system.

"Okay, girlfriend. Take it easy, please. Call us if you need anything. *Anything*. You don't have to be so tough, you know," Tessa said, worried I was straining my mind and body too much, especially after my episode.

"I know. I'll talk to you later."

Once home, I paced back and forth in my living room, debating whether I should open up the conversation to Riley or not. Luckily, the decision wasn't mine, after all, when my cell phone rang, making me jump—Riley's picture flashed across the screen and I took a few deep breaths before answering.

"Riley," I said shakily. I didn't know if I wanted to scream at him because I was angry, or cry because I missed him so much.

"Brooke. Will you speak to me? I know you're mad, but I promise I will tell you everything." He sounded desperate.

"Okay." I swallowed, not sure what to say.

"I want to see you. Can you meet me at Shepherd Park, by the lake?" Riley asked.

"Yeah, I can," I said quietly.

"In half an hour, by the bench near the bridge?"

"I'll see you there." A little part of me was truly excited to see Riley. I did love him. We would work this out, I thought. Shortly after hanging up, I looked at myself in the mirror. My style had been off the entire week. It was very hard for me to care about my appearance when I wasn't talking to the one person I ever wanted to look good for. Summoning the last of my energy, I managed to fix my makeup and hair before heading for the car. Alf followed me to the door, wagging his tail eagerly, but I decided to leave him at home so as not to be a distraction from the conversation Riley and I were about to have; one I felt very uneasy about.

As I pulled into the lake's parking lot, I saw Riley's car parked already. I stalled for a moment, unsure of where to park. Finally deciding on a spot, I made my way to the bench where we'd spent so many beautiful evenings. It got me choked up to think about those times—I missed them. Seeing Riley sitting on the bench set my heart aflame. He looked just as disgruntled as me.

"Brooke," he said, motioning for me to take a seat but being careful to not touch me as if I were off-limits. Riley respected the space I had asked for, but, at that moment, there was nothing I wanted more than to be in his arms again. It was crazy how quickly my will to be mad at him dissipated, like I had no control over my feelings for him.

"Thank you for coming," he said seriously.

"Riley, I'm sorry it took so long. I was… I was mad and hurt. I don't know. And then my episode… it was a lot."

"I know. I know. You don't have to justify anything. I owe you an explanation. An explanation about Ivy…" Hearing her name for the first time made me wince. "We met in college. In a songwriting class. After a few months, we were dating… after two years, I proposed. I'm sorry, Brooke, this is probably hard to hear."

I shrugged. "Tell me, Riley."

He nodded a heavy, slow nod and continued. "We were in different bands and hers was gaining a lot of momentum. They were popular all over the south, not just here, and soon they were booking tours all over. She'd be gone for a few months at a time, nothing too long, but I started noticing changes in her. It was like, every time she came back, a piece of her had faded away. Then her tour bus got pulled over in New Orleans and the next thing you know, I'm bailing her out of jail for stealing and drug possession. I didn't know, I should have known, but she hid it so well. It turned out she'd been using for much longer than anyone had guessed, had been in and out of rehab a few times. Never told me or hinted at it. Her parents didn't know either." He took a breath.

"Oh, Riley." I was shaken.

"Uh, well, once I found out I tried as hard as I could to help her. Supporting her recovery and keeping her away from those who didn't. She never really stopped using, though. No, Ivy always got what she wanted... I refused to give her money, and after a few weeks she came home with a bag of pills and told me she'd slept with one of her fans for it. I meant what I said the other day about recovery from this relationship; it took me years to realize how unhealthy and malignant it had become. I'm sorry, Brooke. It was a dark time in my life that at times doesn't even seem real to me. I called off the wedding. I called off everything. God, she was so upset, but I wanted my life back... all I did was worry. Then that night I ran into you at Impresso I'd been drinking. It was the anniversary of when I'd broken it off." *That explains his foul mood when we first met.*

"I can't even fathom," I said softly.

"At times, I can't either. I was shocked when she called me at your place out of the blue and then to see her

184

at the bar the other night. It was the first time we had seen each other in a year and a half. I guess she is out of rehab now. I'm happy for her if she has cleaned up, but I've learned my lesson. She knows how I feel. I don't want anything to do with her," he said firmly.

"She really hurt you, Riley. I'm sorry."

"Brooke, she took away parts of me that I have only been able to get back because of you. I didn't open up or care about anything except my music for so long until you came into my life. I love you, Brooke. I really do." I couldn't stand the distance between us any longer.

Nearly jumping in his lap, I placed my lips on his and kissed him sweetly. He'd looked so hurt and sad while telling me about Ivy, and all I wanted to do was make him feel better. "Riley."

"Yes?" he said with a starry look.

"You've still got me, baby." He pulled my face to his, kissing me again.

"I don't know what I would do without you."

"I don't know either."

"Are you hungry?"

"Are you ever *not*?" I asked, laughing with a heart so full I thought it might burst. Having Riley back felt invigorating; it felt right. "Come back to my place. I've got food there."

"You don't have to ask me twice, Brooke."

"All right. Let's go." Just like that, our sync was back and the whole thing seemed like a dream. At that moment, Ivy was out of mind, but I couldn't anticipate my reaction if I were to see her with Riley again.

Back at my house, our dinner of sautéed pork and vegetables in a light garlic marinade was cut short by our imminent need for one another. Though it had only been a week and a half since I'd last seen Riley, it felt like much longer. It wasn't until then that I realized how much energy Riley gave me. I wanted to go out, I wanted to explore and do things. I guess he had given me back pieces of me, as well. Parts that I had lost with my dad and my condition. He had me and I was hooked. We would rebound from this and grow, of that much I was sure.

<u>Chapter Fifteen</u>

Fall came too fast, and a new year of teaching second-graders ensued. I missed having more free time with Riley like we'd enjoyed over the summer, but work was work. It was near the end of September, and the weather had begun to cool. On a Thursday afternoon, just after I'd let my class out for the day, Tessa stuck her head into my room.

"Hi, Brooke. Have a good day?"

"Same old same old, but can't complain."

"So, are you and Riley up for dinner tonight? Lowell wanted to get everyone together at Lone Star Steakhouse.

"That sounds nice, count us in." I knew Riley didn't have anything going on tonight and never turned down a chance to go get a good steak.

I didn't go out as much now as before when Riley played. After my night of overdoing it a few months back, he'd asked that I try to call it a night early when I did make a show. I knew he was only looking out for me, and I just felt glad I hadn't had any episodes since. I'd recently had another checkup back in Houston, and Dr. Carlson, after numerous tests due to my most recent episode, found that

187

my vitals and levels were better than he had expected. He still made me promise to take it very easy and take excellent care of myself. It was really my own fault, but I truly hated it, and started to hate that my disease didn't allow me to be with Riley more often, especially when he was doing what he loved to do. He swore that he would tell me if Ivy ever came to one of his shows again. Apparently, she hadn't showed up since that other night. Likewise, Riley never spoke about the record execs that had approached him the night before my episode, nor did he hear back from them. Secretly, I was relieved to have our normalcy back, but realistically, I knew that it was what Riley had been working so hard for. So, for the time being, I decided to act as if that night had never happened, although the thought and reality of it always remained in the back of my mind. Riley always made me feel like he'd do anything for me, that he'd never want to live without me, but if an opportunity came knocking for him, what would we really do? I hoped it would all just work itself out, and denial seemed like the best way to deal with the uncertainty of it all at the moment.

Tessa and I made small talk before we made our way home, and I called Riley on the way, the phone ringing only two times before he answered,

"Hi, Brooke."

"How was your day?"

"Alright. Paying the bills. Yippee." We both knew he only had a day job in order to follow his dreams of stardom and music.

"Want steak for dinner? Tessa said Lowell wants all of us to meet up for dinner."

"Yeah, Lowell said something about that. Did he happen to talk to you this week?" Riley asked. *Why would he?*

"No. Why?"

"No reason," Riley was quick to respond.

"What's going on, Riley?" *What's he up to?*

"Nothing....nothing to worry about. Trust me."

"Hmm, you've really got me wondering now."

"So what time do you want me to come by and pick you up?" Riley questioned, seemingly in an effort to end the conversation before getting himself into more lines of questioning.

"I'll be ready at six-thirty."

"Be there then. Love you."

"You, too." I hung up the phone and spent a brief time wondering what I was missing. I felt like the only one out of the loop regarding my best friend.

Riley arrived to pick me up and we made our way to the steakhouse. Questions lined up in my head. I wanted to drill Riley more about tonight but hesitated. I looked out the window, tapping my hand against my leg.

"Relax, Brooke. What are you so worried about?"

"I smell a rat."

"Well, you shouldn't," Riley laughed, removing one hand from the wheel to stroke his fingers through my hair.

"Will you tell me why Lowell called you?"

"Are we not allowed to talk? Just guy stuff you know."

"Yeah, says every guy trying to hide something… spill it."

"I can't, it would ruin it." That's when it hit me. I felt like such an idiot for not guessing sooner.

"No way!" My eyes bugged out of my head and my voice lifted an octave.

"Damn," he said sarcastically. "You really think you know, huh."

"He's going to finally ask her to marry him."

"Yup, you've got it. Just don't act like you know anything… please?" Riley half-grinned.

"Don't worry about me. Wait a minute," I paused and briefly thought of why Riley was in on all of this. "Why did Lowell tell you and not me?"

"I think I actually don't want to answer that. I think you'll see why when it all goes down." The sincerity in his response led me to not dig any deeper. He was being honest and it showed.

"Okay. But you know I'm dying over here." The drive didn't last but a few minutes longer, but the anticipation I had for Tessa grew by the millisecond. I couldn't have been more excited… The parking lot wasn't too crowded, being a weeknight. My anxiety level was at its peak, and my happiness difficult to contain. I would have to be a good actress for the next hour or so, which made me even more anxious since I was awful at lying. The gravel crunched beneath our feet to the entrance of the steakhouse. Although rustic in appearance, in a log-like building, the interior was much fancier, with tablecloth covered tables and nicely dressed wait staff. Even more eye-catching was the view of Lake Austin behind the windowed walls. It was the perfect setting for Lowell's proposal scheme.

Riley and I saw everyone - Tessa, Lowell, Julie, and a few other friends gathered already at a white-clothed table near the backside of the restaurant where the view of the lake was best. We sat in two empty seats left at one end of the table and exchanged hellos with everyone, trying to mask what was about to unfold but difficult to contain the surprise. I was pretty sure Julie had already figured it out, too because she was almost too quiet, a trait she seldom showed unless trying to hide something. The waiter made his way around the table taking drink orders, and returned promptly with an assortment of wine, beers, iced teas and water.

"So glad you could all make it here tonight, guys. It's nice to get everyone together every once in a while," Lowell said happily.

"Thanks for getting us all together," Riley smiled.

"How about a quick toast?" Lowell spoke again. We all gathered our glasses together at the center of the table. "To a great evening of good food and good friends." Everyone's glasses clinked gently and the voices of everyone exclaimed the happy mood of the evening. As dinner moved along, I awaited the moment Lowell would take advantage and pop the question. He seemed so poised, as if nothing was about to take place. I even gently nudged Riley one time, but he just looked at me with a big grin, squeezed one of my shoulders gently, and kissed my cheek. By the time the main course concluded, and it was quite apparent everyone had enjoyed the wonderful food, my heart pitter-pattered a little harder. Riley suddenly excused himself.

"I'll be right back, everyone."

"Where are you going?" I whispered questioningly.

"The bathroom," he spoke plainly.

"Huh?"

After Riley had left the table, dessert arrived, and a short time later Lowell stood up at one end of the table, clearing his throat. Riley reappeared with his guitar in tow, slowly strumming it in a delicate tune and taking a seat in an open chair just behind Lowell.

Tessa appeared surprised and delighted all at once, beaming in her orange dress. Lowell offered his hand to her and she took it.

"There was a song I wanted Riley to play for you because it expresses everything I feel for you, and, even more importantly, it's our song." Riley strummed his guitar a little more strongly and beautifully sang a rendition of the song *All Of Me*. Tears welled up in Tessa's eyes as she realized what was unfolding. As the song closed, Riley took one last strum of his guitar and Lowell proceeded to get down on one knee in front of Tessa.

"It's been too long coming, Tessa. I love you with all of my heart and want nothing more than to spend the rest of my life with you. Will you marry me?" He then slipped a stunner of a diamond onto her finger. *Wow, what a ring!*

"Of course, I will." Tessa embraced Lowell's face in her delicate hands and he kissed her deeply.

I felt tears running down my own cheeks. Even Julie had one roll down her immaculate face at the amazing moment, and we all expressed happy congratulations as soon as the moment had passed. Riley moved back over to me, setting his guitar down in his lap.

"You did an amazing job, Riley." I kissed his cheek.

"It was all for them. I feel honored to have been asked to help."

"I love you," I whispered in his ear. "You really made this special for them."

"I love you, too." We kissed softly on the lips and then made our way over to exchange hugs and handshakes.

"You've got to let me see this rock," I laughed with Tessa.

"Isn't it gorgeous?" Tessa couldn't stop smiling. Julie joined the moment.

"It's huge, Tessa. Maybe I should give this marriage thing a try, after all," Julie joked. "Now we've got a wedding to plan!"

"Yes, *maybe* you should, Julie. Oh, man, the wedding. I hadn't even thought of that. What colors? Where?"

"Shhh... take it easy, Tessa. Tonight we celebrate, tomorrow we plan," Julie said with a huge grin on her face while Tessa glowed. It was a spectacular night.

***

We didn't end our night there, deciding to all go out and celebrate at a bar downtown, staying out much later than I could manage. I didn't have anything to drink, yet just the thought of having to wake up in a few hours to get ready for work made me eager to head back home. I tugged at Riley's elbow, indicating I was ready to leave. We said our goodbyes and final congratulations and made our way for his car, parked a few blocks away. We strolled hand-in-hand, taking in the joy of the night. Just before reaching the car, ironically enough, was a jewelry store filled with beautifully arranged diamond jewelry displays in a series of small window showcases. I glanced at them, slightly entranced. I suppose it was simply more enticing with the vision of Tessa's beautiful pear-cut ring still etched in my imaginative mind. I could see Riley's head turn slightly toward me as I scanned the exquisite merchandise.

"See something you like?" Riley chuckled.

"How's a girl to choose?" I giggled back.

"Really, though, do you see something that tickles your fancy?" Riley surprised me. His thumb began to stroke the back of my hand softly.

"What? Where did that come from? Not that I should be complaining or anything, you just caught me off guard."

"Well, haven't you thought about it before? I thought nearly every girl has at some point or another." My face felt a little numb. I was dumbfounded. It occurred to me that Riley had gone through ring picking and wedding planning with Ivy, making him more in tune to the desires of females. I felt a slight spark of jealousy go off in my mind, knowing if he did ask me to marry him it wouldn't be his first time around. The feeling quickly vanished as Riley knowingly put his lips to my forehead for a soft peck. The entire topic of rings threw me off-center for a second, but I had had the option in the moment to confess my secret dream ring. Marrying Riley was totally in the picture for me, I just never wanted to screw anything up between us by bringing it up before he did. He was everything to me. What did I have to lose? Maybe this would open up a new door to the prospect of a forever with Riley.

"Well?" Riley smiled down into my eyes, breaking the awkward moment of silence.

"Yes, I do have a 'dream ring' if you'd really like to know. It's sort of different, though."

"I like different. So, will you tell me?" I stepped forward, breaking our locked gaze and Riley followed, walking slowly, matching my steps. I could feel him still looking down at me and I closed my eyes, briefly envisioning the ring I'd always pictured. I never knew where the idea had come from, just that I liked the idea of its meaning.

"It's really not anything like what you see here in these windows," I lifted my hand, pointing towards the jewelry in the storefront. "I've always had a thing for rubies and want to incorporate them into a ring. I see a sparkling white round diamond with two rubies placed on either side of it; the rubies symbolizing the joining of two hearts and the diamond in between being how brightly the love shines. It's pretty cheesy, I know, but it's what I picture."

"It's not cheesy, Brooke." Riley draped an arm over my shoulder and placed his opposite hand in his pant pocket. "It sounds amazing, like something you really want." We picked up our pace, leaving the jewelry store.

"Maybe someday you'll get just what you want."

"Maybe." I smiled as he kissed the top of my head again and proceeded to go to the car. After starting it up, he sat frozen with both hands on the steering wheel.

"Riley? You okay?" I rested a hand on his back. He stared, eyes locked forward.

"I want to be that person for you, Brooke."

"What are you saying?" I took a deep breath. Riley finally turned towards me, taking my hand and looking into my eyes with more intensity that I'd ever seen before, even the first time we'd made love.

"I'm saying, Brooke, that I want to be your everything someday; I hope not far off. I don't know, we've never really talked about it, but seeing Lowell and Tessa made me realize that's what I want, and I hope to get that chance someday with you. That is, if you want me the same way." My lips expanded instantly into a huge smile and I reached for his handsome face, kissing him, wanting nothing but to feel my lips touch his. I grasped that we were every bit on the same page with wanting a future together, forever.

"There's nothing I want more, Riley. There's no one else for me but you." He gave a joyful smile back and kissed me for several minutes, the car idling. It was a moment I'd never forget; the moment we closed the door on his past so we could have a future.

<u>Chapter Sixteen</u>

After the night of Tessa and Lowell's engagement, my relationship with Riley headed for new territory. We were now certain of the direction we were headed, marriage. I sensed moving in together was inevitable, and hoped that with the holidays quickly approaching the perfect time to discuss it would present itself. I didn't for a second doubt he'd say yes.

Riley had been incredibly busy over the fall, with more shows around town; even shows out of town had picked up. The band was gaining more of a following with each passing day, but there was still no word from the record agents who had seemed interested months before. I continued to act as if nothing would ever happen, denying in my head that anything would ever be different, and undeniably content with the present. Riley would continue to play, hopefully get a more secure job down the road, and we'd get married. Perhaps it was selfish, desiring things to pan out just that way, but it's what *I* wanted.

The weather had cooled and the sky was laced with gray clouds. School was out for Christmas vacation and I'd spent the afternoon trimming the small artificial tree I'd used since college. Alf lounged on the large rug under the living room coffee table, drifting off every once in a while. I picked up a box of glass ornaments from a storage container on the couch and strategically placed powder blue and lavender ornaments on the tree already covered in white lights and silver tinsel. The crisp winter evening grew dark quickly, and I awaited a nightly call from Riley. He was playing downtown tonight and I'd decided to take the evening to get a good night's rest before my scheduled appointment the next day in Houston; only planning on driving up for the day, going to the appointment, grabbing lunch with Mom, and heading back the same evening.

At five, my phone rang, causing Alf to perk up then re-situate himself. I set the ornaments on the couch and grabbed the phone from off the coffee table. I scrunched up a sleeve of my oversized sweater as I answered it.

"Hi."

"Hi, baby."

"Are you about to leave for your show?" I asked.

"Yeah, are you sure you can't make it out?" he whined.

"Yes. I want to go, but I have to get up super early tomorrow to drive to Houston, remember?"

"That's right! Your appointment is tomorrow. I'd completely forgotten. Want me to drive up with you? I'll call in sick."

"Absolutely not. I'll be fine."

"Well, it shouldn't be too late a show. If we get out before midnight, I'll head over and leave for work from your place in the morning."

"Sounds great!"

"Love you."

"Love you, too, Riley."

After hanging up the phone, I sat on the couch, admiring my decorated tree, thinking about Riley as he prepped for his show. *I should just go.* But, then again, I knew what I was in for the next morning. My hair had grown and I wound the silky locks into a bun, keeping it in place with a black ponytail holder that had been around my wrist then sat down, intending to rest briefly, but dozed off instead. I awoke on the couch, the news on the television. I grabbed for the cell phone to find the time and saw that it was ten. I set the phone back down, deciding a good hot bath sounded perfect. Almost to the bathroom, I heard my cell phone ring back in the living room. "I wonder who that could be," I muttered, walking back and looking at the phone. Tessa's name popped up on the screen.

"Hey, Tessa."

"Hi, Brooke, what are you doing?"

"I just woke up. I fell asleep earlier after I decorated my Christmas tree. The holidays are positively draining, aren't they?" I said overdramatically.

"Ha, I couldn't agree more!" Tessa laughed.

"Anyways, what's going on with you?" It was a little later than she usually called.

"Well," Tessa said it an enthusiastic voice, "I wanted to see if you'd go look at bridesmaid dresses with me this weekend. You up for it?"

"Of course, you know I'll be there." Tessa had decided nearly everything for the wedding in only a few months. They'd planned for an April wedding at a church they had both attended since college. "As long as I don't have to wear bubblegum pink and big puffy sleeves, you can stick me in any dress you want," I laughed.

"Okay, no problem there, I can assure you," Tessa laughed back. "I'll email you the dress shop info and plan on meeting you there Saturday about two."

"Sounds good. Talk to you soon," I agreed and hung up the phone, feeling a smile on my face, thinking about how happy I was for Tessa. Everything was playing out just as it should where she and Lowell were concerned, and I was honored to be a part of it.

I went to fill the tub, wondering about Riley, imagining his thick arms and toned back. I loved when he picked me up like I weighed nothing. After I had undressed and gotten into the hot water, the bubbles filling the tub flowed over my taught body. I couldn't help but think again of Riley more; undressing him, teasing him. He made me feel like I never had before. While sitting there in the now-full tub, I decided to let my hands explore the parts of my body I'd grown very fond of. Riley had opened me up to that, and I thought of him as pleasure grew within me. I played around for a while before I could no longer control the charge. Panting in satisfaction, I relaxed into the tub, unable to do much else. A total calm fell over me.

***

At some point, I fell asleep, the same recurring dream of my father taking place. Only this time he—my dad—was talking to me from afar, as if trying to tell me something. I tried in my dream state to make it out. Finally deciphering some of it from reading his lips. "It will all be okay, he won't give up…" My eyes jerked open, tears streaming down my face. *I miss you, Dad. So much.* I felt ashamed, realizing I hadn't thought of him much lately. I'd been in my own world, like I'd covered his memory up with my newfound happiness. But why in the world would he try to convey a message to me, and what did it mean? 'It will all be okay, he won't give up.' Was Dad talking about Riley?

I dried my eyes. *What an emotional bath,* I thought as I went to the bathroom to wash my face and take my medicine. After completing the tasks and turning off the bathroom light, a knock at the door startled me.

I guess he had gotten done before midnight, I reasoned, walking to the living room. Alf hopped up and raced in anticipation to the door.

"Sit, Alf." He obeyed. I glanced into the door's small peephole, a result of watching too many true crime television shows to not take precautions, but sure enough it was Riley.

I opened the door, and Alf's barks erupted instantaneously.

"Hey, beautiful." He swooped in, picked me up and twirled me in a circle. While in his arms, I felt his heart beating hard; he appeared excited beyond words. Immediately, alarm bells sounded in my head.

"Hi, yourself! Why so chipper?" I questioned.

"I have so much to tell you, Brooke. We have so much to talk about. I don't even know where to start."

"Well, you have me all worked up now! What is it?" Alf attempted to hop up to get Riley's attention, which he, of course, did as Riley knelt down to hug his neck.

"Hey, Alf, such a good dog." Whatever was going on, Riley was like a kid on Christmas morning. The smile on his face was ceaseless and he had the energy level of someone who'd just consumed an entire pot of coffee.

"What's going on?" I laughed, his energy contagious.

"Oh, my God, Brooke! I don't even know where to begin. It was so unexpected. They came tonight, they were there."

"Who? I'm lost, Riley."

"Let's just say—are you ready to move to Tennessee?" My soul disintegrated into a million pieces, as did my wall of denial. I suddenly had tunnel vision; everything I'd wanted was now slipping away. My dreams and desires tumbled like a house of cards in the wind. My heart sank even more.

When I didn't say anything because I was physically unable to, Riley leapt to scoop me up again, spinning me around.

"We did it, Brooke. We got signed! We're supposed to fly out tomorrow. Are you ready to go to Tennessee and start a new life there?"

"Wha... What? Tomorrow!?" I was careful to stay calm and keep my breathing controlled; I wasn't about to let having an episode every time someone dropped a bomb on me be the norm.

"Yes, baby! It's okay if you come up later, I know you have to notify your work—"

"Riley." I didn't know what to say to him, but I needed to stop him. Every word he said was killing me and I felt even worse for not sharing his enthusiasm. The latter part sounded perfect, it really did. The problem, however, was I didn't believe that I was in any way able to pick up and leave with my condition. Also, if I didn't teach, I wouldn't get health insurance, and there was no way I could get coverage on my own, not with the cardiomyopathy. One slight change in my condition could lead to utter financial ruin. Then I couldn't travel with Riley if they toured; it would be too exhausting to my heart. And look what had happened with his ex-fiancée. The industry changes people.

Still, I couldn't manage to say anything to Riley. I felt my cheeks sag.

"Brooke, why won't you answer? Aren't you happy, too?"

"Of course, I am, Riley. I'm sorry... This is everything you ever wanted." I was dying inside with every word I spoke. My next words would change the course of everything we'd built and I knew it—painfully knew it. I had to be the voice of reason for both of our sakes.

"Riley, I can't go."

"You don't have to go right away, Brooke, but soon enough," he said, trying to assure me.

"No. Riley, I can't go." And realizing the finality in my voice, Riley understood.

"*What*?" His smile faded and he tried desperately to look into my eyes, but I wouldn't look back. I couldn't, it hurt too much.

"Riley, I want to be with you but with my heart condition I can't just pick up and leave. I have insurance, which I get through work. I can't get any on my own; they'd never give it to me. Then there's my doctor here in Texas, he's been my doctor since the beginning and not only that, Riley, I can't travel with you if you go on tour, it's just too much. And what about your ex? Look how that ended. Music is your life, though, so I'm going to do the one thing I thought I'd never do. You need to go. You've waited your whole life. Go live your dream. This is your chance, but I have to stay here."

"Brooke, I won't let you do that. You're everything to me."

"No, I'm not, Riley. I'm second and the music was first, it's how it should be." I tried with all my might to build up anger to make the point clear, yet I hated every word that escaped my mouth. I knew what was coming, and it was easier to be angry and mad than sad and broken. I didn't want to live without him, but I couldn't see any other way that would be fair to him.

"Where are you going with this, Brooke?" He started to pace back in forth in my living room.

"Riley, we can't—"

"Brooke, please don't do this." Riley kept searching my eyes, cupping my face. Still, I wouldn't look at him. Tears formed and then flooded my eyes. I raised my voice,

"Riley, you need to leave. I can't keep you here." I worked my way to the front door, breaking Riley's grasp around me.

"No. Not without you."

"Don't say that. Don't! Please, just leave. You know this is best." I turned the doorknob and motioned for him to leave. "I love you, Riley, but I can't do this to you." He refused to make his way out the door.

"You really want me to leave? Leave you?" Our eyes locked.

"Yes." And my heart was no more, like I'd ripped it out with a knife. As his gaze dropped to the floor, his face was pained. He hesitantly moved towards the door.

"I'm never giving up on you. You're making a mistake." Riley walked out the doorway, turning to me one last time.

"I love you, Brooke." I saw his face tense up, fighting the tears forming in his eyes. "I'm not going to lose you."

"Bye, Riley." I tried not to choke on my words through the tears then closed the door. Hearing him go down the stairs, I slid down the door and dropped to the floor. The devastation was overwhelming, and I sobbed for hours and hours, never moving. Alf sat at my side on the cold floor all night. Life was changed and I felt as if I was dying slowly with every passing minute. *Why? Why take another person I love from me?*

<u>Chapter Seventeen</u>

Time didn't really seem to exist after ending things with Riley. Depression set in as I entered a deep, dark, numb place. For days upon days after Riley had left, he'd call. At first it was at least five times a day, then after a month it dwindled to once per day until, finally, at the beginning of February, the calls ceased, making the weight of my decision slightly easier to bear. Never once did I answer. I wouldn't let myself. I continued to teach, but my spark was gone. I did my job but without the passion for it I'd once had. Life was slowly leaving my once-vibrant soul and I just didn't care—at all. My heart was broken.

Mom nearly had a panic attack when I didn't show in Houston for my appointment the day after Riley had left. She begged me to never do that to her again. I'm not proud of how I responded to her, crying and yelling at her, telling her to leave me alone and let me be. Her mother's intuition sped into overdrive.

"Brooke. Now I know something is wrong. What is it?" she asked gently but firmly. My mom always got to the bottom of things quickly. When I told her Riley had left and that I'd ended the relationship, she appeared to share some of the pain with me, constantly worrying and calling to check in on me numerous times per day.

I put off my appointment with Dr. Carlson, not wanting to reschedule until I finally ran out of my scripts. I didn't want to go and didn't really care. I couldn't bring myself to think anything mattered anymore. I didn't want to live without Riley, yet at the same time, I knew I'd have to keep going for *something*. That's what my therapist had told me after my dad died—although other than Mom, Julie, and Tessa, I didn't know what would keep me going, as my faith in basically everything had dwindled.

I attempted the duties of a bridesmaid, assisting with showers and picking out dresses, all the while putting on a show I knew Tessa could see right through. I didn't want to ruin her happiness, but the depths of my depression grew deeper and deeper, and keeping up the act was a joke.

Julie would stop by my apartment once a week and just let me cry on her shoulder. I had no words, but seemingly infinite tears. *Oh, the never-ending tears.* Each time she'd bring me my favorite take-out dinner from around town, but I wouldn't eat. I'd lost nearly ten pounds and I hated looking at my pale, sickly complexion in the mirror. My energy was completely used up by late winter, and all I'd do after work was sleep. Every waking moment was painfully draining and I'd stopped doing yoga or even taking Alf for the long walks he was used to. I ignored my torn and tattered heart—often feeling faint and ill, but I'd take more medicine, try to sleep through it, and certainly didn't tell Mom or call Dr. Carlson, although I knew I should have. My ignorance was plain stupid, but stupid didn't register with me—not now.

Alf was the best companion to me during the first dark days. He wouldn't leave my side, sensing my anguish. This killed me, too because I could sense he missed Riley as much as I did. The poor thing often stared at the front door for hours while sitting next to me, as if waiting for Riley to come back.

One rainy, winter February Friday, I finally made the drive to Houston for my rescheduled appointment. The drive felt eternal, the air cold and wet, transitioning from rain to sleet, sleet to rain. I made sure to drive slowly as large trucks passed me at racing speeds. I didn't turn on the radio. Music was kind of a tough subject for me to face, so I sat in silence, my face expressionless and my energy non-existent. I couldn't think about anything but Riley; his luxurious smell, dark hair… the way he looked at me. After weeks and weeks of crying, it appeared all my tears had dried up, so I simply drove on with a gaping wound in my heart that refused to heal.

When I made it to Mom's, it had been weeks since I'd last seen her, not since Christmas when I'd forced myself for the first time ever in my life to go home for the holidays. I wouldn't have made her spend Christmas alone, but even that felt lifeless and pointless. The second she laid eyes on me, helplessness and fear appeared on her face and she cried—grasping me in a hug only a mother can give.

"Brooke, you look terrible. You can't keep this up," she spoke softly in my ear, holding me in the driveway. My facial expressions stayed stagnant—lifeless. I was an empty shell of a person.

"I know, Mom." I paused a brief moment in her embrace, "I just don't know where to go from here."

Mom drove to the appointment, at first trying to make small talk. When it failed, she reverted to the topic of Riley.

"Brooke, why don't you just call him? Stop all of this nonsense and just choose to be happy again." I couldn't help but roll my eyes, having developed bitterness towards the world and angry at how simple she believed it would be. *He doesn't need me. I can't be everything for him. Fate betrayed me.*

"It's not that simple, Mom. I mean, look at me—I have to be able to go to a specialist frequently and I can't handle traveling for long periods of time. What do you think Riley will be doing? Traveling, a lot. More importantly, you and I both know I can't get insurance coverage on my own without being employed, no one would touch me with my condition. I won't be able to keep a job if he has to move frequently. And we both know if this condition turns south, the bills will be astronomical. I'd never ask or put you into financial strain even if you wanted to help because I know you're itching to cover some of the bills. It's not fair to him to have to think and worry about me when his dream is finally happening. I hate it, but it's the only way, okay? So stop trying to make it sound so simple. I thought you'd understand my condition's limitations more, Mom. It's like you're totally blind to the obvious! Maybe you should just stop butting in on my love life, okay?" Mom looked at me with a blank stare, knowing I wasn't mad at her, just unfairly taking out my anger on her. When I thought about what she'd put up with I realized she really was a saint. I felt like pulling all my hair out but settled on letting out a small bit of anger by rubbing my hands on my legs quite frantically. I must have looked a sight in a gray sweatshirt, black leggings and tennis shoes—my hair unwashed for days and last night's mascara still on my lashes. My hair was limp and had turned a duller brown from my normal lively color because I had also stopped going to my hair appointments. I could tell Mom contemplated everything I'd just abrasively laid out then she said something I needed to hear.

"Brooke," she said in her most soothing voice, one that had the amazing ability to momentarily abate all my problems. "I see your argument, but you can't keep up like this, it could kill you. Think about the weight of that. You're obviously not taking care of yourself. I believe that if fate puts the love of your life in your path, there is a way to get past anything. Love finds a way if you believe in it,

Brooke. I don't think you gave him the chance he deserved, at least if you had, then you could say you tried and it simply didn't work. Now you'll never know." As Mom completed her argument, we pulled into the parking garage and parked in an empty spot. I turned to her.

"So, you think it's my fault then," I said icily.

"Brooke, I…"

"No, Mom. You're right… you're right. I could kill myself this way, and, yes, I'll regret never knowing what could have been. But I feel like I'm being fairest to him by giving him a one-hundred-percent chance of watching his dreams come to life without me there to slow him down." Though I got defensive, the truth of the matter was that I believed every word of what Mom had expressed. I yearned to call Riley and tell him I couldn't stand to live without him any longer, but my idea of what was best for him stood in my way. I knew deep down he'd come in a heartbeat, but I felt like I needed to let time carry on in the hopes that the pain would alleviate for the both of us—eventually.

"I'm going to say it how I see it, Brooke... I won't mention it again, but I think you're wrong. I believe he needs you as much as you need him." I let out a long, slow sigh then sat in awkward silence—playing dumb. I was not having this conversation again. I needed to conserve some energy for the appointment.

"Well, we better get going. I'm sure Dr. Carlson can't wait on me all day."

"Brooke, just think about what I'm saying, please. I can't say it enough."

"I hear you, Mom, I hear you," I said, brushing off her pleas to rationalize with me. "Now, can we go inside?"

Defeated, she nodded her head. "Yes."

I hardly remember the walk to Dr. Carlson's office. The second he saw me, he frowned, reminding me of Mom's reaction a few hours earlier, but his with more disbelief at my health's digression. Upon completion of the appointment, he gave the prognosis,

"I've got to be honest with you, Brooke; this is not what I'd expected. You've been doing tremendously better. What's changed recently?"

"Life," I sulked.

Mom interrupted briefly, "She and Riley aren't seeing each other any longer. He had to move away."

"Mom, can you not?"

"What, honey?"

"How about tell all my business to everyone!"

"Dr. Carlson needs to know, Brooke. It's nothing personal." I couldn't look at her or Dr. Carlson, as if looking at them would wound me further in some way.

"Oh. I see," Dr. Carlson replied, still frowning.

"Well, Brooke, we're going to have to add a new medication and require that you get some bed rest for a while—*real rest.* I suggest you take some of your medical leave at work. I do not like the direction this is taking;

getting well should be your priority right now. If nothing changes by the next visit, we may need to begin looking into more invasive options, even perhaps a procedure to get things regulated again. I want you to realize the seriousness of what I'm telling you." His words weighed heavily on me—understanding every last one of them. Rest was easy, but without happiness it would only be short-lived. I pictured myself falling back into this dangerous cycle again. I respectfully acknowledged his request because he was only doing his job.

"Yes, sir, Dr. Carlson. I'll call my employer as soon as we leave today. How long are you thinking?"

"Until you get better, there's really no way to know that, but give yourself at least a month."

"Okay." I hung my head. While work had become a lifeless daily repetition, at times, the kids and having something to do helped pass the time more quickly than sitting at home. I wasn't looking forward to all day, every day, to just think. My thoughts were often times too loud. I made good on my promise to the doctor and called my boss as soon as we left, letting her know what was going on. She assured me everything would be fine and to take as much time as I needed. There it was again, the reminder that all I had was time. *Ugh.*

Mom was anything but happy. Not with the diagnosis or with how I was treating myself, revealing her own evident anger as I watched her bite her lip.

It was only four, but with the gloomy dampness of the day it felt hellacious and dark. We didn't say much, but I could tell Mom was brewing up something as she put her energy into mundane household tasks: emptying the garbage, folding laundry, wiping the kitchen counters; things she normally left for the housekeeper but habits of hers when she was thinking something through. As the evening went on, she made some soup and grilled cheese sandwiches. We sat together on the large, leather living room sofa and watched television. As I forced myself to eat, she finally admitted what she'd been fabricating in her concerned parental head.

"Brooke, I think you should stay here with me for a while."

"What?"

"Yes, I think you should stay here, at least for a month like the doctor recommended. It will give you a chance to be taken care of and give me peace of mind. Alf's already here; all you'd have to do is go back to Austin to wrap up anything with work and the apartment, and then I'll take care of you. I'm your mom, it's my job." I didn't like the idea of leaving Austin, and worried that being stuck in the house with Mom for a month might drive me crazy with no escape to be completely alone, but I guess that was the point—not being alone.

"I don't like it, Mom. I think I'll miss Austin too much. Besides, I do have Tessa and Julie; they've been checking in on me."

"Brooke, please, you know that is not the same. Just think it over and tell me tomorrow. I'll plan on riding back with you to help you get your things packed up if you decide to stay here." Mom brushed my cheek with her small hand, something she'd done ever since I was a little kid in moments she wanted me to know, more than ever, that I was her special little girl; convincing me I couldn't tell her no. There was no point in delaying the answer.

"Okay, Mom. I'll stay with you." Right away, the worry in her face lifted. "We'll go back to Austin and get my stuff tomorrow." I was so tired, that night I fell asleep on the downstairs sofa, never showering or changing, awaking the next morning to Mom cooking breakfast. When I made it to the table, she had a plate of fresh fruit and muffins with a glass of orange juice ready for me.

"You're all ready to go, aren't you?" I asked curiously, eyeing her cream velour tracksuit and Coach tennis shoes. She was giddy—too giddy. I speculated it was because she'd technically won and I would be staying with her.

"It's a brand new day, Brooke, and we're on a new road to getting you better. Now eat up, take a shower, and we'll get on the road to Austin, get your things together and drive back tonight." I thought it was sort of a short time frame to be getting my things together, but I didn't possess the energy or remote urge to question her.

"Alright, Mom," I sighed.

***

We made the trip back to Austin in the same type of weather I'd traveled in the day before - gloomy, cold, and rainy, feeling as if Mother Nature were sharing my mood. Mom drove and was much more efficient at the drive than I'd been on the way to Houston, making it to Austin in three hours flat. We had all of my things wrapped up in just two and a half hours, with Mom moving at lightning speeds to help me collect all of the things I'd need. At the pace she was working, I began to really wonder what was going on.

"Mom, are you in some sort of hurry or something? You just seem so raring to get out of here. I don't understand it." I could tell when my mom was hiding something when she would fight a smile, something she was doing at that very second.

"No, honey, not at all, I just want to get on the road before dark, is all." I knew there was more to it, but I'd given up prying it out of her.

Piling back into the car and traveling back to Houston, we reached the house when it was pitch-black and colder than the flippin' Arctic. I was tired just from the packing and loading. Mom was still bright and peppy, fighting a smile and humming occasionally. *Seriously, what is wrong with the woman? I'm devastated, and she's humming away like I'm not even here.* We ate supper then I showered, prepped for bed, took my meds, told Mom goodnight, and climbed into bed – out like a light.

I dreamt of many things, things that didn't really amount to much, things I knew I wouldn't remember. I was startled awake by the sound of a car door closing outside on the typically quiet street. My eyelids fluttered open a few times. I turned over to look at the time on the clock, two in the morning. It struck me as odd because it sounded like the car was close, perhaps even in the driveway. I thought surely I'd just been hearing things, lying back down and closing my eyes. But the hallway light flipping on, shining through the small crevice underneath the bedroom door once again interrupted my sleep. This time I shot straight up in bed, seriously wondering if we were being robbed. I didn't know whether to run, hide or freeze. My heart thumped hard enough that I could feel the palpitations rising from my chest. A small bead of sweat ran down my back underneath my gray cotton cami. My mind kept saying hide but my body wouldn't follow. I was frozen. Then the doorknob turned—my heart beat harder. It opened slowly as if someone attempted with great effort to be impeccably quiet. Immediately, my mind filled with horrific images from scary movies I had seen. Just when I was about to release a bloodcurdling scream, I recognized the familiar figure in the doorway. As if out of some sort of a dream, in the middle of the night, Riley entered the bedroom.

<u>Chapter Eighteen</u>

"Riley?" My throat felt dry and rough. I watched as he softly closed the door and moved warily to the edge of the bed. He didn't say a word, just knelt beside my bed on the floor. Taking my hand, he kissed it once, his soft lips sending shivers up my tired, limp arm. I couldn't make out the expression on his face in the dim room, but I felt something on my skin that revealed why he hadn't yet spoken. Damp droplets fell on my hand still cradled in his. After the tears had slowed, the silence broke.

"Brooke," he struggled to speak before a rush of more tears. "I should've never left you." I reached out my other hand to find his face and wiped tears from his moist cheek.

"I didn't give you much of a choice," I replied with tears filling my eyes too. "How did you know I was—?" He stopped me before finishing.

"Your mom called me last night after you went to the doctor." That explained everything about Mom's perky attitude throughout the day.

"She told me how weak and sick you'd gotten. I couldn't stand it anymore and left Tennessee right then and there. I just made it in. I should've flown, I would have made it here faster."

"I don't care how you got here, Riley. I just can't believe you're really here, not just something I dreamt." My hands left his a brief moment, turning on the small lamp next to the bed, adding a soft glow to the room. I glanced back over to visibly take in the man I loved and would never leave again—no matter the consequences. His eyes were lined with crimson. Tears lingering, he rested on his knees next to the bed. His hair was unusually untidy and his dark jeans and a black long-sleeved shirt were wrinkled, smelling of the leather from his Tahoe. I slipped from the bed and sank down next to him on the floor. Now seeing me in the light, the concern everyone seemed to have for me was plainly evident in his expression. I was sad to think of how I must have appeared to him now compared to when he'd left. I reached out, hugging his neck with every ounce of strength in me. He hugged me back, encompassing all of me in his arms. It was the best feeling in the world. I felt so safe.

"Do know how much I love you, Brooke?" He pulled back and looked straight into my eyes brimming with tears.

"Yes, I do. I am so sorry for everything. I just wanted something better for you."

"You honestly think something is better than you, Brooke?" He stroked my cheek as I thought about my words carefully before responding.

222

"Your music was in your life well before me and I didn't know how my disease could play into your life with everything you need to do for a career in music, especially now that everything you've ever wanted has happened." He looked at me, both sternly and confused.

"Wow, I had no idea that's what you actually think." He looked hurt. "You've got it all wrong, Brooke—all wrong. Music was my life. It made me feel good, happy, but you, Brooke, you make me feel complete. You mean more to me than music ever could, and I'd give it up in a second for one more day on earth with you. I feel terrible that you ever felt you would be worth letting go—for anything." I leaned over his shoulder to hug him again, weeping into his shirt, my tears uncontrollable. I couldn't have felt more bliss and emotional exhaustion all at once. I struggled to calm myself down, intending to make it clearly known that he could have both.

"Riley, I'll never ever ask you to give up your music. Ever. We'll find a way to make both things work," I sobbed, holding him.

"Brooke, we'll make sure you're well taken care of, I promise. There are so many good schools to teach at, and the record label is big enough they even have benefits. You wouldn't even have to work—unless you want to. If things keep going the way it looks now they will, I'll make more money than we'd ever both need. We'd see the best doctors and do everything on heaven and earth to get you as healthy as possible. There's just one stipulation." I promptly let go of my tight grip on him and pulled myself back.

"What do you mean?" I asked, confused.

"Why don't you sit back on the bed?" I followed his request, wiped the tears from my face and took a deep breath. Riley didn't budge from his spot on the floor, reaching for both my hands and looking lovingly at me.

"Brooke, the night I found out we were getting signed, it wasn't the only reason I'd been so anxious to see you. I really had other intentions, but it didn't exactly play out the way I'd imagined. Not even close. Do you remember walking with me that night after Tessa and Lowell's engagement?

"Yes." Beginning to see exactly where he was going with this, I felt suddenly light-headed.

"Well, I didn't forget a word you said that night. I went the next week to have something designed. Just the way you wanted."

Riley placed his hand in his pocket, revealing a dark velvet box. I gasped, shaking my head at how surreal this all was.

"Brooke, you are more than I could ever fully deserve—a woman of such great strength—and I feel more than blessed to have known what true love means because of you. I want to tell you I love you every day for the rest of our lives. Brooke Denton – will you marry me?" He opened the velvet box to reveal an engagement ring, exactly as I'd described it; a perfect round diamond with two rubies placed on either side of it. Everything surrounding me at that moment faded away. My mind hazed, then a moment of clarity hit me. *My dream*. Dad had said 'he'll come back'. This is what he'd meant. Riley would come back. I couldn't believe it. It was as if Dad had foreshadowed everything. In an instant, I snapped myself out of the momentary entrancement, seeing the diamond sparkling in the soft light. Riley filtered back into my eyesight and I could see him waiting, looking worried. I realized I hadn't said anything, hadn't answered his question while every ounce of my inner being cried *yes*.

"A million times yes. Yes, I'll marry you, Riley." He leapt from the floor and picked me up off the bed. My arms clung tightly to his neck. Our lips met with passionate kisses in a moment of pure heaven. Nothing would matter anymore but being with the man I loved for the rest of my life; he was everything. I had never realized how integral a part he played in my life until he wasn't there because of my own stupid mistake. After setting me down, Riley placed the ring on my finger, kissing me again and then picking me up and gently placing me back on the bed in his muscled arms. He laid beside me, staring into my eyes and after a few minutes of letting the realization set in that we were actually going to promise forever to each other, he whispered,

"So, when would you like to get married?"

It didn't take me long to respond. I knew I didn't want to spend another second away from him.

"How about Monday?" I smiled.

"Really? Are you sure?"

"I always thought I wanted a big wedding, but now, I really don't care. I just want to be with you, Riley."

"Well, then, Monday it is. I don't want to wait either." Riley solidified our decision with another fervent kiss that led to much-needed intimacy. These kisses were different. I never thought Riley could taste any better until that moment. He proceeded to kiss my neck gently, taking his time with every movement, driving me crazy. I pressed my body harder into his to make it clear what I wanted, and he reciprocated by pressing back into me. Then he slowly began to remove my clothes, beautifully and naturally. It was like the last few months of depression had never happened at all. Finally, our bodies reunited and euphoria ran through me. Again, Riley had complete control of me. Nothing felt better.

Neither of us truly slept until nearly five in the morning. Light forced its way through the curtains, signaling daylight's approach. As I opened my eyes, I instantly held up the new ring on my left hand glistening in the morning light. Riley was in a heavy sleep after our endless night together, and I didn't want to wake him, but it took all of me not to. It was indescribable the feeling of knowing he was still here and that our reunion was amazingly real. I caressed his forehead with my fingers and kissed his cheek gently—wanting to take him, staring longingly at him in peaceful slumber. He was all I wanted. If I didn't leave this moment, I'd be in pure bliss forever, but my few minutes of bliss were brought to a halt when I heard Mom moving around downstairs, more than likely in the kitchen. I very gracefully exited the bed so as not to wake Riley, quietly making my way downstairs. Stepping into the kitchen, a large plate of pancakes sat in a towering stack on the counter, and for once, food was appetizing.

"Mom," I spoke delicately.

"Brooke. Oh, Brooke!" Mom's face was covered in a smile. "You have to tell me everything." I smiled back at her and gave her an enormous hug then pulled back.

"Well, first of all, Mom, I have to tell you, you've been pretty sneaky. But, I also have to say it was the best thing you could've ever done. So, thank you. Thank you more than you'll ever know."

"Your hurt was too much for even me to bear, Brooke. I really didn't want to betray your trust, but I felt he at least deserved to know about your health, the rest was in his hands." She paused a moment and then a wondering look came upon her face. "Is he still sleeping?"

"Yes." I grinned and then held up my hand to show her what had actually come of Riley's return during the middle of the night.

"Oh, my God, really?" Mom laughed and pranced with joy. "You're getting married? That's amazing. Did you set a date?"

"Well, we sort of decided not to wait. We're going to elope tomorrow."

"Tomorrow!? You don't want a wedding?"

"No, actually I don't. I just want to get married and make it official. I can't wait anymore." I took a shallow breath, followed by a sigh, thinking of how perfect marrying him was going to be.

"If that's what you want, then I am all for it. This is truly an amazing day. We have to go shopping today. Let me buy you your dress." I was relieved Mom hadn't pressed the wedding decision. I know she'd always envisioned an extravagant affair.

"Shopping?" A new voice entered the room. Riley had come downstairs in the jeans and black shirt from last night. He walked straight over to me, wrapped one arm around my waist and kissed the top of my head. Alf rounded the corner at racing speed from the bed I'd placed in the utility room. He barked in a high pitch and ran straight to Riley, jumping up and down with pure delight. I'd never seen him act so happy to see someone. Riley hugged his neck.

"It's so good to see you, boy." It made my heart melt. I realized how quietly Riley must have come in during the night for Alf not to wake. It was touching to see how attached the two of them had actually become. When the moment settled, Mom also made her way over to us and put one hand on each of our arms in motherly fashion.

"I'm so happy for you kids. I can't believe it. Congratulations!" Mom chuckled, turning to give Riley a hug. "I'm glad you came back, Riley. My baby girl sure loves you."

"I'm glad you called." A warm smile lit his face. "So, shopping?" Riley asked.

"Yes, Mom wants to buy me a dress for tomorrow," I grinned.

"Why don't we head out in an hour?" Mom suggested.

"Alright. Do you want to go, Riley?" I prayed he'd say yes, reluctant to let him out of my sight after all we'd been through.

"I want to, but isn't that supposed to be a surprise or something?"

"Yes, but we're not exactly having a normal wedding," I argued, hoping he'd reconsider.

"Yeah, you're right. However, I'm unimaginably looking forward to seeing you in that dress, so let's keep it a surprise. Besides, I have a few surprises of my own to go take care of." He rocked back and forth from heel to toe, and ran his fingers through his unruly hair.

"Of course, you do. You and your surprises. Anything I can know about?" I questioned.

"It wouldn't be a surprise if I told you. Just trust me."

"Okay," I said unenthusiastically. I hesitated to leave without him, but it sounded like I would have to play along with his "surprising ways", knowing he was only doing it for me.

***

Mom and I made our way to the Galleria to shop for a dress over the late morning hours, picking out a gorgeous Alexander McQueen champagne-colored, floral peplum dress. We also found a pair of pastel, flower-print Manolo Blahnik heels with red accents to complement my ring, and then followed that up by a trip to the spa for the afternoon. It was strange, throughout the day, I'd started to feel human again, color re-emerging in my cheeks though still sunken, my energy had catapulted with anticipation, the blissful buzz of love's return not yet worn off. It was as if Riley had brought life back into me in only a day, though I would have a long way to go to completely get back to the health I'd had before. When after what had seemed like an eternity away from him, Mom and I finally made it home. I discovered Riley napping on the couch downstairs, Alf directly below him on the Oriental rug. I rustled my way next to Riley on the couch. Alf's collar jingled as he raised his head from his paws watching me carefully and quietly situate myself on the couch. I woke Riley, softly kissing the end of his nose. He'd changed into a blue sweater and a different pair of jeans. He seemed overall relaxed, but tired. It struck me now that he'd been through a lot, too. I wasn't the only one who had gone through this mess of being apart. I wanted to spend the rest of my life making the pain he'd gone through up to him.

"We're back," I said, lovingly rubbing his back.

"Did you get everything you need?" He yawned widely.

"Yes, but I'm more curious about what you have been up to all day."

"Like you said, me and my *surprises*." He finally started opening his eyes.

"So, are we going to the Justice of the Peace tomorrow?" I joked, but really I knew it was the most realistic option in the hurry we were in.

"Nope," he said, pulling me to him and wrapping me in his arms.

"Hm," I sighed with extreme intrigue, resting into his arms. Before long, I fell into true, really deep sleep. It wasn't until a little while later that the pungent scent of garlic and basil stirred me from slumber. Mom was cooking her famous spaghetti. I'd know that wonderful smell anywhere. *Yum.*

Riley was still on the couch. I moved my head to see that he was very much wide-awake. "Have you been here the entire time I've been asleep?"

"Yes. It was so peaceful to watch you sleep. I've got to drink you in. I've missed too much." I kissed him with a desire for more, but with Mom in the other room, I withheld. He pulled me tightly to his warm body and stroked my chin.

"I love you so much."

"I love you, too, Riley."

"Dinner's ready, kids!" Mom yelled from the kitchen.

Talking and laughing over Mom's amazing meal was a refreshing change from the darkness of the past few months. I began to see how much I'd let my health and myself go. I looked at Riley and his mesmerizing smile as we all talked. I was still in disbelief of the last day, trying to process it all. Mom's decision could very well have saved me from myself. I wanted more alone time with Riley, so I decided to be the first to turn in for the night, especially with the events of the next day—my wedding day. *God, please don't let this be a dream.*

"I am going to go take a shower," I broke into the conversation, followed with a yawn.

"That's probably a good idea," Mom replied. "Big day tomorrow." She raised her eyebrows. "Gosh, I'm so happy for both of you."

"Thanks, Mom," I giggled.

"Yes, thanks for everything," Riley smiled.

I left the table as Mom and Riley continued to talk and headed up the stairs. Even with a nap, I was still tired. While far from where I needed to be, I already felt much better. After entering my room, I made certain the closet door was shut so that Riley wouldn't see the dress. I sat on the edge of the bed, sorting through everything that was happening, making sure not to miss one second of it. Life had changed in an instant, fate playing a different card. For the hundredth time, I peered down at the exquisite ring on my left hand and thought about how absolutely lucky I was to have someone love me this much. I breathed slowly, closing my eyes. When I opened them again, I undressed before reaching the shower, leaving my last strip of clothing in front of the tub then turned on the faucet and watched steam fill the room. I stepped in and let the water therapeutically run over my skin, when, as if expected, I felt a hand wrap around my hip and then lips lightly kiss my neck.

"I hoped you'd come in," I spoke, turning around to meet Riley's eyes, pulling myself to his wet skin and kissing him with deep want.

"I should've known better," Riley whispered in my ear. "I want you more than I think I ever have."

"So, what are you waiting for?" I replied, kissing his shoulder.

"Tomorrow. I want it to be perfect."

"Wow, you're really going to make me wait? You know how to really get a girl going."

"I think I like your answer," Riley leaned in to kiss me again but sought nothing more. I slept, tightly ensconced in his embrace, desperately longing for tomorrow to come.

Chapter Nineteen

I made my way downstairs as the early morning sunlight filled the large baroque bay windows of the living room. With each step, a conversation became more distinguishable. Alf met me at the base of the stairs, tail flopping back and forth. After scratching the large tuft of peppered hair on his head, I attempted to glide quietly across the wood floor in the living room in slippers, my gray pajama pants skimming the floor. If not for Alf's jingling dog tags at the base of the stairs, they may not have known I was there. *Damn.*

"Good morning," Mom grinned. "Are you ready for the big day?"

"Without a doubt," I beamed. Riley's face glowed as he looked into my eyes, something I'd missed terribly.

"Your mom and I were just discussing the plan for today," he said, followed with a sip of coffee.

"And what is that going to be?"

"Well, first of all, just enjoy your morning." He rose from the table as Mom took a bite of fruit on her plate. Moving towards me at a slow pace, he continued, "Then

234

after you get ready here, your mom is going to take you to meet me at four." He rested his hands on my shoulders. "After that, we'll be saying 'I do'."

I laced my hands around his neck, "So, still no hints, huh?"

"Nope," he replied with a peck on my lips.

"Well, then, I wish it was four now."

"Me, too," he smiled.

"I've arranged to have someone come do your hair and makeup today, Brooke," Mom said, rising from her chair, empty plate in hand.

"I don't know, Mom. Really? I can do it." I was fairly particular about my beauty routine. However, I knew that it would be very difficult to focus today so I welcomed the invitation.

"You should feel like a princess today," Mom smiled.

"Well, I definitely do already."

"Brooke, you're going to be pampered today whether you want to be or not." I smiled at my mom's bluntness.

"Okay, okay. Thanks, Mom."

Riley seemed so calm, too calm throughout the morning, getting some things together in a small suitcase he'd brought from Tennessee. I felt so happy, any part of feeling weak or tired was virtually gone and the last thing on my mind. I couldn't have felt more hopeful for what forever would bring. When it was almost noon, Riley prepped to leave the house for whatever he'd so quickly and thoughtfully planned. I walked him outside to his Tahoe and leaned against the cool metal of the door. The air was still frigid but the sun shone so brightly it created a little warmth on my face. The idea of locking his keys in the car briefly entered my mind. I didn't want him to leave, just wanting to go with him and never leave his sight for as long as humanly possible, but then again I knew that he'd put a lot of thought into whatever he'd managed to pull together in less than twenty four hours so I'd have memory of some sort of authentic wedding ceremony, not just in front of a judge in some cold, stark room. I couldn't get over how much he showed he loved me. He raised his hand to my cheek; it was warm and I laid my face against it, returning the gesture by softly kissing it.

"It's not long now," Riley spoke softly.

"No, it's not," I whispered, looking into his dark, affectionate eyes. "I appreciate all of this, Riley. You care so much, and I can't believe I get to spend my life with a man like you." He pulled me in close, so close I could feel the gentle thud of his heart in his chest against my ear, and rested his chin on my head.

"As long as you know you deserve the world and more and that I will never put you second to anything."

We embraced in a quiet moment but realized it was time to part. We gave one last loving glance then exchanged half a dozen 'I love you's' before he loaded himself into the Tahoe. He rolled down the window to give me a kiss, my last kiss before I'd see him in what felt like an eternity of hours to exchange our vows. He put the Tahoe in reverse, backing out of the long driveway slowly then driving off into the distance. I crossed my arms, rubbing them now, realizing how cold it actually was out of the grasp of Riley's warmth. The sun showered rays of light on my face and I smiled incessantly, taking a long deep breath before returning to the house. Mom was stepping out of her room, peppy and high-spirited.

"Well, Brooke, I bet you can't wait. He's really planned a wonderful little ceremony for you two."

"I'm so ready to get this shindig on the road, Mom," I replied with certainty. "I can't wait to see what he has in store."

"Well, the hairdresser and makeup artist should be here very soon. I would pack a few things; you'll be staying the night somewhere."

"Oh, okay." I didn't know what I'd expected. I knew we would probably spend the night somewhere, but I hadn't really thought about it. I headed back for the stairs. "I'll go get some things together." I trotted to my room and gathered a small Louis Vuitton overnight bag and gingerly folded a few items in it. I had no clue what to pack. In the back of my mind, I assumed I may not be wearing much of anything anyway. I giggled aloud at the thought. Ironically enough, I packed way too much, barely able to close the bag, forcing the zipper shut. A girl can never be too

prepared was my motto. Afterwards, I walked to the mirror
in the adjoining bathroom and washed my face, brushed my
hair, and lost my train of thought for a few minutes. My
mind drifted off to a thought that hadn't even touched my
mind with all of the drastic life-changing events of the past
weekend—Dad. I realized he wouldn't be there to give me
away. Suddenly, every childhood memory of him jogged
through my mind at racing speed. I felt slightly dizzy.
"Breathe, Brooke," I said aloud to myself and then again,
"Just breathe." I forced myself to calm down. This was not
a day I wanted to express any more tears. Although he
wasn't there with me physically, he was in my heart, my
soul. He had always been there in some capacity, even if it
was my dreams. I looked up at the ceiling as if the wall of
the roof above didn't exist, and, instead, the clouds of
heaven above were there. "I love you, Daddy, always." I
glanced back at myself in the mirror and was jolted out of
the moment with the ring of a doorbell. Alf's barks and the
click of his nails on the floor shortly followed as he
accompanied Mom to the door to answer.

"Brooke, come on down!" Mom hollered.

"Be right there!" I took a deep breath and meandered
back downstairs.

***

After an hour and a half of makeup applicators and
rollers, I hoped all of the poking and prodding would be
worth it. I could see the colors on my face from the corner

of my eye; they were so vibrant, and the wavy curls placed strategically on my head didn't budge from all of the hairspray. Mom handed me a mirror as the makeup artist and hairdresser stepped back to admire their work.

I held the mirror up to my face, hardly recognizing the vision before me. The frail, weak-framed woman from only a few days earlier was gone. I looked full of life and felt stunning, exactly as a bride should feel on her wedding day.

"Wow," I smiled.

Mom walked the few feet over to me and patted my shoulders.

"You look amazing, Brooke."

The makeup artist chimed in, "Truly a vision."

"No doubt," the hairdresser confirmed.

I felt like a doll in a china cabinet with all of the eyes on me in such a made-up state.

"Well, thank you, ladies, so much. You did a great job." To which they both thanked me.

I got up and walked to Mom's large bathroom mirror to see the full details of what had been done. As I did, the ladies packed up their things and Mom escorted them to the door. By the time she returned, I was in the bathroom, astounded at the transformation forty-eight hours of bliss and two beauty professionals had accomplished. She headed straight for her closet where I could make out the sounds of ruffling and boxes opening. When Mom reemerged, she carried something in her left hand.

"What is that, Mom?" I cocked my head to the side.

"This is something that belongs to you now." Mom reached for the hand at my side and placed a small shiny object in it. "I have faith it will fit."

"Mom." I was in awe for a moment, touching the wedding band once belonging to my father. It was so comforting to feel something tangible of his. The gold was slightly dulled, but more special to me than the newest ring I could have given Riley. I had completely forgotten to get him a ring in the rush but now I was thankful for it. I closed my fingers around it in a gentle fist and looked up from my hand to Mom. "Thank you, Mom. This means so much to me." I gave her a tight hug, hoping she'd understand how much the gesture really meant.

"He'd definitely want you to have it and I know he'd have loved Riley." Tears began to collect in Mom's eyes.

"Please, no tears, Mom, it will make me cry and I can't afford to ruin my makeup." We laughed together in the moment.

I was hell-bent on getting this show on the road after what seemed like an eternity. I wanted to snap my fingers and magically be wherever he was. I set my bag and wedding dress on the sofa, eagerly waiting to depart and said my last goodbyes to Alf, hugging him like a mother hugs a child. "I'll be back soon, Alf baby, and Riley will be with me," I reassured him. Mom appeared dressed in a lavish black dress, looking absolutely stunning. I felt so silly in jeans and black sweater tunic with my hair and makeup to the nines and Mom looking so complete, like a wrapped present, but I didn't want to risk wrinkling or staining my gorgeous, crazy-expensive dress. We piled all of our things into her sporty Mercedes and made our way to the freeway in the direction of the downtown area. I twiddled my fingers in my lap.

"Nervous, Brooke?" Mom spoke, soft but reassuring.

"No, not even a little. I'd never been so ready for anything. "I just want to see Riley, to call him my husband. I want to be with him more than anything, with all of my being."

"We'll be there really soon, honey, only about two more blocks." Mom freed one hand from the steering wheel and gave my jittery hand a loving squeeze.

Buildings towered all around. I assumed it would be a hotel, based on the locale. Mom made a turn and began to slow down the car, the direction of her car blinker the final indicator as to where we were going as she pulled up to the valet of the towering Four Seasons Hotel.

"We're here," Mom smiled widely.

"You've got to be kidding. He deserves an A-plus for this." *Especially on such short notice.*

The valet took the car away and, after collecting our things, we approached the reservations counter and were greeted by a man dressed in a sharp black blazer.

241

"Good afternoon, ladies, how may we serve you today?"

"We're here for a wedding ceremony. This is the bride-to-be, Brooke Denton." Mom turned and laid a hand upon my shoulder. I stepped in her place to the counter.

"Ah, yes, Ms. Denton, we have everything ready for you."

"Oh, really?" I said, giving a half crooked smile.

"Yes, ma'am. Mr. Proctor has arranged everything. Here is your room key."

"Thank you."

Mom had mentioned on the way up that Riley's and my room was elsewhere in the hotel and he wanted it to be a surprise until after the ceremony. Not wasting a moment, I eagerly dressed in my exquisite Alexander McQueen dress and made final touches to my hair and makeup, and then Mom had the concierge take my bags to Riley's room for after the wedding. I didn't ask questions, just simply went along with the magical flow of the day. A knock came at the door and a lady with a florist logo on her polo and a small bouquet of flowers appeared when I opened it.

"Mr. Proctor asked that we deliver these to a Ms. Brooke Denton."

"That's me," I grinned with unbearable anticipation, thanked her, and closed the door. The bouquet was full of the most beautiful crimson roses I'd ever laid eyes on.

"Oh, Brooke, they're beautiful," Mom smiled.

242

"They're perfect." I smelled them, unable to contain myself, when a ring of the room's phone broke my attention from their sweet scent. Mom stepped over to pick it up as I stared back down at the exquisite shimmer of the red and white diamond ring.

"Hello? Okay, we're on our way down." She gently set the phone down and grinned, "He's ready for us to make our way down."

"Alright, let's go," I replied without a second thought and followed Mom out of the room to the shiny brass doors of the elevator. We made our way down several floors. It felt like I was floating in a sea of no worries, fearless, but quickly I was reminded that my feet were planted firmly on the ground when the elevator doors opened again. We made our way across the lobby floor, my floral Manolo Blahnik heels sinking into the heavy carpeting. Mom guided me the entire way through a maze of hallways that passed ballrooms of varying sizes. Finally, after the last leg of what felt like a never-ending journey, she stopped outside a room more than likely designed for smaller intimate affairs. I could hear a piano beautifully playing music that grew more distinct with each step. A large door opened, the scenery breathtaking, boasting a fireplace with a heavy mantelpiece and assortment of cream colored candles of all sizes lighting the room with an incredible glow. Then Riley approached, reaching for my hand. His dark, wavy hair was perfectly placed, his skin gleaming, and he sported a perfectly fitted black suit, cream paisley dress shirt, and black tie. He guided me a few short steps to the pastor awaiting us, not once taking his eyes off me, and I couldn't help but do the same to him.

"You're breathtaking, baby," he said under his breath.

"I'll give you everything, Riley, you know that," I whispered back to him.

"Ready?" Riley beamed.

"Months ago," I winked at him.

We exchanged our vows beneath the dim romantic light as tears were shed, sealed with a finalizing kiss.

<u>Chapter Twenty</u>

Approaching the hotel room door with our hands interlocked, the smile of a newly-wedded bride was swept across my face. My dream of having a life with this amazing man was real. The angst to feel each other's lips couldn't be contained any longer. Riley pressed my body gently against the door and covered my lips with his, then traced his fingers from the back of my neck along my shoulders and ended at my waist. I kissed him back, my chest as close as physically possible to him. I had never wanted him more, and seconds felt like hours. I tugged at his shirt collar and his hands responded by grabbing my bottom through the dress, lifting me to him.

"Brooke?" he managed to get out between the long, passionate kisses. I hastily responded.

"Yes?"

"This is already better than I imagined. I'll give you everything."

"Good," I grinned. I couldn't contain myself any longer. "No more talking then. Let's get in this room."

"Yes, ma'am, Mrs. Proctor," Riley laughed.

245

I had no will left to keep from feeling every part of him, and I knew he could sense it, too. He managed to reach a hand behind me and insert the hotel card key into the lock. The instant we heard it unlock, all bets were off. Still holding me in his arms and kissing me feverishly, we stumbled through the dark room, finally making it over to what felt like the edge of a bed. At that moment, I was sure the intensity would further ignite, but, to my dismay, Riley halted his hands at my waist.

"Wait!"

"What, wait for what?"

"I want to make this last as long as possible—make sure I don't miss one part of you," he said hungrily. I laughed.

"You're killing me," I said as he made his way down my body to the bottom of my dress. "This needs to come off," I begged.

"Let me undress you." He made his way up my body but not before grazing softly over my tender parts with his hands, kindling my already-lit-with-passion body.

"Okay," I softly whispered in his ear followed by a soft kiss to his earlobe. "Do as you want with me," I whispered again as he stood me up before me, turning me around while running his fingers gingerly over my back and legs, savoring every moment.

Without missing a beat, his fingers gently slid down the middle of my shoulder blades until they met my zipper,

slowly pulling it down and letting it fall to the ground. I
stepped out of the dress, turned back to Riley and wiggled
his tie loose with my fingers until I was able to slide it over
his head, dropping it on the floor. As if a game of my turn
your turn, we undressed each other, anticipation growing.
Facing each other in our underwear, Riley in snug briefs
and me in a new matching cream ivory lace bra and thong,
I guided his hand to my panties and he pulled them to the
floor. I leaned on him for balance. He stood back up and
slowly pressed his chest to mine. He skillfully unclipped
the bra, tossing it to the floor, as well. Remaining in
nothing but my heels, he lifted me up in his arms and softly
laid me on the cool sheets of the enormous bed. Even in the
darkness of the moonlit room, I searched for his
mesmerizing eyes and then led his face to mine. The kiss
began innocently, but he soon used his mouth to tease me
with small kisses that started on my neck and progressed
downward. I slowly glided my fingers along his skin as he
worked his magic. It was one of the purest moments of my
entire existence. Soon, desire within our wanting bodies
took over. We rolled, intertwined, across the bed, never
letting go, frantically keeping as close to one another as
possible. Finally, the frenzy grew in both of us, past the
point of no return, where we succumbed to our primal
nature and made love to each other over and over again.

***

With the light of day peering in on my skin, partially placed beneath the covers, I slowly opened my eyes. Riley's body was so warm against mine. I sat up slowly, trying not to wake him but my effort was curtailed.

"Lie back down. Where do you think you're going anyways? I want to hold you longer."

"I can't say no to that," I responded, putting my head gently back on his chest.

"Well, we did it… we made it official." I let my lips graze his bare skin. Je followed suit, kissing the top of my hair.

"We sure did, wife. I get to call you my wife for the rest of our lives. Was there ever a luckier man?"

"Oh, shhh…" I said, laughing.

"So, yesterday was all right."

"Just all right, Riley?!" I exclaimed.

"Brooke, my wife, my beautiful, fashionable wife, was it everything you could have asked for?"

"No." I briefly paused then laced my fingers across his chest, perching my chin on top of them to meet him eye to eye. "It was more, *so* much more."

"Then I'm happy. I love you."

"I love you, too, husband." I sat for a moment, and a wondering look must have crossed my face.

"What is it? What are you thinking?"

"Nothing, just curious. Did you happen to bring your guitar?" I hadn't even paid a bit of attention to a stitch of luggage in the room.

"Yeah." Riley stroked my cheek with his thumb.

"Could you maybe play me the song you wrote for me? I haven't heard it in a long time."

"There's nothing more I want to do right now than play that for you, Brooke." He slipped on a pair of athletic shorts and then went to one corner of the room to pick up the case I knew very well. I slid next to him after he'd returned, sitting on the edge of the bed, resting my head on his shoulder, wrapped only in a sheet from our bed. He graced me with his beautiful song—my song.

After finishing, I had no will left in me to hold back. I peppered his neck with my swollen lips and he set the guitar down beside the bed. He swept me into his arms and I knew there was no escaping, but I didn't want saving. Not after months without him. All I wanted was him. We let our passion get a little rougher than yesterday, slowly exploring the boundaries of our bodies. It was exhilarating, and I felt a growing addiction to the feeling. The following day and night were heaven. We made love over and over again, never feeling that there could be an end to the want for each other. Hours were spent lying in bed or soaking in the massive Jacuzzi tub in the amazing room Riley had gotten, knowing full well how much I loved being with him in a tub. The rest of the hours were spent ordering room service when we realized we were famished but didn't want to leave the room, too immersed in each other. These past few days were incomparable to any other exquisitely happy moment I'd ever had in my life. I wasn't ready to leave, longing to stay in the dream-like existence. To my dismay, we knew the time to leave was upon us and we began discussing what would happen from here. Over our last breakfast in bed we finalized our next move.

"We'll head back to your mom's after this and get your things together," Riley said, sipping his coffee.

"Then what?" I swallowed a piece of fruit and followed it with a sip of orange juice.

"We'll wrap everything up in Austin with your apartment, hopefully by the end of the week, and drive back to Tennessee with Alf. Does that work for you?"

"Hmm, everything but the wrap everything up in Austin part. I just want to go, leave it all behind— everything; everything but Tessa and Julie. They're going to be so excited for me though. I haven't even thought to call them. Riley, I'm just ready for our new life right now." The memory of how upset I had been the last time I was there was enough to make me want to leave Austin for a while.

"Me, too, Brooke. Me, too." He smiled and kissed me on the lips.

We checked out, having all the plans in place, and I knew I'd always be with Riley come hell or high water, so, as sad as I was that our brief honeymoon was ending, I was eager to start our life as husband and wife.

After Riley had put our bags in the Tahoe, we set out for Mom's house. I held Riley's arm as he drove, unable to take my eyes off of him, mesmerized by the reality that he was all mine—only mine.

I raised my hand to run my fingers gently through his hair, as I'd always loved to do.

"You know I can't quite figure out how a few days ago I was lonely and lost," I proclaimed, "and now this." With his eyes fixed on the road, he reached for my hand resting on his arm and kissed the back of it.

"It should've happened before it got to that point. I shouldn't have left. I'm just praising God I didn't lose you."

"I love you so much, Riley. You're never going to lose me."

He glanced away from the road for only a moment towards me in the passenger seat.

"I love—"

<u>Chapter Twenty-One</u>

A bright light filled my eyes and reached over every crevice I could see as my eyelids flickered at the gushing illumination around me. I forced myself to sit up, resting my weight on my forearms. The grass under my fingers was deep green and lusciously soft to the touch. I felt my chest rise as I forced myself to breathe, slowly getting my bearings. I peered to my right, following the noise of what sounded like running water. It was a creek full of perfectly blue water and its gentle fluid movement was soothing.

"Hey, kid." The voice coming from behind me was familiar, but why? Like something I knew but just hadn't heard in a while. From out of nowhere, a hand gently squeezed my shoulder.

"Need some help up?" I turned my head up towards the still-blinding light raining down and saw the outline of a man, without the face in focus. He was dressed in crisp khaki pants and a pristine white pressed shirt. Eventually, a face came into focus as his hand reached for mine. My heart began thudding rapidly in my chest.

"Daddy?"

"Yup, it's me bugger bean." I hadn't heard that nickname since childhood. My hand met his and its warmth instantly comforted me as he pulled me upward. As soon as I was upright, I leapt into his arms, hugging his shoulders with all my might. He unexplainably felt so real, exactly as I remembered him.

"How is this possible?" I questioned. "I don't understand."

"You don't need to worry, Brooke. You're going to be just fine."

"What?" I felt my eyebrows rise as I questioned him. "Don't worry about what, Dad?"

"Just trust me. You trust me, don't you?" I was instantly reminded of when Riley had asked me that. Suddenly, a sharp pain shot through my head as a large crashing sound deafened my ears. Dad pulled my focus back to him, looking at me he said, "My beautiful girl is all grown up." Looking down, I finally noticed I was dressed in a white long-sleeved shirt and jeans—I didn't recognize them or the brands. "I can't believe how truly beautiful you are." I was a little lost inside, knowing I typically appeared frail from my heart, yet, at his words, I took notice that my skin looked healthy, almost glowing.

"You have no idea how much I've missed you, Daddy."

"You, too, honey." Dad smiled down at me, wrapping his arm about my shoulder, guiding me to walk slowly in the direction of the creek I'd heard. As we walked what seemed a long while along the water's edge, we laughed and talked as he told me about all of the memories—good memories, he had of me as a little girl and teenager. I basked in the still-magnificent bright light raining down on us, feeling lost about where I was yet not for a second desiring to leave the strange place or my father. It was like time had stopped, and, although I knew something significant was occurring, my mind was unclear of a sane explanation for it all. Leaning on his arm and matching him step for step, I noticed a bridge off in the distance, and a million thoughts converged in my mind.

"I know this place, Dad."

"Of course, you do," Dad smiled.

"Yes, this is where you are in my dreams." I felt my face scrunch, wondering why my former dreams had never felt this real. It was definitely different than before. I looked up at Dad again.

"Is this a dream?"

"Bugger bean, this is going to seem more real than any dream you've ever had. It's a moment to…" he paused, as if he knew what he wanted to say but was searching for the best words to explain it. "It's a time to come together and have a sense of closure or a very real memory." He sighed and gave me a reassuring smile. "Let's keep walking, there is someone waiting for you."

"Who?" I was scared. I felt out of control again but in an awful way, only staying calm because I was with my dad. He rubbed my shoulder, pulling me towards him.

"Someone who loves you very much." As we finally approached the bridge, I saw someone else—another man, materialize, and immediately I knew from the dark hair waiting for me.

"Riley?"

"Yes, Brooke," Dad verified.

"But wait? How do you know—" Dad chimed in before I could finish,

"Oh, we met before you arrived here. We've had a while to talk. I like him tremendously, Brooke."

"I knew you would, but why is he here?"

"Why don't you two just have a talk; he's been waiting for you." Dad's hand met mine one last time and escorted me to the foot of the bridge. He gave one last squeeze to my hand. "I love you very much, Brooke."

"You, too, Daddy." I grabbed his hand firmly, afraid I may not see him again but knew to follow his instructions and let myself go. He gave a nod and walked off in the distance, fading away after several steps. It was all so surreal for a second. Resetting my concentration, I looked up at Riley and those deep dark eyes hypnotically beckoned me to the crest of the bridge. He extended his hand as I walked to meet him.

"There's my wife," he confirmed, his enormous smile sparkling.

"This is all so confusing, Riley, but I'm so glad you're here. So happy you're with me wherever I go. Always." I reached for more of him, locking my arms around him. He was dressed as I was used to seeing him in nice jeans and a black shirt—untucked. I felt his lips kiss the top of my head and then he rested his cheek in its place.

"There's a lot to say, Brooke, but I really don't know how long I have, so I just need you to listen and know that whatever happens I love you more than life itself." He pulled back a short distance to look me straight in the eye with his hands nestled at my waist and I could feel something in the gut of my soul rise up that scared me to death. My chest tightened and my head spun. It took all of my might not to leap into his arms and stay there forever. I reluctantly took a deep breath and made myself focus on his eyes.

"Okay, I'm listening."

"First of all, Brooke, whatever happens, please don't give up. There is something ahead of you, you may not see it at first, but it's very important that you stay strong. Things may be very different and scary at first from here on, but no matter what—and I mean no matter what—I'm always with you, wherever you go, whatever you do."

"I'm getting scared, Riley. Why are you talking like this?" A sense of urgency overcame me, and with what little poise I retained fading away, it suddenly came to my realization that Riley was slipping away from me, literally fading. My breathing shortened as it became apparent that I was currently not in control of my life. Riley caught my chin gently and pulled my lips to his for one long kiss like I'd never felt him kiss me before. When I pulled away, slowly, he placed a hand over my heart.

"I'm here, Brooke. I'll always be right here."

Again, all at once, everything was black.

....
....
......

Wherever I'd just been was gone and the tremendous pain I had felt in my head returned, along with shock and fear as my eyes opened, but unlike last time, the scenery wasn't quite so inviting. Tubes, everywhere there were tubes going into my arms, sticky things all over my chest, machines everywhere surrounding me. This place immediately felt like hell compared to where I'd just been. Confusion again set in as I glanced around the room and saw cold white walls. This time another familiar voice greeted me and touched my hand.

"Oh, my God, Brooke, baby." It was Mom.

Gasping for breath, I felt a horrible pain ping in my chest and responded by reaching for the source, feeling it covered with some sort of bandaging. Unsettling fear set in and I felt myself wanting to scream.

"Brooke, it's okay. It's okay." I felt Mom trying to comfort me, rubbing my arm, and then heard her call for assistance as I started screaming and yelling.

"Where is he? I need to see him!" I screamed for Riley, piecing together my dream with the reality of what was happening to me. As terror set in, I felt my heart beat uncontrollably.

"Nurse… nurse!" Terror pierced Mom's voice as she cried for help. That's all I remembered of my first trip back to consciousness, and then all went black again into nothingness. I experienced episodes like that several more times until, finally, I awoke, understanding what would be awaiting me. I woke fearful but calm. It was dark in the room and I guessed it must be nighttime. Mom was there and I reached out to her.

"Mom, what's going on?" My mouth felt like sandpaper.

She took my hand and with my free hand I slowly placed it on the spot of the pain still sharp in my chest. It was still covered with the bandage I remembered feeling before.

"Brooke, honey, you're in the hospital and there is a lot to explain, but for now just know that you're okay. Everything is healing really, really well. I will let Dr. Carlson explain more when he returns."

"Explain what?" I definitely felt terrified now, inconceivably afraid of the answer I may receive, especially when I saw tears begin to well in Mom's eyes. *Stay calm, Brooke.*

"Do you remember *anything* that happened before you woke up here?" I tried with all my might to rummage anything from my memory, but only the seemingly real dream—or place—with Dad and Riley was still fresh. "I... I only remember a place... I think it was a dream. Dad and Riley were both there." A tear dripped now from Mom's cheek onto the sheet of the hospital bed. Then it registered. If I'm in a hospital, where is Riley, and why isn't he here?

"Mom, where is Riley? I need to see him." Dr. Carlson appeared in the doorway of the uninviting room. "Well, will someone please give me some answers? That's my husband!" I pleaded with all my might and saw Dr. Carlson give a glance over to Mom, as if silently inquiring, *who first*?

"Why don't we have your mom start? It may be best coming from her." He moved next to the bed opposite Mom. Dr. Carlson took a slow breath and continued, "It's just crucial, Brooke, that, despite what you are about to learn, you try to stay as calm as you can. Your heart is in a fragile state right now. I know this is scary, but I need you to try, okay?" He gave a slight nod of the head to Mom, and she proceeded,

"Brooke, the day you and Riley left the hotel after the wedding, someone ran a red light at an intersection and they hit Riley's car." I raced through memories of that day, not remembering, only wanting to know where my Riley was.

"Then where is–" I winced in pain as my mom quickly stopped my questioning.

"Honey, when the car hit you, you were both taken to the hospital. The doctors told us immediately that you were probably not going to make it; your heart just wasn't strong enough with your injuries, and your body was just so fragile already. They put you in an induced coma."

Dr. Carlson chimed in, coming to Mom's aide, as it was getting increasingly more difficult for me to stay calm.

"Brooke, it was best to put you into a medically induced coma in the hopes we could find a suitable heart donor. Because of the state of your injuries and heart, you were immediately placed at the top of the donor list. Your death was imminent without the transplant. Go ahead, Mrs. Denton."

"Well, how do I even tell you this, when there are just no words?" She was on the verge of sobbing but forced herself to take a calming breath. "When Riley was brought in with his injuries, he was already... he was already brain dead." My chest felt like it would just burst as I fell into a pit of deep despair. Tears started spilling from my eyes.

"How am I supposed to stay calm? What?" I heard one of the several machines attached to me begin to beep over and over, louder and louder.

"Brooke," Dr. Carlson spoke. "I know this is devastating, there's nothing we could say or do… but I really need you to take a deep breath or I will need to give you a sedative." Right then it was the only thing that could possibly sound good compared to this hellish, palpable nightmare.

"There is one more piece of crucial information your mom needs to tell you," he finished.

I couldn't imagine what else I needed to know and tried with all my strength not to hyperventilate. After a few minutes, I calmed as much as possible, feeling all expression leave my face. My world felt instantly empty, until what Mom said next changed me forever—just when I'd thought all the damage was done.

"After the accident, Riley's family flew down from Chicago, but shortly after they arrived, he… he didn't make it." Mom paused. "Riley's family knew he'd always been open to being an organ donor. God, I'm so sorry, honey." Mom couldn't finish, trying to fight back tears. Dr. Carlson gave a supportive pat to her shoulder, coming to her rescue.

"I'll explain the rest for you, Brooke. Really, from my standpoint, what happened next was a medical miracle of sorts." Dr. Carlson placed his hand on mine. "Brooke, Riley's heart was a perfect donor match and…" he sighed, "You now have Riley's heart. He was your donor."

"What? WHAT? I can't even, I can't—" Tears flowed uncontrollably. "You put my dead husband's heart into me?" I cried, horrified. "What am I supposed to do from here? Why would you do that to me?!"

"Brooke, try to calm down," Dr. Carlson advised. I couldn't. "I'm going to have to sedate you." Still, I refused to listen. Seconds later, a blanket of relief came over me. For the next few days after that, everything felt numb. I was given sedatives off and on to keep me calm, reliving the news with each trip back to clear consciousness in a living hell. The worst pain fathomable was cast over me, but in conjunction with the devastating news, I was also bestowed the responsibility of staying strong for Riley because he'd given me the one thing keeping me alive—my heart. But how could I ever really live without him? It was all too horrific and I couldn't stand it.

Eventually, I muddled through details in small doses, learning that the driver of the truck that had hit us never even hit the brakes, then the explanation that Riley never felt a thing, as if that scenario would somehow help me to feel better about it. Worst of all, I had been deprived of the chance to say goodbye at some sort of a service for him. His family had made the decision to have him cremated, and I'd been in the hospital recovering from my numerous injuries and the transplant for nearly a month. Mom said his family wanted to wait for me to be able to attend the service when I was still in a coma, but, after nearly two weeks, it was decided it couldn't be postponed any longer. It was worse than when Riley left for Tennessee, the emptiness. It wasn't fair, I argued from the depths of my soul. The most important part of him was beating inside of me, but it wasn't the same. I wanted him here, with me, to comfort me, hold me... love me.

When the initial phase of the pain of losing him finally subsided, I was able to think back to my final lasting memories of him, the bridge in the dreamlike heaven. Whatever it was, I would have rather stayed there with him. I understood now that he was saying goodbye as I placed my hand over my heart, stitched up and bruised.

'I'm here, Brooke, I'll always be right here.' He wasn't lying; he'd meant it in every capacity. In that moment, in the dark of night, confined to a hospital bed, I made a decision, not because I wanted to, but instead because I was left no other choice. The promise that I would pull it together as best I could for Riley because of how much he'd loved me and because this was his heart keeping me alive. He would want me to see this as a blessing, but my soul would always cry for the heart beating in me. Grasping it all, there was one thing that heavily puzzled me, something else Riley had told me when he was saying goodbye on the bridge.

'There is something ahead of you,' he'd said. What else did he say? I struggled to remember the rest, 'you may not see it at first but it's very important you stay strong.'

What did he mean, I may not see it at first? I hung on to his words because he'd never steered me wrong, and now I didn't know how to exist without him.

Chapter Twenty-Two

Six weeks after the accident, I was released from the hospital but was told it would be best to stay nearby for a few more months. Meaning I would be in Houston for the foreseeable future. Dr. Carlson wanted to keep me closely-monitored.

Mom had taken care of all my affairs in Austin while I was in the hospital: paying my bills, rent, and notifying the school of the circumstances. I felt like the lone surviving victim in some horrific movie.

Entering Mom's house forced me to revisit loss: first Dad, now Riley. The sadness was, at times, crippling. What on earth would I do without either of them? Upon entering, the familiar sounds of paws and collar were the only things that comforted me as Alf bolted into the living room, slobbering me with hundreds of kisses and shrieking barks of excitement. I'd missed him tremendously. After reuniting, I managed my way up the stairs—winded. Yet, although I felt weak after the stairs, in reality, I had been growing stronger with each passing day. Dr. Carlson couldn't have felt better about how the transplant had gone, and expected me to heal well, that is, if I took care of myself, which was much easier said than done, especially in this wretched situation. After entering my room, untouched from the day I'd left for the wedding, I laid back on the partially made bed, Alf jumping up alongside me in his loyal, loving way. I stared up at the ceiling until all was calm and quiet. Feeling the beat of my heart, I closed my eyes following each thump. Riley's heart in me was now the only thing I had left of him. Feeling tears well up in my eyes, they eventually ran beneath my closed lids, and I cried myself to sleep, thinking about the beautiful times we'd shared together. Fate had unleashed the ultimate betrayal.

When I woke, both the afternoon and night of the previous day had vanished. A fresh new sun seeped through the window shades.

Making my way to the kitchen, Mom had a strained smile on her face, attempting to comfort me with a hug followed by a breakfast of toast and fruit. I actually had an appetite; strange too, because prior to having the transplant, when I'd been sad and depressed, the last thing I wanted to do was eat—you'd think I'd stop eating completely now. We both quietly retreated to the living room after eating, Mom sitting on one side of the large sofa, me on the other.

"Brooke, I'm not sure what you want or need me to do from here, but I'm here for you and will support you. I wish I could take your place with all of this—really. I just can't

imagine losing you, too; you're my baby girl." She
struggled to hold back the tears dammed up in her eyes. In
reality, she was the only other person on earth who'd ever
understand, who would ever know what it meant to lose
your other half, the part that completes you because she'd
experienced it, too. I shifted over to her, needing my
mother's comfort, laying my head in her lap while she
stroked my hair. I had no words to reciprocate, just needed
some sort of soothing. All I could do was cry. Thus, this
became my pattern for the next full week: breakfast, tears,
sleep, repeat. Alf was there each day, snuggled up to me
when I wasn't being comforted by my mother. Pain in me;
in my soul; in my mind—pain.

Then, one early Sunday morning, several weeks later,
Mom came up to my room and gently nudged me awake.

"Brooke?"

"Yes?"

"You have some visitors on their way here." I already
knew who it was, of course, but gave Mom the opportunity
to tell me herself. I owed her some appreciation for just
being there for me, and hadn't been much for conversation
lately.

"Who is it, Mom?"

"Tessa and Julie. They've wanted to see you terribly.
They came to the hospit—" she stopped mid-sentence, as if
deciding bringing that up wouldn't be the best option and

then rephrased a bit. "Well, you weren't conscious yet, that is, when they last saw you."

"Oh, okay, thanks for letting me know. I guess I should get in the shower, then." Mom placed a piece of my hair behind my ear before returning downstairs. I really wasn't sure I was ready to see anyone yet, but I concluded it may be better to start somewhere, and it might as well be with my closest friends. I hoped it would give me a dose of the world I'd have to face eventually anyway.

It was really the first time I'd really gotten ready for anything in nearly two months. Taking my time in the shower, I wondered when the horrible lonely feeling might ever let up, even if it was just for a moment, it was better than this. I felt like I was living in torture; wanting to see Riley, feel his warm embrace. I pondered the life we would have had, the family—God, this is so wrong. It's not fucking fair! I just wanted an answer given to me in some form I could accept, reconciling with myself that surely something would become clear at some point in my life as to the reason for this because technically, I was left with no other choice. I either had to live for something or I'd wither away and die. What good would the latter do? How fair would that be for the ultimate sacrifice Riley had paid?

"I miss you, Riley. I love you *so* much. I'll hold it together only for you, but how do I live without you?" I both whispered and cried, collapsing to my knees, water running over me. I couldn't get that question out of my mind. On my knees, I looked in horror at the long scar on my chest. After my back began to feel on the verge of burning from the hot shower, I pulled myself slowly back to sanity, washed my face, and hoped I could reduce the puffiness of my tired eyes with a warm wet washcloth. The evidence in the mirror after I forced myself from the shower still showed, the washcloth having served little purpose, my eyes still puffy and red. I got myself ready as best I could manage, half-fixed my face with makeup, put a headband over my damp hair, put on a pair of jeans and found a green long-sleeved shirt. Putting on the shirt, my finger snagged on the sleeve and I realized I'd completely forgotten about the ring on my left hand for the last few weeks. I contemplated removing it but couldn't bring myself to do it, and had no idea when I'd ever be ready to do so. Like a bolt of emotional lightning, for the first time since I last saw Riley in the heaven-like place, his voice felt clear as day all around me.

"I'm here, Brooke, I'll always be right here. There is something ahead of you, you may not see at first, but it's very important you stay strong." I felt a cool breeze against my ear. Like a whisper. Riley's whisper.

It sounded so real, I caught myself glancing all around me, expecting to see him, but nothing was there. It had now been the second time the words seemed to reiterate in some form since regaining consciousness in the hospital, like Riley was reminding me to push on—keep moving. I hugged myself for a moment, imagining myself in his arms and, for the first time in a very long while, prayed to God for strength instead of anger. "God, show me your purpose before I get lost in this grief."

Alf moved into the bedroom and sat at my feet, reviving me to reality. I bent down to scratch his head, but, instead, he rolled onto his back as if to tell me he wanted his furry tummy rubbed. I giggled. I actually did something half-heartedly happy for once, and it reset my mood enough to put forward a better demeanor, at least to make it through my meeting with Tessa and Julie.

I spent an hour mulling around downstairs, snacking on an apple, crackers, and cereal. I felt famished, and ended up eating half the box of cereal and the entire package of Saltines. Mom left to run a few needed errands, so I sat on the back porch in the cool crisp air, wrapped in a fleece blanket and just let the sun hit my face. I closed my eyes and, just as I felt myself on the verge of slumber, the sound of a car braking in the driveway forced my eyes back open. Alf, who'd been sunning next to me, began barking. I got up from the patio chair and walked over to the driveway. Julie, in a gorgeous beige leather jacket and black jeans leapt out of the passenger side of Tessa's white sedan, sprinting towards me.

"Oh, Brooke, I've missed you!" For the first time I could ever remember, Julie looked like she could sob at any moment. "I can't believe all of this. I wish I knew what I'm supposed to say," she paused briefly and continued, "Goodness, I just love you." She proceeded to hug me until I thought all breath had left my body.

"Brooke, I can't believe it. You're okay. Oh, babe..." Tessa piled onto the hug, and, surprisingly, it felt comforting to have them here. We moved into the house after our reunion, out of the cool weather, and settled in the kitchen, talking over coffee and tea where they gingerly asked questions, and I'd catch them glancing at one another, as if gauging each other's questioning. I felt like some special piece of china everyone was afraid to touch for fear of breaking.

"So, how are you feeling? I mean, are you healing okay?" Tessa asked.

"Well, my doctor is happy with the recovery. I will have to see him every week for a while longer, and then I can start going less often, maybe once a month."

"How are you doing with the loss of Riley?" Julie followed. Now the elephant in the room was out in the open. I breathed long and slow and forced myself to look up at Julie.

"I'm grieving pretty hard—I don't know. I cry a lot. I try to see myself moving forward, but I'm just going to have to force myself to take one day at a time. I mean, I can't depend on my mom to nurse me through this forever, but I'd be lying if I said I could just pick up the pieces and move on right now. I feel so broken."

"I would imagine that's very normal, given all you've just lived through, Brooke," Tessa added softly, her hand reaching for mine.

"We're both here for you, always. We'll be here for you through *anything*." Julie smiled and added her hand to ours on the table. We were all teary-eyed, so I lightened the conversation.

"Well, ladies, would anyone like to grab some lunch?" I asked forcing a grin.

"Oh, yes, that would be nice," Tessa replied, wiping a tear before it could run down her cheek.

"Where to?" Julie asked.

Wow, a normal activity. It had been so long since I had gone out, not since my wedding day, really. I searched my mind for anything that sounded appetizing, having just eaten a lot.

"Pizza? Yes, pizza sounds good."

"Well, then, pizza it is. I'll drive," Tessa offered.

A little while later, we were sitting and eating pizza. It was like a trip away from my depressed reality, almost therapeutic. We discussed what they had been doing and when the conversation felt right, we talked about when Riley had returned from Tennessee and the wedding. It was horrifically painful to relive aloud, but it was also a reminder of happier times. They were the few people in my life who understood my anguish and loved me like family. A little bit of weight left my chest. Maybe this is what would help, being around people I loved, and talking things through. It was no miracle cure, but a way to inch my way back to the land of the living.

Taking notice of Tessa's engagement ring as she took a bite of pizza, I realized I'd completely forgotten about her and Lowell's wedding, blinded as I was by my own grief.

"So, when is the big day?"

"Oh, we don't have to talk about that, Brooke. It would feel wrong."

"Don't, Tessa. I need to be a good friend to you, too. So please, fill me in."

Tessa twiddled her thumbs for a few seconds.

"It will be next month in Austin."

She looked like a person who felt they were walking on broken glass, so I attempted to make her feel better about it by forcing a smile, as I'd often had to do lately, now grasping that my natural ability to smile felt foreign where it once was second nature.

"Well, can I still be a part of it? That is if you want me to be," I asked.

"Oh, Brooke, my cup runneth over." She sprang from the table and wrapped her arms around my neck. Seeing a wedding would be unbelievably difficult with everything still fresh, but this was about more than me. Tessa's happiness at my request to still be part of her big day made a seed of new life sprout in my heart, Riley's heart.

The next half-hour, Tessa filled me in on the many final details necessary of the wedding fast approaching: the bridesmaid dress, shoes, rehearsal. That is until Julie caught notice of something I hadn't paid the slightest attention to the last few hours.

"Good Lord, Brooke, I think you've eaten almost an entire pizza. I've never seen you eat so much—ever. I guess that's a good sign of your regaining strength."

"Oh, my gosh, you're right. I wasn't even paying attention, although, you know, earlier, I was really hungry, too. Weird. I guess you're right, I'm gaining strength." Until today I hadn't even been thinking about food nor had I ever eaten like this before, but, then again, I hadn't had a heart transplant either.

"Well, that's good, then, Brooke. You need to get some meat on those bones." Julie jokingly jostled my arm.

"You're absolutely right, Julie. I can't even imagine how frightening I must look."

Tessa stared at me intently.

"You're beautiful, Brooke. Always have been, always will be."

They were my best friends, restoring some hope by showing me true friends' love. Not the love Riley had given me, but love that reminded me I was still alive and cared about. A spark of light flickered in my soul and I reminded myself again, I would push on. I had to keep living.

Chapter Twenty-Three

A month later, I made the trip back to Austin, the first time I'd seen the city in months. Mom came with me, of course, having taken better care of me and been there for me in a way I felt was never truly repayable. She'd taken care of bills, medical expenses, and anything in between. The first thing she set out to accomplish when we returned was to tidy up the apartment that was covered in layers of dust that wafted around when we'd first arrived. I was more thankful than anything to have someone to face Tessa's wedding with. I needed all the love and support feasible. There was another feat looming in the air, however, both of us realizing that in only a few more months I wouldn't be as strapped to the doctors in Houston, and would need to begin moving on with my life again, learning to be on my own. It was both terrifying and lonely, but reality. I couldn't imagine starting over.

My medical leave would soon be up and I needed a game plan. I'd corresponded with my boss about coming back and was told "you have a job when you're ready, we'd be glad to have you back," which at least supplied me with

275

my next move. Teaching would keep me focused on something, but my love for it had changed after losing Riley. It was as if that part of me had died when he did, leaving me longing for something new in life. I just wasn't sure what that "something" was, so, for the time being, teaching would have to suffice. Most of all, I missed Riley every second of every passing day, but emotionally, I was improving at a snail's pace. My appetite, on the other hand, never really subsided. Since Tessa and Julie's visit to Houston, I must have gained eight or ten pounds by the way I looked in the mirror. My skin looked brighter, but my eyes, well, they were still dim and tired with grief.

Three months, nearly three months, since losing the love of my life, but somehow, here I was still standing. I believed the latter part was only because of Riley's haunting words. Still, I wanted desperately to discover the 'thing unforeseen' I supposedly had to live for, left with only the option to wait—waiting is excruciating when all you're left with to contemplate is being alone.

Staring out of the apartment window at the spot Riley would park, my longing memory was broken when Alf ran into the living room, seeking attention. I released my eyes from the parking lot and scratched his ears, and then filled his empty water bowl in the kitchen. Just as I sat it back on the floor, Mom darted around the corner, carrying a cloth and glass cleaner.

"All spic and span."

"Thanks, Mom."

"Think it's about time to head over to the wedding?"

"Yeah, I'd better."

Looking at the clock in the living room, it showed nearly twelve in the afternoon, and Tessa had requested that everyone be there by one. It was time to vacate if I planned to make it in time. Gathering up a small bag of essentials and the baby-blue tea-length bridesmaid dress, I called out from the doorway, "I'm headed out, Mom!"

She walked over and rested one hand on my shoulder and the other on my face.

"Brooke, I love you, and you are doing a really strong thing today." She bowed her head a moment and then searched my eyes. "I mean, you're a good friend for doing this. Don't forget that. I'll meet you there in a little while."

"Thanks, I needed that." I kissed her on the cheek then departed.

The afternoon was frenzy-filled. Tessa supplied hairdressers and make-up artists to doll up the five bridesmaids and herself. I filtered through flashbacks of my own wedding day. *Stay focused, Brooke. It's Tessa's day.*

Tessa deserved it, after all; this was something she'd waited years for and I understood now in a way I never would have before Riley what marriage truly meant. As the time neared for her to take the walk down the aisle, before a quaint crowd, she looked vivacious, focused and ready.

"Ten minutes 'til go-time," the planner announced before darting off to some other pre-wedding preparation. A few seconds later, a faint feeling struck me like lightning. It wasn't nerves, more like a bad bug that hits suddenly—crappy timing. I hoped I could pull it together in the next few minutes, or I might be passing out or losing my lunch with Tessa at the altar. I wanted neither as an option. Quietly sneaking over to a far corner of the large room, out of the commotion, I hoped to stay under the radar until I could pull it together. I dipped my head between my legs, fanning myself with one hand, holding my bouquet in the other. Just when I thought I'd escaped everyone's watchful eye, Julie walked over and bent to my level.

"Don't let Tessa see me like this, please, Julie," I begged, sweat forming on my face.

"I can do that, but more importantly, are you okay?"

"I don't know. It's the craziest thing. I feel faint and sick." Continuing to fan myself, I added, "I was fine all day. I don't know if it's from the heart or something else."

"Alright, well, take some slow breaths for now, okay. I'll be right back." She left and came back a few seconds later with a bottle of water and opened it. "Here, sip this."

"Thanks."

I took the water and sat up slowly, taking small sips. The faint, dizzy feeling left. *Thank God.*

A lingering nausea took its place but just enough to be annoying; I could at least force myself to get through the ceremony slightly nauseated. I steadied myself while Julie made sure Tessa didn't pay attention, and the nausea subsided just as the planner returned.

"Alright, everyone, let's line up."

Tessa had an aura about her that emitted pure elation. She was beautiful in her lace-embellished wedding gown, hair loosely curled and her veil covering her face. It reminded me of my own happiness when I had promised eternity to Riley, recalling how perfect a day we'd had and that I'd carry it with me forever. I glanced at the shimmering wedding ring I still wore as a reminder of my soul mate, and I saw his face, making me smile inside. Memories, I learned, were the things the outward world couldn't take away. The heart carries them on forever. He'd always be my Riley.

***

The wedding was beautifully orchestrated and well organized, just like Tessa. She and Lowell beamed throughout the exchange of vows, with a traditional ceremony complete with their family and friends.

At the reception, Mom and I sat at a table with Julie and her date, who seemed like a pretty decent guy—easy to talk to. I was really thankful not to be sitting with perfect strangers, being that I didn't want to rehash my life's recent events, and Mom and Julie made the conversation fun and lighthearted. Julie's date even made me giggle a few times.

Enjoying the main course of prime rib, sautéed vegetables, and garlic mashed potatoes; I once again proved I could pack it away, now having finished my plate before anyone else at the table.

"Wow, Brooke, you're at it again," Julie laughed. "I still can't believe how much you can eat now."

A part of me was now annoyed with Julie's reminder of my appetite, but, on the other hand, she was only telling the truth. It was a quality I admired in Julie, even though at times it might sting. I mean, I'm glad I have the urge to eat and all now, but it's starting to seem a little over the top, transplant or not, so what was the deal with my crazy appetite?

"I know," I said, deciding to play along. "I just can't seem to help it lately."

"You look a lot healthier, Brooke, even your color's improved," Mom said, laying her napkin on the table. It was true. For once, I felt my body looked healthy.

Evening settled in with the various wedding traditions, first dance, and cake cutting. With each passing thing, my emotions tanked, and I sat, watching all of the happiness around me all the while crying inside. I would spin the ring on my left finger, desperately hoping it would somehow allow me to sense Riley right next to me, but it only made the anguish worse. It wasn't the same as having his arms around me, or his kiss on my lips. *Stay focused, Brooke, it's Tessa's day*, I reminded myself yet again.

Just before I felt the tears begin to force their way to my eyes, the urge to be sick washed over me. I bolted from the table, half-hunched in desperate search for a restroom. Finally, I located a bathroom sign on the door a few seconds later and was grateful I'd found it just in time to see my dinner resurface. Flushing the toilet, I heard the door open as I sat back against the wallpapered wall. It was Mom and Julie with concern on their faces.

"Oh, my God, Brooke!" Mom yelled.

"Brooke," Julie followed.

"I don't feel so good. I haven't felt right all day." Shakily, I moved, resting my head on my knees.

"Do you need to go to the hospital?"

"No, Mom, not a hospital. I just want to get into a warm shower and bed."

"We should get you to the doctor first thing Monday."

"I think your mom is right," Julie agreed.

"Something's not adding up." Julie wet a paper towel and dabbed my face.

"I'll help you get her to the car, Mrs. Denton."

"Alright, I'll go pull my car around."

After being corralled to the car and then up to my apartment, I showered and lay in bed. As much as I had wanted to sleep, it just didn't happen as curiosity flooded my thoughts. I filtered through everything I'd experienced physically the last month, trying to pinpoint an answer, only able to justify that it must be from the transplant, but still I couldn't be sure. As much as I wanted to be with Riley in heaven, not having to deal with the world and all its heartache, I would feel even more ashamed to just give up on the part of him that gave me life. What would be worse, complications from the transplant and dying leaving my mother all alone in the world or failing Riley by not being able to survive his final life-giving gift?

Minutes turned to hours and I sifted through it all over and over until it hit me like a Mack truck. I sat straight up in bed. Could that really be it? Was it really possible?

Chapter Twenty-Four

Sitting on the examination table, I felt an unshakable anxiety take over my body; not because I believed my heart was the answer for my recent troubles but for an entirely different reason I could not believe I'd missed.

Mom had no idea what I was thinking, and I didn't let on to what I believed the real culprit to be. What would've been the point? If it weren't true, it would make Mom terrified for no reason. So I let her continue to think as she'd suspected, that it was my heart. She sat tensed and patted her foot on the floor.

"Mom, hey, it's okay. Look, I'm okay. You're okay. Things are good, alright?"

"Sorry, Brooke." She shifted in her chair and crossed her legs. "I'm just being a concerned mom."

"Well, don't worry—I'm not worried." Boy was that a lie. I was terrified. Terrified because if what I thought was true, it would mean an entirely new journey. I smoothed a crease in my cream pants and tucked a loose lock of hair behind my ear when the door opened and Dr. Carlson returned with test results on a clipboard in front of him. It was obvious by his facial expression that he was concerned, but he maintained a professional boundary by keeping a straight face.

"Alright, I've gotten the results back from the lab." He planted himself on the stool and then focused in on me, our eyes meeting.

"Well, it's not a virus, and it's not because of your heart."

I couldn't resist any longer.

"I think I know what you're about to tell me, Dr. Carlson. It dawned on me Saturday night. Am I right?"

"What on earth are you talking about, Brooke?" Mom blurted out and leaned forward in her chair. If she wasn't already confused, she definitely was now.

"Am I pregnant?" I blurted out.

"What?" Mom exclaimed and turned white as a sheet.

"Yes, you're right, Brooke. You are pregnant." I knew it, the appetite, the random bouts of nausea, and the faint feeling all made sense. I felt the muscles of my cheeks hurt from the gargantuan grin on my face. Dr. Carlson, however, didn't share my expression, and he looked serious.

"Here's the thing, Brooke. This is a very dangerous thing to consider. There are so few documented cases of pregnancies with transplant recipients, let alone heart transplant recipients. Even more importantly, with the timing so close to the transplant itself. It could put an enormous strain on your heart."

"So, what are you saying?"

"I don't want to tell you this is impossible, but it's going to be incredibly dangerous; not only for you, but the baby, as well."

The baby, I thought as everything else around me momentarily faded away. *My baby. Riley's baby.* A thousand pictures of life with a baby flashed like a storybook in my head. The first bottle, first day of school, sports practices, graduation—a living, breathing being that Riley and I had created. He'd now left me two miracles, and I refused to quit on them for anything.

When Mom's face unfroze from initial shock, she asked Dr. Carlson,

"So, what are you saying she should do?"

"Well, it's more or less considering the options."

I came back from my brief trip to dreamville upon hearing "options".

"I don't understand. Why the hell would you suggest options?"

"What I am telling you is that, in my medical opinion, the safest option in this situation is to consider termin—"

"Absolutely not! No! I would *never* give up this baby."

"What if she keeps the baby, Dr. Carlson?" Mom asked in a serious tone, all expression vacant from her face.

"We would need to keep her very closely monitored, and I'd work alongside the obstetrician. We're talking a daily effort to ensure you and the baby progress with minimal complications. There are many issues that could arise; the heart is going to be overworked, and the delivery would be very dangerous. Do you understand all that I'm saying?"

I gathered my words, glancing back and forth between Mom and Dr. Carlson.

"I know I'm taking a risk. You're saying this could be harmful, even potentially kill me—but, let me be clear, I'm keeping this baby."

"Brooke, why don't you take a few days to let it all sink in?" Mom suggested.

"Look, I'll tell you both right now, I won't change my mind, not in a million years, but, if somehow you both think a few days is necessary, then fine. However, I'll see you in a few days with the same answer." Inside, I was livid at what had just been suggested. How could I simply give up a life when one had just been given for me? I'd never be that selfish. Without the restraint to continue sitting, I stormed out of the office and waited by the car for Mom to emerge.

"Brooke?" Mom reached for my arm.

"What do you want me to say?"

"You don't have to say anything. I already know the answer, honey." She rubbed my arm and it felt comforting.

"Understand Dr. Carlson was merely telling you his medical opinion. It's his job to give you all options available to you. It's your choice, only your choice, your body and your baby."

"I haven't felt alive like this since losing him, Mom."

A smile spread across Mom's face and while I knew her first worry had been for me, she truly understood what this baby meant to me.

"Well, then, let's get you to the house. You have a lot to prepare for. You'll have the doctor's appointments to schedule and perhaps start reading up on pregnancy. Maybe we can stop by the bookstore on the way home."

I hugged her with all my might, wanting her to grasp all of my appreciation.

"I love you, Mom."

"Baby, I'm always here for you. We'll do this together. I'm going to be a grandmother."

Back at mom's, I evaluated how much my life was about to change in conjunction with considering all I'd just lived through. Where would I live now with a baby? Austin, where I'd be forced to be independent or stay in Houston and have Mom help me raise the baby? What would I do about teaching? So many questions and no clue as to the answers. Then a more important thought, what would it be like to hold a baby in my arms?

A baby in my arms… time halted and I succumbed to my own little dream world, attempting to picture a baby in my mind when Riley's message in the dreamlike heaven after the crash finally became crystal clear. He'd said,

"There's something ahead of you, you may not see it at first but it's important you stay strong."

He was trying to help me hold on for this baby. He knew, my God, *he knew*.

"Riley, I get it now. If you're listening from somewhere, I see it now." The words came out, and I felt as if he were standing right next to me. Tears of joy ensued. The love of my life had given me life. He'd given me a baby and more than anything restored my hope in the world. I didn't know just how much more I could stand to take in how bitter-sweetly blessed I'd been. I collapsed on the carpeted floor at the foot of the bed and let my emotions run their course until the ring of the doorbell broke my sentimental trance.

Mom reached the door first and I could hear conversation exchanged, briefly followed by the close of the door just as I reached the base of the stairs.

"Who was it, Mom?"

"It was a courier." She glanced at the label. "It's addressed to you." She handed it to me. The sender's address was in Chicago, the last name 'Proctor'.

"What on earth?" Blood could be felt pumping through every vein in my body.

"You alright?" Mom rubbed my back.

"I think so. I'm just going to step outside and get some fresh air."

"Okay, find me if you need me."

"Alright." I walked swiftly to the back door in desperate search of fresh, open air. After the door had shut, I leaned against it, taking one deep breath before resting on a large cushioned lounge chair. After setting the package next to me, I sat still as a statue for what felt like an eternity, just staring at the package, afraid to reveal its contents. Finally, I convinced myself I was being stupid and anyone else would've ripped it open already.

"Just open it," I said to myself, both frustrated and confused. At last I picked it up and forced a finger into one corner, tearing it open neatly. Sliding my hand inside, I pulled out a handwritten letter and another smaller envelope. I set the smaller envelope beside me and unfolded the letter displaying feminine penmanship. It read,

Brooke,

I don't know where to begin. I suppose first I'd like to say thank you for loving my son. We are devastated at losing our wonderful Riley, but I cannot begin to fathom what it has all meant for you.

When we learned that his heart was a perfect match for yours I was positive God

had given him life to be lived on in his soul mate, an enormous miracle that's helped me through the grieving. There are often no right answers to life's mysteries. I struggle daily to understand, but it's crucial to me that you know this: The heart that you now carry inside of you is a bittersweet blessing. You have to know there is no one else he'd ever have wanted his heart to live on within. Please find the will to live on for him and for the life that fate still has ahead of you. We believe now that his heart was always meant to be yours.

Lastly, the envelope. It contains his estate from various financial matters, royalties his bandmates wanted you to have, and a small life insurance policy.

We felt as a family this belongs to you. Please accept it.

Love,
Sally Proctor

Tears sprinkled the letter as I set it down, reduced to sobs. I used the sleeve of my shirt to wipe my face and then reached for the smaller envelope and opened it, revealing a check for nearly three hundred fifty thousand dollars.

Everything surrounding me faded away, and I breathed one long breath, astonished.

I set the check on top of the letter and stroked my belly in soft circles, pining for the little life growing inside of me, and then turned my head towards the sky, knowing with all of my being he was there, watching, listening.

"Riley, I love you now and always. I will give this baby a wonderful life, and I know I will make it through this because I know your heart won't fail me. You were my fated love. A love I'd live for all over again." A cool breeze whipped through the air. I shivered knowing he was with me, in me, all around me.

Epilogue

"Reese, honey, be careful." The olive-skinned, brown-eyed little girl looked up, attempting to climb backwards up the steep slide.

"Mommy, I can do it."

"You know it's easier to go around and back up the ladder."

"I know, Mommy." But she went right back to attempting to climb the slide.

She reminded me so much of her father, with those deep dark eyes and olive skin. Her vivaciousness was contagious, and she excelled at nearly everything she put her mind to. It was impressive for a four-year-old. Her teachers even wanted to start her in kindergarten early, but more than anything, she showed signs of musical talent. She was always singing in the car, and recently begged me persistently for piano lessons. I'd caved, and we now housed a beautiful grand piano in our living room.

The park was empty for a Sunday afternoon, but it was getting late in the day, dinner just around the corner. After making it to the top of the slide, Reese slid down and came running over.

"Mommy, can we go get ice cream?"

"I think we need some dinner first."

"Aww, Mommy."

"No, baby, dinner first."

"Okay, well, can I play a little longer?" I couldn't help but laugh at her adorable attempt to negotiate.

"Yes, but just a little longer."

"Okay." She hopped off, this time for the monkey bars. I settled into the park bench with Alf, who hadn't budged from the spot next to it since our arrival. Arthritis had taken its toll on him in his old age and he looked ragged, rarely letting me trim his fur. I reached for the notebook in case a creative thought came along when a voice from across the playground broke my train of thought.

"Brooke?" I glanced in the direction of the voice and made out a male figure in a ball cap, worn khaki shorts, and a gray t-shirt.

"Yes?" I called back. The man walked from a trail and across the playground at my response.

"I thought that was you, Brooke," he said, approaching the bench.

"Do I…" the man removed his cap and his identity registered before I could finish. It was Riley's old roommate. "Troy… oh, my gosh, how are you?" I stood up and we exchanged a casual hug. Alf raised his head briefly to glance up at the stranger, but had energy for little else and rested it back on the ground.

"Mind if I sit down?"

"No, please." I motioned him to sit.

"What are you up to?" he asked. I pointed over at Reese, now reverting back to the task of tackling the slide instead of the monkey bars.

"Is that your daughter?" His eyebrows squeezed together, confusion on his face. I stared at her and then at Troy, our eyes meeting.

"Yes, she is." I broke our stare and looked back towards the playground at her. "She's Riley's." The memory of the wonderful man who was her father washed over me.

"Oh," he sighed and then stared at Reese, but more intently this time. "I had no idea, Brooke. She's really beautiful." He paused and set a hand on my knee and our eyes found each other again. "Listen, I'm so sorry about Riley, he was such a great person."

"Yes, he was." We sat in silence a brief moment until Troy shifted on the bench and put the cap back on his dirty-blond hair and then pointed at the notebook.

"Are you journaling or something?"

"Oh, this?" I held up the steno notebook. "I take this thing with me everywhere, gives me a chance to jot down my ideas. I'm a children's author now. I started writing when I was pregnant, and finally got published two years back. That's when I decided to come back to Austin."

"That's really great, Brooke. I can't say I've ever known anyone who's an author."

"It's fun, not something I never expected to take up, but I ended up loving it."

"I guess there are a lot of things in life we never expect."

"What do you do now?" I questioned.

"Well," he started and leaned back. "I'm a realtor, randomly enough. I sell in this area. Actually, I live right around the corner."

"No way! I live in a house about three blocks from here."

"Small world," he laughed.

Reese ran over, no doubt finally bored with the slide. She hopped up in my lap.

"Hi, who are you?" she smiled at Troy.

"Hi, there. I'm Troy. Who, madam, are you?"

"Reese." She kicked her legs back and forth.

"Well, that's a very beautiful name."

"Thanks. I like it, too."

"I'll tell you what, Reese."

"What?" she giggled.

"Why don't you and your mom come over this weekend for burgers at my house? That is, if you and your mom don't have any plans."

I looked up at him, a little flutter hitting my stomach as I sat unprepared but flattered.

"Oh, can we, Mommy?" Reese tugged at my arm.

"Sure. I'd like that," I replied with a smile.

We exchanged phone numbers and talked a few minutes before he got up to make his exit.

"I look forward to this weekend," he nodded, pulling the tip of his cap.

"We do, too," I grinned and then he walked off the way he'd come.

Reese looked up at me after he was out of sight.

"Mommy, how do you know that man?"

"Let's just say we both knew someone very special. I'll tell you all about him someday."

Acknowledgments

What a journey bringing this story to fruition has been.
Years ago it began and, over numerous drafts, evolved into
more than I'd ever dreamed.

To Diana Schalk, what fabulous life you've instilled in the
characters. A fresh eye and deep appreciation for the story
truly brought Fate's Betrayal to an entirely new level.

Barbara, thank you for helping me brave the waters on this
one. I would have never brought this to fruition without
your faith in the project.

My closest friends, you have helped embolden my
confidence to dare write on a deeper level, to be
courageous with words and step out of my comfort zone.

Always, I have to thank my husband. Your love never
ceases to amaze me and your support on my writing
journey is irreplaceable.

Finally, Shelia, I envision you looking down on me from
the clouds. What you said never left me. You told me years
ago that if I really wanted something I should go after it.
Well, I never forgot and never will. That's a promise.

Author Bio

Beth Ann is a wife, mother, blogger, and book-lover from Texas. Her passion is writing stories that draw the reader into a world where they can become the characters and experience a gamut of emotions. When she's not writing, Beth Ann loves to be home with her family and their two yellow labs. In addition, Beth Ann is a sucker for super-sappy romance movies, loves trying out Texas wines, is an avid hot tea drinker, and loves to check items off of her ever-growing bucket list.

A communications graduate of Texas A&M University and active in the corporate world, in 2010, Beth Ann began writing as a bucket list dream and discovered writing to be her true calling. She hasn't looked back since, and has numerous projects on the horizon.

In addition to *Fate's Betrayal*, Beth is also the author of the New Adult Romance *Diverted Heart*.

Website: www.BethAnnStifflemire.com
Blog: http://www.thewritingtexan.com
Twitter: @BASAuthor
Facebook:www.facebook.com/BAStifflemire
Pinterest:@BethStifflemire